"Stay

Lynn screeched.

"Stay out of it!" Don't you dare treat me like some witless child, Sam Russell. I've let you get away with it since the minute I said 'I do,' but it stops. Right here. Right now."

Sam stared at her as if she had lost her mind. Indeed, he thought that might be a distinct possibility, given the pressure she was under.

"Lynn—"

"No. This time you're going to listen to me, Sam." She came around the opposite side of the bed from where she had been sitting. "I—" she poked a finger at her own chest "—am not your child. I'm *having* your child. And if you care one tenth as much about this marriage as you say you do, then you'd better wake up and listen to me, or you can kiss it—and me—goodbye."

Sandy Steen is acknowledged as the author of this work.

Special thanks and acknowledgement to
Sutton Press Inc. for its contribution to the concept for
the Crystal Creek series.

ISBN 0-373-82534-X

SOMEWHERE OTHER THAN THE NIGHT

Copyright © 1994 by Harlequin Enterprises B.V.

Sandy Steen

SOMEWHERE
OTHER THAN THE NIGHT

Harlequin Books

TORONTO • NEW YORK • LONDON
AMSTERDAM • PARIS • SYDNEY • HAMBURG
STOCKHOLM • ATHENS • TOKYO • MILAN
MADRID • WARSAW • BUDAPEST • AUCKLAND

Dear Reader,

It's Christmas in Crystal Creek, and Brock Monroe and Amanda Walker are finally about to say "I do!" What's more, the McKinneys are planning their annual celebration, and all the family will be on hand. Until, that is, one of the youngest family members mysteriously disappears. Sandy Steen, author of the critically-acclaimed *Shameless*, promises to keep Crystal Creek fans on the edges of their seats during this heart-warming—and heart-stopping!—Christmas Eve tale.

Next month, Ruth and Tyler McKinney are once more at center stage, and all of Crystal Creek is wondering if their marriage can survive the recent blow it sustained. Amid preparations for another set of nuptials—those of Lisa Croft and Tony Rodriguez—Ruth and Tyler need to determine if they can ever get past the pain, the guilt and the suspicions that are wreaking havoc with their relationship. Margot Dalton, who so sensitively depicted Ruth and Tyler's courtship in *Cowboys and Cabernet*, returns with her seventh remarkable contribution to the Crystal Creek series, *The Heart Won't Lie*.

Spend Valentine's Day in Crystal Creek—home of sultry Texas drawls, smooth Texas charm and tall, sexy Texans!

Marsha Zinberg
Senior Editor and
Editorial Coordinator
Crystal Creek

A Note from the Author

Shakespeare was right. Parting *is* such sweet sorrow. I will miss Crystal Creek and all of its inhabitants. For me, the series has become much more than just stories and characters. On a recent trip through the little town we used as a prototype, I had difficulty thinking of it as anything other than Crystal Creek. As my fellow travelers and I drove around the square, I pointed out where the Longhorn Café should be and the newspaper, bank and real estate office. I showed them where the carousel had stood and where the sheriff's office should be. I even rattled off the directions to the Double C! No, I haven't lost my mind; just my heart.

From now on, the matchless beauty of the Texas Hill Country will always remind me of Crystal Creek. And when I do return to the blue skies, rolling hills and streams that wind their way through the bluebonnets and live oaks, it will feel like a trip to visit old and dear friends.

I couldn't say goodbye without offering my appreciation to all of the writers in this project for their hard work and their generosity. But special thanks go to four ladies who shared their time, talents and even an occasional shoulder to cry on: Phyllis, Sally and Penny. And to Marsha, the heart and guiding light of Crystal Creek.

Sandy Steen

Who's Who in Crystal Creek

Have you missed the story of one of your favorite Crystal Creek characters? Here's a quick guide to help you easily locate the titles and story lines:

DEEP IN THE HEART	J. T. McKinney and Cynthia
COWBOYS AND CABERNET	Tyler McKinney and Ruth
AMARILLO BY MORNING	Cal McKinney and Serena
WHITE LIGHTNING	Lynn McKinney and Sam
EVEN THE NIGHTS ARE BETTER	Carolyn Townsend and Vernon
AFTER THE LIGHTS GO OUT	Scott Harris and Val
HEARTS AGAINST THE WIND	Jeff Harris and Beverly
THE THUNDER ROLLS	Ken Slattery and Nora
GUITARS, CADILLACS	Wayne Jackson and Jessica
STAND BY YOUR MAN	Manny Hernandez and Tracey
NEW WAY TO FLY	Brock Monroe and Amanda
EVERYBODY'S TALKIN'	Cody Hendricks and Lori
MUSTANG HEART	Sara Gibson and Warren
PASSIONATE KISSES	J. T. McKinney and Pauline
RHINESTONE COWBOY	Liz Babcock and Guy
SOUTHERN NIGHTS	Lisa Croft and Tony
SHAMELESS	Rio Langley and Maggie
LET'S TURN BACK THE YEARS	Hank Travis and Mary
NEVER GIVIN' UP ON LOVE	Brock Monroe and Amanda
	Neale Cameron and Clint
GENTLE ON MY MIND	Betsy Holden and Hutch
UNANSWERED PRAYERS	Howard Blake and Eva

Available at your local bookseller, or see the Crystal Creek back-page ad for reorder information.

To Mary Ben,
who punctuates my life with her wonderful friendship

CHAPTER ONE

THE DAY WAS GRAY and limp with the residue of a thunderstorm that had swept the Hill Country the night before. Feeling as thick and heavy as the air around her, Lynn McKinney Russell slipped from the front seat of her pickup truck and stood for a moment, her right hand braced against the door, her left hand massaging the small of her aching back. Her fingers kneaded the area that was—at least from a rear view—still relatively narrow, despite the fact that she was barely eight months pregnant. The full frontal view was another matter entirely.

Lynn glanced down at the denim maternity shirt tented over her belly. These days she felt as if her stomach preceded the rest of her body like some mammoth ocean liner—with her navel pointing the way—towing a tugboat in its wake. She didn't walk; she pitched and rolled, stem to stern. And despite the fact that she was thrilled and excited about the soon-to-be newest Russell offspring, she had to admit that the drastic changes in her body, coupled with her roller-coaster emotions, were sometimes hard to get used to. Today, for instance, she felt as if she weighed at least fifty pounds more than the number indicated on her bathroom scale, and Lord knew that number was high enough.

Stop complaining. The baby's healthy. You're healthy. So just knock off the whining.

If she were honest with herself, Lynn had to admit she had been doing a lot of whining lately. Too much. Oh sure, everybody said pregnant women were entitled to a certain amount of mumbling and grumbling, and perhaps so. But that sort of behavior wasn't in her nature, and she detested the way she had done nothing for weeks but, well . . . bitch.

About everything. From sunrise to sunset. Day in and day out. No topic, object or person escaped her bitchy target practice.

Her morning eggs—cooked by her own hand—were either too runny or overdone. The paper boy *maliciously* threw the newspaper into the bushes. Couldn't Detroit make a truck cab that didn't require a ladder to reach it? Surely she wasn't the only petite, pregnant woman to ever climb into a pickup. Why was it every time she closed her eyes for a teeny-weeny nap, Sam's daughters came storming in from school like cowboys just off a trail drive? And who, in the name of all that's holy, decided that pregnancy impaired a woman's judgment just because her rationale for some things was emotional? Could she help it if the check and subscription for Sam's silly old dental journal got mixed up with the payment of the electric bill? Nobody's perfect.

"O-o-o-o-oh," Lynn groaned out loud, and leaned her head against the open door of the truck. "Would you listen to yourself? You're beginning to sound like a real nag."

And that was another thing. Not only was she vying for the undisputed title of Bitch Queen of the Lone Star State these days; she had also begun to talk to herself.

Stop it! she thought in defiance of the new and annoying habit. *A month from now you'll be rocking your baby, and none of this will matter. Everything will be fine once the baby comes.*

As if to signal agreement, her baby kicked. Lynn smiled and gently patted her belly. "Sweet pea," she murmured. "I can't wait to hold you in my arms." She stood for a long time, savoring the feel of the baby as it moved within her, strong, eager. Each tiny movement reaffirmed the joy of the present and the promise of the future.

No, she was being unfair to blame her ill temper on the stress of pregnancy. In truth—after the initial shock of discovering she had conceived on her honeymoon—she loved the whole idea of giving birth. The real source of her irritation was nothing more than pride. Wounded pride. Well, dented was probably a more accurate description. Dented, because she had been forced to take a back seat in the achievement of the goal she had worked so hard toward—racing her horse Lightning in the Triple Crown. Because Sam, her father and Ken Slattery feared the rigorous preparation schedule she had always maintained would be too much for her, they had insisted she hand over the actual training to someone else. Now, a stranger was working with her horse. Someone else was doing her job.

Lynn pushed away from the truck door, slammed it with a resounding whack and headed for the stables.

And not just *someone,* but Walt "Tag" Taggart, a drifter with a gift for handling horses. A man whom Lynn disliked intensely. She hated the whole idea of having to deal with him five and often six days a week, and she suspected the feeling was mutual.

It didn't matter that he handled horses like a man born to the task. It didn't matter that he had the devil's own way with Lightning. What mattered was that Lynn didn't like him. She didn't like the way he looked, or talked, or anything about him. Especially the way he bragged about his reputation with women. The first time she had laid eyes on Walt Taggart, the hair on the back of her neck had prickled, and every instinct in her body had practically shouted that he was bad news. She couldn't explain it, she only knew she felt it. And she felt something else.

Evil.

Walt Taggart had an aura of evil around him.

Not the occult, demon-possessed kind of evil the media so enjoyed exploiting, but a cold, insidious, calculating kind of evil that seeks to rot everything it touches. These feelings were nothing substantial, nothing Lynn could prove any more than she could prove the notion that Tag mistreated Lightning from time to time in order to get him to behave. The fact was, she feared and distrusted Tag. Although she did an excellent job of hiding her fear, she would definitely breathe an enormous sigh of relief when the day arrived that she would be able to resume training Lightning herself. When the day arrived she would no longer require Taggart's help. That day couldn't arrive soon enough to suit Lynn.

Of course, when she had expressed her feelings first to her father, then to Sam and asked—begged— them to find another man to work with Lightning, she had expected a more positive response. In fact, she had expected her father to send Tag back to working cattle and find her a replacement. But that hadn't happened. She had been outvoted because Tag was good—maybe one of the six or seven best J. T. McKinney had seen in the past ten years—and he was available. She had been outvoted because the men in her life thought she was overreacting and too emotional. All of which they attributed to Lynn's state of impending motherhood and frustration over having to give up control where Lightning was concerned. All of which Lynn considered on a par with the piles of ready-made fertilizer amply supplied by the Double C livestock.

So, on the subject of Taggart, Lynn kept her mouth shut and her eyes open.

She was running later than usual this morning and most of the hands were already gone. Ken Slattery's truck had been parked at the main house when she drove past so she suspected Ken and her father were discussing ranch business. Otherwise, the stable area was almost deserted. Almost. Just as she entered the stables, she heard Taggart's voice raised in anger and the unmistakable sounds of a panicked horse. Her horse. She rushed down the row of stalls, then stopped dead in her tracks.

Lightning, wild-eyed, snorting, stomping and thrashing his head, was backing away in fear. In one hand Walt Taggart held a lead shank, hooked to Lightning's halter and stretched across the big animal's velvety nose. In the other hand, raised above the trainer's head, was a riding crop poised for striking.

Lynn's reaction was instinctive and immediate.

"Get away from my horse."

Taggart whipped his head around and at the same time gave the lead a vicious jerk. The rough rope painfully scraped Lightning's tender nose and the horse made a sound that was a cross between a whinny and a screech. Tag's usually narrowed gaze widened momentarily as he lowered the riding crop. "And let this—" Lightning tried again to rear and back away, but Tag gave the rope another hard yank

"—pampered nag get the upper hand? Not in this lifetime. There ain't a horse born I can't control."

"I won't tell you again, Taggart."

"He knows who's boss." Tag turned his attention back to the horse, who had quieted some at the sound of his mistress's voice. "Don'tcha, knot-head?" The even tone of Tag's voice belied its cold hardness. A hardness the fractious horse seemed to recognize. Still, Lightning continued to snort and blow, refusing to be completely stilled. "Don't make me haveta teach ya some manners, ya hear?"

Whatever initial fear Lynn might have had was now shoved aside by anger. "If you lay one hand on that animal, so help me, God, I'll—"

"Hey, now, Duchess. Don't get so riled up." In a well-practiced move, Tag unhooked the lead shank, scooted backward out of the stall and closed the door. Lightning whickered his relief, but his agitation didn't completely abate. Now Tag gave all his attention and a one-sided grin to Lynn. "You're in no position to be threatenin' anybody."

Even though he was smiling, Lynn knew Tag wasn't joking. She also knew that, given her present shape and gait, she probably looked like the least threatening person on the planet. But she had no intention of backing down. Lightning was hers. Her pride and joy. He was not only the embodiment of a hard-fought goal, but she loved him. And no one was going to hurt him if she could help it.

"I'm telling you straight out that if you use that crop on Lightning, you'll be off the Double C so fast it'll make your head swim."

"Ain't we the sassy one!" Somewhere along the line Tag's grin had drooped into a sneer. His dark-eyed gaze traveled over Lynn like a snake slithering over its favorite hunting ground. "You forget somethin', Duchess. You don't do the hirin' and firin' around here. And just 'cause this fancy nag comes whenever you call, don't make the same mistake about me." He took a step toward her.

Lynn stood her ground, but every instinct screamed for her to run. "I may not have the authority to fire you, but I do have some influence with the man who does."

"Slattery won't let me go." He tapped one end of the crop against his palm and took another step closer. "I'm the only one around here that can handle that highfalutin nag of yours." He stepped closer still.

When he did, Lynn caught a strong aroma of alcohol on his breath. "Just because you're good with horses doesn't mean—"

"I'm good—" Tag reached out with the crop until the end lightly touched the swell of Lynn's right breast "—with anything wild."

Lynn's whole body flashed hot and cold, trembling with a mixture of fear and rage. For a moment she didn't know whether she was going to throw up or laugh in his face. The man must be drunk... or have a death wish to come on to the boss's pregnant daughter. J. T. McKinney would have Taggart's head mounted and stuffed when he found out about this. The idea bolstered Lynn's courage, and with more calm that she thought she possessed, she pushed the crop away from her and stepped, not back, but to the side.

She lifted her chin a notch higher. "*I* am Lightning's owner and *I* say who handles him and who doesn't. From this minute forward, you don't. I don't want you anywhere near my horse."

"Well, now, ain't you the feisty one! I always did like a gal with spirit."

"You've had your fun now, Taggart. I suggest you get on out of here and go sleep it off."

"I'm in no hurry."

Suddenly, Lynn realized that while they talked Tag had skillfully maneuvered himself so that a stall was at her back and he was positioned to prevent her escape to either end of the stable. He saw the realization flash across her face, and the grin that curled his lips could only be described as triumphant, like the look of a hungry cat when he knows the stalked mouse is cornered.

Lynn swallowed hard. "Well, I am. I've got better things to do than stay around a hungover cowboy—" She started to step around him, but his right hand shot out to stop her while he slipped the riding crop into his back pocket with the other.

"That man of yours takin' good care of you while you wait on that baby?"

Now the smell of alcohol on Taggart's breath was distinct and foul. Was he so drunk that he didn't know what he was doing? "I—I don't know what you're—"

"You know, some men don't like to even touch a woman when she's breedin'. Now, you take me. I ain't that particular. That city fella you married strikes me as re-e-eal particular. But I can help you there."

He was crazy. And dangerous. A genuine sense of panic began to inch along her nerves. She tried to take another step, but he cut her off. "Let me pass."

"Yes, sir, just you and me and a big ol' pile of hay. Don't that sound good?"

"No."

"Sure it does."

Lynn straightened her shoulders, gathered all her courage and looked him in the eyes. "You lay one finger on me, and I'll scream loud enough to bring every ranch hand within ten miles in here."

"They're all gone till noontime. Ain't nobody gonna hear us."

"Daddy and Ken are—"

"Too far away."

Suddenly the truth of his words cut through her bravado, and for the first time she realized the extent of the danger she could be facing. Taggart was definitely drunk and he was right. Ken and J.T. were too far away to hear any cries for help. Lynn swallowed hard. She would just have to rely on her wits. "I'm telling you for the last time. Get out of my way. Let me pass and we'll…just forget this incident ever happened."

"Now ain't that decent of ya. The grand duchess handin' down favors." Before Lynn could blink, Taggart's hand snaked out, grasping her by the throat as he pushed her back against the stall door. His thumb dug into the tender spot beneath her jaw and his fingers caged her neck in a steel-hard grip until she thought she might pass out from the pain and lack of breath. Her slender fingers clawed at his hand.

Taggart's eyes narrowed to slits and a drop of spittle oozed from a corner of his mouth. "Well, let me tell you somethin', Duchess. I go where I want to. Whenever I want to. Nobody tells me what to do. Especially not a little spoiled, know-it-all, rich bitch like you. Women got no business around horses. You think 'cause you got money you can do anythin' you want, then you come in here every day lordin' it over me like I was trash. And I've had enough, do you hear? Now it's my turn to call the tune."

Fighting for breath, Lynn doubled her fists and beat on Tag's chest, trying to push him away. But he was too close to her and too strong for her. In the futile struggle her hand slipped past his rib cage and touched the riding crop sticking out of his hip pocket. In desperation, she yanked out the crop and struck it against his back. Once, twice, three times. As hard as she could. As quick as she could.

"Why, you little..."

Taggart didn't release her completely but slackened his hold enough for her to breathe and to put a few inches of distance between them. Not much, but enough for her to raise her knee.

She missed her target, but the threat was sufficient for him to release her.

"You bitch!" he yelled and lunged for her again.

Lynn struck him full force with the riding crop, catching him across the right side of his face. A line of blood appeared instantly. Momentarily stunned by what she had done, Lynn stared as the bright red slash beginning to ooze then drip blood down his cheek.

Taggart touched a finger to his face and looked at the blood, then looked at Lynn. "I'll kill you for this."

Suddenly, with startling clarity, she knew he meant to do precisely that, and she ran for her life. He caught her before she reached the door to the stables, and grabbed a handful of her thick auburn hair. Lynn screamed, and down the row of stalls Lightning went wild, his hooves stomping the stable floor so loud they sounded like rumbling thunder. She jerked free, but in the instant before she thought Walt Taggart would capture her again, throw her to the ground and do God-knew-what to her, she heard a sound that could only compare to a chorus of heavenly angels—the noise of boots hitting the ground on a dead run and Ken Slattery's voice.

"Lynn! Lynn, you in here?"

Taggart released her just as she called out. "Ken!"

"What was all that screamin'—" Slattery ground to a halt at the sight of Lynn McKinney Russell, wide-eyed with fear, facing off with an angry Walt Taggart. "What the hell is going on here?"

Instinctively, Lynn stepped closer to Ken. The action was enough to tell him that something was dead wrong. He glanced down at her, noticing that her face was flushed and she was breathless. Given her state of agitation, and the fact that she held the crop like a weapon, he was almost positive she had been in the midst of, or on the verge of, having to defend herself when he walked in. "You okay?"

She nodded.

Ignoring Slattery, Taggart glared at her.

"You sure?"

"Y-yes," Lynn said, responding to his gentle concern with a weak smile.

"What happened?"

"She didn't like the way I handled her precious goddamn horse," Taggart said before Lynn could answer.

The look Ken turned on the ranch hand was lethal. His usually soft blue eyes were now as cold as the Arctic in the dead of winter. Lynn and Tag had disagreed several times over how, when and how much training the Thoroughbred needed, but the disagreements had never become heated. Although, truth be told, Ken knew if it had been up to Lynn, Tag would have been fired long ago. He turned back to Lynn. "That so?"

Her heart still racing, Lynn stared at Tag. All she had to do was say the word and he would regret these past few minutes more than any in his life. She knew Ken suspected Taggart wasn't telling the truth. All she had to do was answer "No, he's lying through his teeth," and she knew Taggart would be picking his teeth up off the ground.

Then she looked into Tag's eyes and saw more hate than she had ever thought it possible for one human could feel. A white-hot flame of hate so deep it consumed his soul. Moments ago, he had threatened to kill her and she had believed him. She still believed him. Walt Taggart was a dangerous man. She wanted him away from her, away from Lightning, away from the Double C. Thank goodness Ken had shown up when he did.

She glanced at Ken, waiting for her answer, waiting for her to confirm his suspicions. "Y-yes, that's so. We . . . we couldn't agree. And I know it's not my place, but...I—I lost my temper and...fired him."

Ken watched her closely for several seconds. She wasn't telling him the whole truth. Neither one of them was. Slattery knew it the way he knew the sun would come up tomorrow morning. The question was, why?

Suddenly, he had what he figured was a clear picture of what had happened, or almost happened. The scruffy-looking wrangler had a reputation for womanizing, and Ken had heard enough talk among the other ranch hands to know Taggart's reputation wasn't built on charm. "And that's all there was to it?"

Lynn swallowed hard. "That's all."

One corner of Taggart's mouth lifted in a half smirk. A self-satisfied smirk. Lynn had to suppress the urge to scream out the truth, to tell Ken to kick the guy out on his tail. But she didn't, because for once she didn't allow her usual urge to leap before she looked overrule her good sense. Tag *was* a dangerous man, and there was no sense antagonizing him. Life was too precious to waste on looking for trouble when it could be avoided.

"All right, Taggart. If Miz Russell says you're fired, you're fired."

"She's got no right—"

"No, but I do. And I'm telling you, you're fired."

As the ranch hand turned to leave, Ken caught sight of the line of darkening blood across Taggart's cheek. "What's that?"

"What?" Taggart snapped.

"Your face."

Taggart's gaze darted to Lynn's as he touched his cheek. "Accident. Cut it on a nail in the stall."

Taggart took two more steps before Ken Slattery's voice stopped him cold. "I think you're lying."

The ranch hand spun around to face the Double C's long, lean foreman. "Just what the hell—"

"I think you got outta line and she put you in your place. With that." Slattery pointed to the riding crop.

"You got no call to go accusin' me—"

"That mark on your face is proof enough." Ken turned to Lynn. "That how it went? You tell me, Lynn."

She didn't have to answer. Ken saw the truth in her eyes. For a fleeting moment he actually considered taking the crop from her hand and finishing the job. He turned on the ranch hand, his lean body tense, his expression hard.

"I'm callin' Wayne Jackson, and you better hope I don't decide to kick your worthless ass clean outta Claro County before he gets here. Or worse."

"No." Lynn stepped forward and put her hand on Ken's arm. "He's not worth it. All I want is for him to be off the Double C for good."

"I think you're letting him off too easy—"

"I'm not hurt," she assured him. "Shook up, but not hurt. There's no reason to make a federal case out of this. In fact—" she glanced at Taggart, hating to give him even this much satisfaction "—the less said about it, the better."

Ken Slattery shoved his hat back on his head, thought about the situation for a moment, then said,

"All right, but only because you insist." He looked at Taggart. "You got ten seconds to get outta my sight, and ten minutes to get off Double C land. If I find you here after that, then you better hope the sheriff gets to you before I do. And if I ever see or even hear that you've bothered Lynn again, I'll personally make you regret the day you were born. You got that?"

Taggart didn't say a word. He just glared at the other man. He had hated Slattery since the first day on the job, and he'd like nothing better than the chance to bust the foreman to pieces.

Without even a glance at his watch, Slattery said, "Nine seconds and countin'."

Taggart continued to glare for what to Lynn seemed like minutes instead of seconds; then he simply turned and walked out of the stables.

When he was out of sight, Lynn saw the tension ease from Ken's shoulders as he turned to her. "I think I should call Wayne all the same and let him know—"

"Please, don't do that," she insisted. "I just want to forget about the whole thing. I'm not hurt. Taggart's gone. Let's leave it at that, okay?"

"I'm not sure your father will leave it at that."

·"There's no reason to tell him. Or Sam. Like I said, it's over."

"And what about when J.T. asks why I fired Taggart?"

"Tell him the truth. I walked in, found him abusing Lightning and wanted him fired. You backed me up."

Ken looked doubtful. "You sure this is how you want it?"

"I'm positive."

"All right, but it's against my better judgment. And if that worthless piece of trash ever shows his face around here again, all bets are off."

"Fair enough." If Taggart ever showed his face around here again, Lynn would be only too happy to have Ken, or anyone for that matter, introduce him to the business end of a boot. "And thanks, Ken."

"You wanna go up to the main house and sit down for a minute or two?"

She shook her head. "I think I'll...just go on home."

Ken smiled and Lynn reflected on how he had changed since he'd married Nora. He had always been something of a loner, reserved and aloof for the most part. Not that he had become gregarious since his marriage, but he smiled more, seemed more relaxed, more content. Yes, content was the right word. Ken Slattery was a contented man.

"Thanks, Ken. I don't know what I would have done if you hadn't come along. You're one of the few men who could have handled the situation as well as you did."

"Happy to oblige." As always, uncomfortable with praise and appreciation, he settled his hat back down on his head. "Can I walk you back to your truck?"

She shook her head. "I'm fine, now, thanks."

He nodded. "Then I reckon I'll see ya'. Drive careful." He strode off in the direction Taggart had disappeared.

Lynn watched him go and thought about how strange it was that she had known this man since she was a child, but this was the first time they had ever related to each other on an adult-to-adult basis. For years she had only been the youngest McKinney, and he the foreman of her father's ranch. After today, she would think of him as a friend.

And, thanks to Ken, after today she would never have to deal with Walt Taggart again.

I COULDA KILLED 'EM both and never looked back. Now cold sober, Tag glanced in his rearview mirror and watched the dust swirling behind him, almost obscuring his last look at the Double C. *If that son of a bitch Slattery hadn't showed up...*

As far as he was concerned, Ken Slattery was nothing but a kiss-ass lackey for the McKinneys, always making himself out to be better than he was. *Well, his time's comin'. Nobody treats me like that and gets away with it. He's gonna pay, all right.*

But first, he would take care of little Miss High-and-Mighty Lynn McKinney Russell.

She had ordered him around for the last time. Ever since he had taken over the training of her fancy-shmancy racehorse, she had done nothing but cut him down at every turn. Telling him—*him,* one of the best horsemen in the state—how to handle a piece of high-strung dog meat like that horse of hers. Well, he was sick of it, and she could just go to hell.

For weeks now, she had pushed and nagged, telling him *don't do this* and *don't do that.* Every day was worse than the one before.

She'd been a burr under his saddle since the first day he had walked, flat broke and needing a job, onto the Double C. No matter what he did or how he did it, nothing was ever good enough for her. *Oh, she always bitched with a smile on her face. Always made it seem like I was to blame 'stead of her just wantin' everything her way.*

Well, no more.

He'd have taken care of her today if he hadn't been so hungover from last night. And if that sorry foreman hadn't stepped in to take her part. Tag touched his cheek with one hand. The other doubled into a fist.

Yeah. I shoulda killed her. No woman makes a fool outta Walt Taggart and lives to tell about it.

Several very depraved ideas began to take shape in his nasty little mind. Ideas designed to make Lynn Russell regret the day she'd ever thought about crossing him.

CHAPTER TWO

"DID YOU FINISH your math homework and study for your test?" Allie Russell asked as she fixed herself a bowl of cereal.

Fully launched into demolishing her own bowl of sugar-coated crunchy something-or-other and attuned only to the sounds coming from the headphones of her portable cassette player, her sister, Sandy, was nonresponsive.

"If you didn't, Lynn's gonna be furious."

Still no answer.

"Hey." Allie snapped her fingers in front of her sister's face.

"What?" Sandy said without removing the headset. She continued to crunch cereal to the beat of whatever tune she was listening to. Probably some classical piano piece, since she was currently in what Allie called her "snob phase."

"I said, did you..." Irritated at being ignored, Allie reached across the table and jerked the headphones off Sandy's head.

"Put those back!"

"You little dork, you didn't hear a word I said."

"Who cares? All you ever talk about are stupid boys and who you saw at the mall. Gimme those back," she demanded, reaching for the headset.

"I asked if you did your homework and studied for the math test you're having today. If you didn't, Dad's going to be mad, and Lynn will be fit to be tied. Now, did you?"

"Did I what?" Sandy asked, deliberately baiting her sister.

Allie shot her sibling her best expression of loathing. The one designed to imply she was acting like a child. The one she knew Sandy hated. "You are so juvenile."

"Am not, Miss Smarty Pants. You just think because you're two years older you can tell me what to do. You're not in charge, and when Dad comes down—"

"When Dad comes down, what?" Sam Russell inquired, carrying an empty coffee cup as he walked into the kitchen.

"She thinks she's in charge of me." In a flash, Sandy snatched the headset from her sister's hand.

"Well, somebody needs to be," Allie insisted.

"Somebody is." Sam poured himself another cup of coffee. "Now, what's the problem?"

"She didn't finish her math homework."

"I did so."

"Why, you little..."

"Hold it," their father commanded. "Did you, or did you not complete your math homework, Sandy?"

She slipped two sheets of notebook paper from between the pages of one of the schoolbooks stacked on the kitchen table. "All done."

"What about the test?"

"I studied for two hours last night."

Sam had to smile at the so-there grin his younger daughter bestowed on her sister. "Then I don't see what all the fuss is about."

"But Daddy, she—"

"Allie, I appreciate your concern, but in this case, it looks like everything is under control. Now, I suggest the two of you get your things together so I can drive you to school." He pointed at the headpiece reconnecting Sandy to her electronic concert. "And that stays home."

"Aw, daddy, can't I just—"

"No, you can't. Now scoot, or you're going to be late."

Sandy started to pout. "I wish we could go back to our old school. Moving here is a bummer."

The cup of hot coffee halted halfway to Sam's mouth. "I thought you liked your new school. You were the one who thought moving from Austin to Crystal Creek was going to be 'cool.'"

"Oh, Daddy," Allie said, gathering up her books and purse. "She's just yankin' your chain."

"She's what?"

"You know. Punching your buttons. Trying to make you feel guilty so she can get her own way." The explanation was delivered as though he were the child and she the parent.

"I am not," Sandy said from the doorway.

"Oh, yes, you are."

"Stuff it."

Sam put down his cup, and a shrill whistle rent the air. "Time out," he said, matching hand signals to his words. "I can see this is not going to be one of our more pleasant days, so I'll just separate the two of you like I had to do when you were babies. Sandy, you get in the back seat and, Allie, you ride in the front."

"How come she always gets to ride up front? Why can't—"

"Enough."

Sandy recognized the tone in her father's voice as one that meant business and decided not to push her luck.

When the back door closed behind them, Sam sighed with relief. The whole household seemed to be stressed out these days, he thought.

Despite the fact that Christmas was less than ten days away, everyone seemed to be lacking in holiday spirit. Tension was hanging in the air of the Russell household like smoke over a battlefield.

To begin with, Allie had started making noises like a rebellious teenager. Nothing serious, or constant. Stubbornness mostly. But Sam could see trouble not too far down the road if something wasn't done. But what? He was totally out of his depth where this teenage thing was concerned. Over the past year so many things about her had changed. Her language—half of everything she said sounded like Greek to him. Her appearance—she was much too concerned about how she looked. And boys. She was much, *much* too concerned about boys. He was trying so hard not to put too many restrictions on her, but neither was he willing to let her run wild. Most days he thought he handled his concerns well, but other days...

Thank goodness we've got Lynn, or the "other" days might outweigh the good ones.

But lately his and Lynn's good days had also been less frequent.

Sam frowned. More and more she seemed distant, and he worried she might even be depressed. He knew how much she had suffered over the loss of her beloved great-grandfather, Hank, and he had tried to be sensitive to her needs. Considering her grief and her new life, plus being eight months pregnant, she had managed better than he had a right to expect. Still, something was wrong. The distance between them remained, in fact, grew wider as the days passed. He had racked his brain trying to figure out what was wrong and still hadn't a clue.

Everything will probably be all right once the baby comes, he reassured himself. *Maybe she's just tired from preparing for the holidays.*

Lynn *had* gone all out for their first Christmas. Decorations graced every room, and the tree in the parlor—covered with handmade ornaments and ribbons—was nothing short of outstanding. He had to admit she had turned herself inside out to make the move to Crystal Creek as easy as possible and the new house feel homey. And she had worked a miracle.

But all her hard work and determination—all of her almost frantic need to have everything perfect—made it that much harder for Sam to share his problems with her. She was trying so desperately to make everything and everyone as comfortable and happy as possible that he didn't have the heart to burst her bubble.

He stared into the cooling coffee and asked himself for perhaps the hundredth time if he was being fair to his wife by not sharing the particular problem that had been occupying a great deal of his time and energy for the past three months. While a part of him insisted Lynn deserved to know, another part was equally insistent that knowing would only cause her needless distress. At this point, there was nothing she would do *but* worry, and he feared how the strain might affect the baby.

Rationalizations, his conscience warned him, but still he hesitated to tell her the extent of his current financial difficulties. *His* difficulties. He still didn't think in terms of *their.* In fact, he had always considered money matters—at least worrying about them—a husband's province.

Marta always trusted me to handle everything, he thought, reflecting on his comfortably balanced relationship with his late wife. *My life felt so organized then.*

Softspoken, even-tempered and possessing the patience of Job, Marta *had* kept his life running smoothly, and she'd appeared to do it effortlessly, particularly in light of the fact that her own practice was as busy as his. As a skilled ophthalmologist, she had developed a talent for reconstructive surgery, specifically trauma cases. But even her emergency trips to the hospital were handled with a minimum of disruption to her husband and children. Home and family were always her top priorities despite the demands of her career. She was a caring, attentive mother and an old-fashioned wife who still believed the husband was head of the household. She was quite simply the most well-organized person Sam had ever known.

Their life was predictable, comfortable. They had developed a simple, compatible partnership: Marta took care of him, his home and his children, and he took care of everything else. Sam knew the formula was considered outdated and even chauvenistic, but it had worked beautifully for them.

He was beginning to wonder if he and Lynn would ever achieve such harmony. And dumping his problems on her certainly wouldn't help. If Lynn knew all the details, she would definitely insist on sharing the responsibility, and he couldn't allow her to do that. Right now, she needed less stress, not more. The most important thing was having a healthy, happy baby.

Of course, the big question was how much longer he could keep his little secret from her. How much longer could he try to protect her?

She's out there right now, spending time with one of the things she loves most in this world. How can I tell her there's a possibility she could lose everything she's worked for?

The mere thought was enough to pitch Sam even further into the depression that had been threatening to drag him down for weeks.

Closing his eyes, he sighed. *No, I can't tell her about the money. I can't—*

"Daddy?" Allison stuck her head in the back door.

Sam's eyes snapped open. "What?"

"We're going to be late if you don't hurry."

"Coming." He set the cup in the sink and followed her out.

Today was another chance, another attempt to borrow enough money to see them through this crisis. He prayed the savings and loan in Austin, where he had made an application more than three weeks ago and where he had an appointment today, would be more generous than the two banks he had already contacted. The two banks that had already turned him down. Flat.

LYNN WAS FLAT WORN-OUT by the time she arrived home, and the sheer quiet of the empty house was wonderfully soothing. She paused just inside the back door, resting her head against the doorframe, as if the effort it would take to reach the chair by the kitchen table was too much. The run-in with Taggart had left her drained emotionally and physically, and at that moment a hot bath and a nap sounded like a little bit of heaven.

Thank the good Lord she didn't have to face Taggart again. Of course, now she would have to face her father and Sam and explain why she had to resume Lightning's training. It wasn't going to be a piece of cake, but she could do it. She hadn't failed yet when it came to making sure Lightning received the best care, the best training. Mostly because she had always been the one to give the care and do the training. Lightning's workouts must proceed, and she had to be the one to handle them.

"And that's just how it is," she said out loud, punctuating her statement with a determined bob of her chin. Sam, of course, would probably object.

But then, Sam objected to a lot of things these days, she thought as she pushed herself away from the door frame and headed for the bathroom. They both did, and the objections usually led to arguments. Not major ones, but arguments nonetheless.

To be truthful, she was worried. She and Sam had grown—what was the word she wanted—stale? No, after only nine months of marriage she could hardly use the word *stale*. What then? Was the honeymoon truly over?

As Lynn drew a tub of bathwater, and sprinkled it liberally with scented salts, she thought back to their honeymoon on the island of Maui. She and Sam had spent glorious days under the tropical sun, playing like children in the surf, and spent their nights making passionate, tender love.

That time had been idyllic, blissful, she thought, after undressing and sliding down into the delicious water, and far too short. Looking back now, she could almost believe it was two totally different people on that honeymoon, not she and Sam. Not the people they were today. Lately she felt as if those feelings of love and devotion she had known on Maui might never be recaptured. Something was definitely wrong between them.

And it was her fault.

It had to be.

Sam was the kindest, gentlest man Lynn had ever known, and she loved him totally, body and soul. And deep in her heart of hearts she knew he loved her, but something had changed between them. Lynn had racked her brain trying to fathom a reason for his preoccupation of late, his self-absorbed worry, and came up with what she had decided was a logical answer.

Overload. Specifically, responsibility overload.

When she and Sam first met, he had only had to concern himself with his thriving dental practice and the rearing of his two daughters. Those concerns alone were enough to keep any normal man busy for a lifetime. Now, he had remarried, moved from a large, upscale house in suburban Austin to an eighty-year-old farmhouse that, for all its charm, needed work, uprooted his children to a new environment, opened a branch office one day a week in Crystal Creek and, last but not least, discovered that he would soon become a father again. Talk about responsibility. No wonder he seemed distant of late. The man was overwhelmed.

Maybe he isn't ready for a new baby, not ready to start all over again. Maybe, even though outwardly he's accepted the idea of a baby, deep down he resents it. What if it were true? How would she handle it?

She straightened her legs, forcing her shoulders and upper body out of the fragrant water. *This is ridiculous. You're making yourself crazy. Sam loves you. He loves our baby.*

Of course he loved her. And of course, he loved the baby. No husband could be more solicitous of how she felt, what she needed. He treated her like a treasured piece of fine porcelain. But even that behavior seemed to be part of her unease, part of their problem. The only time she felt that her husband was the man she had fallen in love with, the man she had married, was at night.

Lovemaking was everything Lynn had dreamed about all her life and more. Sam was a tender, compassionate lover, always making her feel as if she were the only woman he had ever wanted or ever would want. While she was in his arms, all their differences seemed to melt into oblivion and the effort of discussing them seemed a waste of their special time together.

Daylight brought little arguments, disagreements and a series of confrontations over things so insignificant that afterward, Lynn always wondered how she could have attached the slightest importance to any of them. But the night was their time. And somehow over these past few months their bed had become their sanctuary, a place—the only place, it seemed—where intimacy and trust flourished between them.

She needed more than the hours between sundown and sunrise. *They* needed more if their marriage was to survive. Lynn shivered. The thought of life without Sam was incomprehensible. She shivered again, only then realizing that the bathwater had gone stone-cold. Quickly she climbed out of the tub and toweled off.

She probably was overreacting, she cautioned herself. The added anxiety over the short time left to do most of her Christmas shopping didn't help. *I wonder if I could talk everyone into moving the hol-*

idays to July, when I'll have more time? She sighed. *Pull yourself together and stop being such a Gloomy Gus. Everything will be all right once the baby comes.*

But deep in her heart Lynn knew that after the baby arrived, there would be new pressures. And somehow, some way, she and Sam had to find their way back to each other before the nights were all they had.

LYNN WAS still ruminating over her troubles two hours later when the phone rang.

"Hello."

There was no answer, only breathing. Heavy breathing.

"Who's calling, please?"

Still no answer.

Unexpectedly Lynn's whole body felt chilled, as if a blast of frigid air had swept into the room. Her heartbeat jumped, keeping double time with the heavy breathing at the other end of the line. Suddenly she knew the caller meant her harm. It wasn't a conscious thought, but more of a feeling. A frightening feeling and incredibly powerful. She hung up, jerking her hand from the telephone receiver as if she had touched something foul, ugly.

Probably some kid, she thought, trying to calm herself. She really was tense if a prank call could upset her the way this one had. Maybe there *was* something to Sam's notion that she was overreacting.

By the time the school bus was due to drop Allie and Sandy at the end of the lane leading up to the Russell house, Lynn had put the call out of her mind. She had enough to worry about without looking for more.

"Hi," she said brightly as the younger girl trooped in the front door.

"Hi," Sandy answered just as brightly. "Great dress." She pointed to a new maternity dress, a gift from Cynthia, her stepmother.

"Thanks. Cynthia has great taste, doesn't she? Where's Allie?"

"She's coming." Sandy headed for the kitchen. "What's for dinner?"

"Baked chicken and veggies."

"I'd rather have french fries," the girl called over her shoulder.

"So would I, but this is better for us." Lynn waited for Allie to make an appearance and, when she didn't, decided to check for herself. She walked to the front door and glanced out of the oval-shaped beveled Victorian glass pane in the door. Twelve-year-old Allie Russell was standing at the end of the driveway talking to a boy. A boy behind the wheel of a pickup truck!

"That kid looks awfully young to be driving," she muttered to herself.

Digging into a bag of potato chips, Sandy reentered the room, and came to stand beside Lynn.

"Him? That's Ronald and he's not a kid. He's four-teen."

"Fourteen? And driving?"

"Sure. He drove us home."

"Wait a minute," Lynn said. "You're supposed to ride the bus home every day. You know neither of you is allowed to accept rides with anyone. Ever."

"Allie met me before I got to the bus and said Ronald was taking us home."

"What happened to the bus?"

Sandy shrugged. "Beats me."

"I don't think Sam would like this," Lynn muttered under her breath. "If he knew, he'd—"

"Freak," Sandy supplied.

"That's putting it mildly."

Lynn knew that it was common practice for the young men around Crystal Creek to learn to drive at an early age, even though it was illegal. Country roads were seldom subject to speed traps, and most of the boys drove as a matter of course in order to help out on their parents' ranches. Her own broth-ers had been driving since they were thirteen or fourteen, and she had never thought much about it. Now, viewing the practice from the perspective of a parent, she wasn't so sure it was all that great an idea. And she could almost guarantee her husband would share her judgment.

Sam was fiercely protective of both his daughters and, to Lynn's way of thinking, a little too naive when it came to Allie in particular. The girl was maturing rapidly and it had become clear to Lynn that Sam wasn't ready for the inevitability of her young womanhood. Her own position as a new wife and stepmother made it difficult for her to be as forthcoming as she would like to be about Sam's head-in-the-sand attitude. In six days, Allie would turn thirteen. Whether he liked it or not, she would officially become a teenager, with all that the label implied. Perhaps because Lynn herself had been little more than a teenager when her mother died, her sympathies tended to go with Allie. Growing up was hard enough, but to attempt it without an occasional bit of guidance from another woman was ten times worse. Lord knows what she would have done without her Aunt Carolyn and Beverly, her cousin. She wanted desperately to be there for Allie, but so far, the girl had been less than eager to accept anything but superficial overtures. Lynn told herself not to push, not to expect too much, but she was beginning to wonder if Allie would ever fully accept her the way Sandy had.

"She thinks he's awesome, but he's dumb looking if you ask me," Sandy announced, licking her lips after her impromptu meal.

"Well, awesome or dumb, he's too old for Allie. Not to mention the fact that I doubt he has a driver's license."

"You gonna tell Daddy?"

Lynn glanced at the eleven-year-old. "You think I should?"

Sandy shrugged again.

Lynn's first instinct was to do precisely that, but then she changed her mind. Running to Sam was a surefire way to erect more barriers between her and Allie. "Nobody likes a tattletale," she told Sandy. "Besides—" Lynn gave a last look at the two intense young people "—I'm not worried. Allie's got a good head on her shoulders." A few seconds later the boy drove away and Allie came inside the house.

The instant she walked through the door, Allie knew that Lynn and her little sister had been watching her. They were standing only a few feet from the front door, and the look on Lynn's face said she was not completely thrilled with what she had seen.

"Did, uh, Sandy tell you about the grade she got on the math test?" Allie asked, hoping to divert attention away from herself.

"No, but she told me a young man by the name of Ronald brought you home."

Allie's gaze shot to her sister, and if looks could kill, poor little Sandy would have been bleeding profusely.

"What happened to the bus?"

"It—uh . . ." Her gaze slid away. "It broke down, I think. I mean, I think that's what I heard one of the other kids say. Anyway, Ronald offered to bring us home, and I just thought . . ."

Lynn's determined stare forced Allie's gaze back to hers. The girl was lying through her teeth. Lynn knew it as well as she knew her own name. The question remained: what did she do about it? If she confronted her, an argument might follow. If she let it pass without any comment, the girls might get the idea she was a soft touch. She loved Allie and Sandy, but this parenting business was still so new, and discipline—when and how much—was one of the areas she was the most unsure of. As far as Lynn was concerned, there had been too much petty arguing in the Russell household lately, and she decided this incident wasn't worth a battle. They were dealing with an error in judgment here, not the end of the world.

"Well, the next time the bus breaks down, or leaves without you, you should call, and either your father or I will come and pick you up," Lynn said, looking from Allie to Sandy. "Okay?"

"Okay," Sandy responded.

Allie simply nodded.

"You wanna see my math test paper now?"

Lynn smiled. "Sure."

Sandy headed for the kitchen and Lynn turned back to Allie. "What do you say we sneak a piece of chocolate cake? I know I'm supposed to watch my calories, but I won't tell if you won't."

Allie's mouth dropped open, then quickly closed. "Sure. Yeah, okay." Relief was so evident in the girl's clear blue eyes that Lynn couldn't help but smile.

They joined Sandy in the kitchen, and Lynn could tell that Allie didn't quite know how to handle this unexpected turn of events. *Bless her heart,* Lynn thought, *she probably expected me to go straight to Sam and—what is it the kids say?—rat on her.*

Ever since she and Sam had decided to marry, Lynn had worked hard to win both of the girls' trust and friendship. And she had made terrific headway, or at least thought she had, until they learned about the baby. At Lynn's suggestion, she and Sam had deliberately not informed them about the baby until she was almost three months pregnant. She had successfully managed to hide her daily bouts with nausea since her "morning sickness" actually occurred just before the noon hour and Allie and Sandy were in school. At first, both girls had been excited over the news, and in some ways still were. But gradually they had begun to realize just how the new addition to the family was going to affect their lives.

For one thing, Lynn's previously high energy took a nosedive, ending the shopping trips for the three females and hours spent at the Double C Ranch— hours that had helped forge the tenuous basis for the budding relationship. The vivacious, energetic woman they had come to know and accept as part of their lives suddenly didn't have enough energy to cook, much less take them shopping. Lynn felt desperately guilty about it, but there was absolutely nothing she could do about it.

But more upsetting than the blow to the fragile relationship with Lynn was the change in their relationship with Sam.

Because of the morning—or rather—afternoon sickness, Sam had missed one of Sandy's cello recitals and an open house at the school. Then there was the field trip he had promised to chaperon for Allie's biology class. Try as he might to make up for them, the disappointments had been difficult, and both of the girls had developed a distrustful attitude where their father's word was concerned. If they were unable to resolve these problems as a family, Lynn feared both Allie and Sandy might grow to resent the new baby. Then what?

The ringing of the telephone brought Lynn out of her musings.

Sandy answered it. "Russell residence." After a second or two, she said, "Hello." Then another second passed and she hung up.

"Who was it?" Lynn asked.

"Nobody. Wrong number, I guess."

Another one? "Did they say anything at all?"

"No. Just somebody breathing on the other end."

Lynn shivered.

At that moment the kitchen door opened. "Hey," Sam Russell said. "How are my three favorite girls?"

Allie and Sandy raced to greet him. Lynn waited her turn.

"Hey good-lookin'," he said a moment later as he pulled his wife into his arms.

"Hey, yourself." She smiled up at him.

He kissed her tenderly at first, then deepened the kiss. Lynn kissed him back, passionately. He drew back slightly and grinned. "I guess you're glad I'm home."

"Very. And early too." Lynn rose up on tiptoe, wrapped her arms around her husband's neck and hugged him. Over his shoulder she caught sight of the now silent telephone resting on the counter top, and another shiver danced down her spine. She couldn't shake the feeling of doom hanging over her like a storm cloud on the verge of bursting. "I'm very glad you're home," she whispered and held him tighter.

IT HAD TAKEN Tag the better part of the day, but he had finally found just the right place. A perfect hideout. A little spot down by a bend in the Claro River, and the beauty of it was, the location was actually on McKinney land. In fact, the area of the Double C actually ran like an alleyway along the back of the Circle T, then made a dogleg up toward the exotic animal compound on Scott Harris's property. This particular section was used for grazing, but rarely supported more than forty or fifty head of cattle at one time, and seldom saw a cowboy.

He had set up a makeshift camp with a Coleman stove and lantern, bedroll and coffeepot he kept in the back of his run-down 1983 Jeep Scrambler. Not too much—the less there was to notice, the better he liked it—but just enough to provide a place for him until he finished what he needed to do.

He had driven to a big chain food store on the outskirts of Austin where he wouldn't be noticed, and had stocked up on coffee, cigarettes and some staples—the main staple being beer. Then he'd set up camp, expertly built a small fire that minimized flame and proceeded to chow down no less than three giant burritos he had bought at a fast food drive-through on his way back.

Home, sweet home.

"Not bad," Tag said out loud as he surveyed the rocky overhang that was high enough and long enough to at least shelter the bed of the Scrambler. The most important thing was for him to be able to sleep dry. Having to camp out was bad enough, but damn, he hated to have to do it when it was raining. Nothing irritated him more. But he would sack out in a downpour and sleep like the dead if it meant getting his revenge against Lynn Russell.

And it was gonna be so sweet.

The whole idea of making her suffer was tasty as hot corn bread and molasses on a cold winter morning. Just thinking about it almost made him drool. He pitched the half-eaten third burrito into the campfire. Instantly, the paper wrapper blazed into lighter-than-air ashes and was carried away on the soaring heat waves. The tortilla and its remaining contents sizzled, popped and spit as the flames ate away at it like some invisible, ravenous monster. Casually, he reached inside his boot and withdrew a knife.

The weapon—a long-standing favorite that had seen enough action to satisfy a New York city gang leader—had a wide, six- to eight-inch blade encased in a thin leather sheath. He pulled the knife from its sheath and held it up so that the firelight caught the almost mirror-smooth surface of the blade. Mesmerized, he watched the shades of red, gold and orange reflected in the polished steel sway and jump like a band of brilliantly dressed dancing gypsies.

Oh, yeah. I got big plans for you, Duchess. Big plans. You're gonna regret the day you crossed old Tag.

There wasn't a woman born that could best him. Not the longest day she lived. Enough had tried, but none had ever made it. He always paid them back. Always.

And always the same way.

That sassy-mouthed teenager hanging around that truck stop in El Paso. The blond waitress with the big tits in San Saba, and that honkey-tonk barfly in Port Arthur. They were all the same. They all needed to be taught a lesson.

Like that little Spanish gal down in Juaréz. He ran the flat of the blade over his palm from fingertips to wrist, then back again, savoring the feel of the tempered metal on his skin. *Little whore thought she could get me too drunk to notice she was riflin' my pockets. I got her good.* He repeated the mock sharpening motion as if he were honing the blade in preparation for use. *Ain't nobody gonna pay her for it with that scar on her face.*

The memory of the dark-eyed, dark-haired prostitute screaming for mercy, seconds before he had left his mark on the smooth skin of her cheek, made him smile into the flickering light of the campfire. All women were whores as far as he was concerned. Good for only one thing.

And you're no different, Duchess. Just you wait and see. You're gonna scream just like the rest of 'em.

He had plans to make. The two piddly phone calls he had placed this afternoon were nothing. What he needed was something to show her a little blood. Something small, but to the point, so when the time came she would know he meant business.

Yeah. 'Cause when your time comes, Duchess, you're gonna beg and plead just like they did. And I'm gonna give you the same answer I gave them.

With a flick of his wrist, Tag flipped the knife around and caught the handle securely in his palm. Then he expertly grasped the tip between his thumb and forefinger, held it for several seconds as if testing the balance, then sent it singing through the air, over the flames and into the knothole of a piece of freshly cut firewood.

Dead center of the knot hole.

CHAPTER THREE

LYNN DECIDED against telling Sam about resuming Lightning's training until after her checkup at Dr. Purdy's office. As she drove to her appointment, she reasoned that so far she had been in perfect health with no problems concerning the pregnancy; she'd continued to ride, although for the past week or so, riding had become marginally uncomfortable. As long as she was careful, she saw no reason she shouldn't ride Lightning right up until time for her to deliver. Other women had done it. So could she.

But Nate Purdy quickly shot down her reasoning like the first covey on the opening day of dove season.

"No more racing the wind for us," Lynn said later to the only other being who could understand her disappointment. Lightning snorted as if he were in complete agreement.

"I know, fella. But Dr. Nate said, 'no more.' Can't fight city hall." Actually, she *had* thought about defying Nate's orders until he had reminded her of how unbalanced a woman becomes during her last trimester and that riding a horse—no matter how well acquainted she was with this particular horse—was literally riding for a fall. And at this stage of her pregnancy a fall could be fatal to her baby. The minute he said *fatal*, Lynn had completely dismissed the idea of disobeying.

Admittedly, she had handled the first few months of her pregnancy with a somewhat cavalier attitude, as though nothing much had changed, or would change. Though thrilled at the prospect of becoming a mother, Lynn had deliberately avoided the kind of gushy sentimentalism that many women seemed to fall prey to while they were expecting. She decided that kind of behavior was silly and, frankly, obnoxious. So, outwardly at least, she appeared to be very nonchalant about the fact that her life was on the cusp of a drastic change.

And then two things happened that altered her feelings to the point that she would never again be nonchalant about babies or pregnancies.

First, she felt her baby kick. From that wondrous moment on, her whole mind-set about the baby and being a mother had been transformed.

Second, her sister-in-law Ruth suffered a traumatic miscarriage at the end of her seventh month of pregnancy.

The whole McKinney family was devastated, and for the first time Lynn realized how precious her unborn child was and how much she wanted this baby, Sam's baby. Terrified of suffering a similar fate, she found it difficult not to think about such a possibility. In fact, the thought preyed on her mind. And although she did her best to keep her fears hidden, particularly whenever Ruth was around, she couldn't help but feel blessed and guilty at the same time.

Partly because the entire family was so sensitive on the subject of babies at the present, and partly because of the strain between her and Sam, Lynn didn't confide her fears to anyone, not even to her Aunt Carolyn or Beverly. Carolyn and Vernon Trent hadn't been married much longer than she and Sam, and acted as if they were still on their honeymoon. Lynn was genuinely happy for them. And envious.

Beverly, the one person she had always turned to, the one person she had shared secrets with since girlhood, was suffering terribly after the death of her fiancé, Jeff. She herself was in need of comfort and support rather than in a position to offer them.

Strangely enough, the only person Lynn felt could even come close to understanding the fears and anxieties churning inside her was her father's new wife, Cynthia.

"Who would have thought the woman I didn't want in our family would turn out to be the only one I can talk to?" Lynn said out loud. And thankfully, Cynthia had listened, to as much as Lynn had been willing to share. Twice now, she had called her stepmother for small tidbits of advice concerning the care and feeding of pregnant women and been pleasantly surprised at Cynthia's openness and eagerness to talk. They weren't exactly bosom buddies, but at least now there was hope for friendship. For one thing, Cynthia understood about Lynn's...*feelings;* those strange intuitive sensations that seemed to come over her at unexpected moments.

For instance, the overpowering feeling that the child she was carrying was a boy. She simply *knew* it. There was no doubt, no possibility for error. Her baby was a boy. She was so certain that she flatly refused to buy anything pink. Cynthia had understood. Sam had not.

In fact, he had insisted her "feeling" of certainty was nothing more than wishful thinking on her part. Particularly after a sonogram indicated that the sex of the baby was probably female, while still allowing for the possibility of an error. Lynn stubbornly refused to accept the results. Probability or possibility be damned. Her baby was a boy. And that was that.

Knowing the baby's sex and feeling him move within her had given her a new perspective on the present and the future. For the present, all her energies were centered on having a healthy baby son. As for the future, well, that remained a big question mark in her mind.

She gently stroked her protruding tummy. "But don't worry, little Hank, I won't let anything hurt you. I just wish..." Her voice trailed off and she sighed.

The big horse whickered softly and nuzzled her neck almost as if he were trying to comfort her. She stopped stroking her tummy and reached up to stroke his powerful jaw and neck. "Thanks, boy."

"Hey there, Miz Russell." Bucky, one of the cowhands, approached Lightning's stall. "You talkin' to Ol' Fireball just like he understands evr'y word you say."

"I think he does." She patted Lightning's well-groomed neck. "Sometimes I think he's the only one who understands me."

Bucky spit tobacco juice out of one side of his mouth. "Well, then do me a favor and tell 'im I'm a real nice feller, so he don't try to eat me alive when I feed and brush 'im."

Lynn looked at the cowboy. "What do you mean?"

"The ramrod told me to help you out. Said Tag was gone."

"I'm afraid you're going to have to do more than help out, Bucky. As of today, it looks like you'll be feeding, grooming *and* riding."

"But you always—"

She splayed both her hands over her stomach. "Not anymore. At least, not for a while."

Bucky grinned. "Yes'm. You just tell me what you want and how you want it, and it's as good as done."

"Thanks, Bucky. I guess for now, just the regular workout. Take him for a run so he can burn off some of his excess energy, but don't push him. I'm going up to the house to talk to Cynthia and I'll check back with you before I leave."

"Good enough." Bucky tipped his hat and went to fetch a hackamore for Lightning.

With one last rub of the big horse's downy-soft nose, Lynn turned and headed for the ranch house, feeling more depressed than she'd ever been in her life. All the stresses and anxieties of the past few months had pyramided, stacking one on top of the other until she had just about reached her limit. Today, Dr. Nate's no-riding rule had been a harsh blast of reality she didn't need.

As she walked in the back door and into the kitchen, she felt an immediate easing of the tension that had furrowed her brow and knotted her shoulders ever since she left the doctor's office this morning. She had lived all but the past nine months of her life in this house and it still felt like home. And if the house itself felt like home, the kitchen felt like heaven. Lynn took a deep breath, savoring the deliciously familiar aromas that brought back happy memories of both the long-ago and recent past.

One of Lettie Mae's famous stews was simmering on the stove, but the Double C cook was nowhere in sight. Then Lynn heard the washing machine kick into a cycle and decided Lettie Mae must be in the laundry room. She glanced around and noticed a plate of cookies on the counter that looked suspiciously like the pecan wafers her mother used to make. Concocted from little more than sugar, flour, butter, eggs and pecans, the delicately thin wafers were pure melt-in-the-mouth perfection and one of

Lynn's all-time favorites. She couldn't resist taking one.

As she murmured a groan of delighted satisfaction, Cynthia walked into the kitchen. "Aha!" Cynthia tapped the edge of the counter with her hand. "Caught you."

"Guilty, Your Honor. And I throw myself on the mercy of the court." She helped herself to another cookie. "I don't know what Lettie Mae does to these cookies, but mine never turn out this well."

"For your information, my dear, Lettie Mae can't claim credit for those. I made them," Cynthia announced proudly.

"You did?" A piece of pecan fell from the corner of Lynn's mouth as she attempted to polish off the treat. "These are great. It *is* Mom's, uh..." Lynn had been on the verge of asking if her mother's recipe was indeed the one used, when she remembered that not too long ago her dad had told her that Cynthia was rather sensitive where the subject of the first Mrs. McKinney was concerned. The concept was one Lynn could identify with, considering Sam's first wife, Marta, seemed to fall into the category of paragon, as far as she could tell.

"Your mother's recipe? Yes. Well—" Cynthia held her right hand in midair, fingers splayed, and rocked it back and forth "— kinda, sorta. I added a little something." At Lynn's quizzical expression, she added, "Chocolate. Actually, cocoa."

"You're kidding."

"Cross my heart," Cynthia replied, marking an invisible cross over her heart, then holding up her hand as if to swear her oath. "Even Lettie Mae approves."

"Well, you can add me to the list. These are absolutely wonderful." Lynn reached for two more.

Remembering her own battle with pounds while she was carrying Jennifer, Cynthia hesitated for only a second before offering, "You know, I found a new brand of really delicious fat-free chocolate cookies the other day. Would you rather have one of those?"

Lynn's hand halted in midreach. She sighed. "What's another pound, more or less? I already look like the Goodyear blimp."

Ah, thought Cynthia, it looked like a severe case of prepartum depression. She had guessed so when she heard the almost forced brightness in Lynn's tone of voice. "Feeling a little down?"

Lynn's narrow shoulders lifted in a silent answer.

"Want to talk about it?" Cynthia poured two cups of decaffeinated coffee and handed one to Lynn.

"Talk about what?"

Although they were closer than they had been, they had yet to reach a mutual comfort level for any depth of sharing in their relationship. Despite this, Cynthia felt strongly that something was bothering Lynn. She took a risk and hoped Lynn would confide in her. "Feeling fat, depressed, even a little hopeless, maybe?"

Over the rim of her cup Lynn eyed her stepmother carefully. "What makes you think I'm depressed?"

"I've been there. Besides, I saw you walking up from the stables," Cynthia admitted. "And the expression on your face was not exactly sunshine and roses."

When the younger woman didn't comment on the remark, Cynthia didn't push the matter. Their relationship had gotten off to a rocky start when J.T. first brought his Boston-bred fiancée home, and it was only over the past six months that things had changed between them. Cynthia didn't want to put a kink in the budding friendship and destroy the progress they had made to date, but her heart went out to J.T.'s oldest daughter. Obviously, Lynn had something on her mind, and Cynthia could tell whatever it was weighed heavily.

"Does it show that much?" Lynn asked softly.

On an impulse, Cynthia reached over and touched her hand. "Only to someone who's been where you are now."

Lynn looked up, her eyes glistening with ready-to-shed tears. "Oh, Cynthia," she whispered, her voice breaking along with the dam holding back her tears, "I'm so miserable." She buried her face in her hands and cried.

Momentarily stunned at the outburst, Cynthia quickly recovered, slipping her arm around Lynn's trembling shoulders. "Oh, sweetheart, I know it feels like the end of the world at the moment, but I promise it will get better." She stroked the silky auburn hair and let Lynn cry until finally the sobs subsided into sniffles and an occasional sob.

"For the most part, having babies is wonderful, but it can take its toll on you. But, hey—" Cynthia placed her fingertips under her stepdaughter's chin and lifted the tear-streaked face "—if I can muddle through and come out with a reasonable amount of sanity left, anybody can. Everything will be all right once the baby comes."

"Y-you r-really think so?"

"No question about it." She crossed to the far side of the kitchen, retrieved a box of tissues and handed it to Lynn. "You are looking at a former basket case. And, I might add, from the not-too-distant past."

Lynn blew her nose none too delicately and grabbed more tissues. "But it's not just the baby. I mean it is, but... Now, Nate says that I can't ride or even train Lightning anymore. I'm too *big*."

"I'm sorry. I know how much you enjoyed the training."

"Even that wouldn't be so bad if...if things at home were better. Nothing is working out like I thought it would."

Oh no, Cynthia thought. *Not Lynn and Sam, too.* It was certainly no secret among the family and close friends—and Cynthia supposed a good deal of the town by now—that this year's Thanksgiving feast at the McKinneys' had been something less than festive. Ruth had lost her baby a few days before the

holiday and was so distraught and depressed that she
and Tyler had stopped communicating all together.
The argument resulted in Ruth's leaving Crystal
Creek. Tyler had gone after his wife, but they were
both still in California and the situation was yet to be
resolved. At last report, they had reached a common ground of understanding, but the marriage was
still less than stable. Cynthia and J.T. had talked long
and often about the situation, both wanting to help
and both expressly forbidden to do so by Ruth *and*
Tyler.

"You don't mean you and Sam, do you?"

Lynn nodded.

"Oh, well, every couple goes through a period of
adjustment—"

"I-it's serious."

Cynthia gnawed on the inside of her lip. Talking
about pregnancy and childbirth experiences was one
thing, but talking woman to woman about marriage
with her stepdaughter was not a subject she was prepared for.

"You know, your daddy's in his study. Maybe
you'd feel better if I called him—"

"No! I don't want to talk to Daddy. He's as bad
as Sam. They're both so hung up on having everything just the way they want it. Everything in its place
and a place for everything. It drives me crazy."

Prepared or not, Cynthia decided, it appeared
talking about husbands was definitely on the agenda.

"No question about it, men can be infuriating at times. But Sam loves you—"

"I thought so, but now I'm not so sure."

"Oh, you can't actually think—"

"No. I'm serious, Cynthia. I don't think that Sam has completely gotten over the death of his first wife. I think that deep down, he's still in love with her and he's decided that he made a mistake marrying me."

Cynthia started to pooh-pooh the statement until she saw the sadness in Lynn's eyes. *Good Lord,* she thought, *the girl really believes what's she saying.* Of course, it wasn't true. It couldn't be. Rarely had two people fallen in love as hard or as fast as had Lynn McKinney and Sam Russell. But then, strong relationships weren't built overnight. Hers and J.T.'s marriage was certainly a perfect example.

Neither were relationships forgotten overnight, and maybe there was a grain of truth to what Lynn said about Sam's late wife.

"Have you tried talking to him?"

"He just keeps saying everything is fine, and I know it isn't. He won't talk to me."

"About anything?"

"Nothing that matters."

To you, or to him? Cynthia wondered, fully aware how couples who loved each other desperately could often be at cross purposes. "What do you think is wrong?"

Lynn shrugged. "When he asked me to marry him, I'm pretty darn sure he never expected me to get pregnant on our honeymoon."

"But he seems to be very happy about the baby."

"He says he is. But we argue. All the time. About little things mostly, but I hate it. And then, there's Allie and Sandy. It was bad enough when I was the only other thing they had to fight for Sam's attention, but now with the baby on the way..."

The hopeless shrug of her shoulder said more about her depth of depression than all the words she had spoken. Cynthia looked at Lynn and thought how incredibly young she looked, how incredibly young she *seemed* compared to most of her contemporaries. According to Lettie Mae, Lynn had grown up around men, but had almost no practical experience with them on a man-to-woman level. To say that her life had been sheltered until she'd met Sam was an understatement. For the first time Cynthia realized that, despite all her straightforward, speak-from-the-heart talk, Lynn probably suffered from an inferiority complex. Practical tips on how to manage an infant and still find a minute or two to organize a much needed evening together, Cynthia could handle. But she was way out of her depth trying to deal with low self-esteem, mostly because she still suffered from the same malady herself occasionally.

"You think they'll resent the baby even more once it's born?"

"I don't know, but I worry about it all the time."

"I think," said Cynthia, "that worrying all the time is your biggest problem." Once again she put her arm across Lynn's shoulders. "I'm not trying to make light of your feelings, but I know from personal experience that being pregnant is an emotional roller-coaster ride you can't stop. Maybe you're just worrying too much about things that will all work themselves out once the baby comes."

"I don't think so."

Feeling defeated with nowhere to go, Cynthia decided to try and change the subject to something—anything—that would help Lynn out of her doldrums. "Will you promise me something?"

"What?"

"Take a little time each day for yourself. Take a long soak or read a book—anything to help relax you."

"I'll try."

"Good, and in the meantime, maybe I could talk you into helping with the Christmas party."

"O-o-o-oh, Christmas," Lynn groaned.

"Only eight more shopping days."

"And I'm not anywhere near finished with my shopping."

"You *are* your father's daughter." Cynthia grinned. "He gets up every morning announcing that today is the day he's going to drive into Austin and finish his shopping. So far, his truck is not exactly burning up the road between here and the city."

"Dad has always been a Christmas Eve shopper. You think it's in the genes?"

Cynthia laughed. "Oh Lord, I hope not. That means Jennifer's got a fifty-fifty chance of being just like J.T." She rolled her eyes. "Heaven help me."

Lynn laughed, then realized how good it felt. "Thanks. I'm glad I stopped by."

"So am I. And," Cynthia said, her gaze meeting Lynn's directly, "you have a standing invitation. Any time you need to talk, or if you just want to get away for an hour or so, consider this your destination. I'm not, and probably never will be an authority on marriage, but I'm a terrific listener."

"Thanks. I feel better." Lynn smiled and headed for the door.

"Then, as Lettie Mae says, 'we done good.'" Going with her instincts, Cynthia gave her stepdaughter a gentle hug and was surprised to have it returned. "Take care of yourself."

"I will. And thanks again." With that, Lynn left.

Standing at the kitchen door, Cynthia watched the other woman walk toward her truck and prayed her problems would work themselves out.

"Was that Lynn?" J. T. McKinney walked into the kitchen, then over to where his wife was standing.

"Hmm." Cynthia continued to watch until Lynn climbed in her truck and drove away.

Noting her concentration, he asked, "Something wrong?"

She turned and looked into his eyes. How she hated to be the one to even mention that another of his children was unhappy, but better she than someone in town—an inevitability the next time Lynn sported a long face and a sad expression. "She told me that she and Sam are having problems."

For a moment Cynthia thought J.T. was going to cry. Only the night before, in the intimate darkness of their bedroom after making love, he had poured out all of his anxieties about his family and confessed to feeling at least partially to blame for some of Ruth and Tyler's problems. She had lain beside this man she loved so much, and her heart had almost broken as she listened to him speak his fears about his own inadequacies as a father and his worry for his firstborn.

Tenderly, she touched his cheek. "I won't have you blaming yourself, J.T."

"I haven't set a very good example, have I?"

Because of the basic truth in his words, Cynthia thought for a moment before responding. "Like everyone else, you've reacted and made decisions based on the values and behaviors you were taught. That doesn't make you a bad parent."

"Look at me, Cynthia. It's taken me more than fifty years to realize what's really important to me. I don't want my kids doing the same thing."

"Of course you don't. But J.T., they're all grown, making their own mistakes, which they will have to correct or learn to live with themselves. The best you—we can do, is to love them, and hopefully in the long run, they will be able to profit by our mistakes."

"I know," he said, but his words lacked conviction.

Cynthia had never seen her husband down and she didn't like it one bit. But, since Ruth and Tyler's separation, more than once she had caught him in deep contemplation, somber and obviously worried. "Sweetheart, as far as Lynn and Sam are concerned, I really don't think it's anything more than the kind of adjustments all couples have to go through. We lived through it and they will, too." She slid her arms around his waist and pulled him close. "Besides, I'm sure everything will be fine once the baby comes."

J.T. smiled, wanting to believe her. "Yeah. Everything will probably be fine once the baby comes."

THE HOLE IN THE WALL Dude Ranch was not exactly on her way home, but Lynn decided that she should check on the new boots she was having made for Sam and the girls for Christmas. At least, they were three presents she wouldn't have to be concerned about.

She drove through the main gate, bypassed the sprawling lodge and recreation center and several of the guest cabins until she came to the Old West–style building that housed La Herencia, the bootery owned by her brother Cal and his wife, Serena. Some of the finished boots were displayed and sold at the lodge, but the actual construction took place here at the recently added workshop. Each pair of boots was custom designed and handmade to order and visitors and guests could wander in and witness the boot-making process firsthand.

Serena had started small, depending on word of mouth and a reputation for quality to be her best marketing tools, and Cal had joined the business after retiring from the rodeo circuit. Their patience had finally paid off. La Herencia was fast gaining a reputation as maker of some of the finest quality boots in Texas. But the bootery wasn't the only iron Lynn's brother had in the fire. Recently, in partnership with Ken Slattery and his old rodeo buddy, Rio Langley, he had joined in a stock contracting ranch, had also invested in Tyler's winery and was, to use one of Lynn's great-grandfather Hank's phrases, "rollin' in it." But even though Cal and Serena were now financially comfortable, La Herencia remained their favorite endeavor.

Nestled between the beauty parlor and a general store—all for the exclusive use of the guests, and all with a Western facade—La Herencia was by far the most popular of all the shops set up on the Old West-style street. But instead of stopping in front, Lynn drove around to the back of the workshop and parked. As usual these days, she slipped rather than climbed out of the front seat of the pickup. She took several steps toward the back door of the workshop, but suddenly stopped and glanced back over her shoulder.

Someone's watching me.

She could feel the watcher's eyes on her as surely as she could feel the cotton shirt she wore next to her skin. Again, a chill swept over her body like an icy wind. She squinted her eyes against the late-morning sun, her gaze scanning the thick stand of live oak trees at the back of the property. Except for an almost imperceptible breeze, nothing moved. Seconds passed into minutes while she waited, straining to see if she could see anyone, but...nothing.

Don't be such a silly goose. Who would be watching you?

She turned back toward the workshop but couldn't completely shake the feeling that she was being watched. When she reached the door, she turned for one last look. But again, she saw nothing and so she stepped inside.

"Hey, Wylie, how are you?" she yelled, greeting one of La Herencia's craftsmen.

Wylie Crump was one of Serena's part-time workers and a true artist with leather. At age seventy-two, his eyes weren't what they once were, but his hands were as nimble as ever. "Fine and dandy, Miz Russell. And you're lookin' fit as a fiddle. Won't be long now 'fore that baby gets here, huh?"

"Not long. Are Cal and Serena around?"

"No ma'am, I'm pinch-hittin' for a while. Serena and Tracey Hernandez come by here early this morning on their way to New Braunfels. One of them charity fashion shows wanted to spotlight the boots, so off they went. Cal's over to the Langley place. None of 'em stand still for very long.''

"I know." She was disappointed at not being able to see Cal and Serena but, after all, that hadn't been the main reason for her visit. "Wylie, maybe you can tell me if the special order I placed with Cal is ready? There were three pairs of boots. One for my husband and one pair for each of his daughters—"

Wylie snapped his fingers. "I 'member Cal tellin' me when he first put that order in. You know, he keeps all the information in that fancy computer machine of his. Got lots of charts and schedules and such, but not me. I keep everythin' in this here book. Write it down in longhand myself. Lemme check."

"Thanks."

Just then some guests wandered in and wanted to watch the boot maker at work. "That's all right, Wylie, go ahead. I'm in no hurry," Lynn assured him.

"Now, if you folks'll step up to the workbench you can see how we do it. This here's our only vice," the old man said, pointing to what looked like an antique sewing machine. "We glue the sole pieces together, then stitch 'em. Then we stitch 'em again for strength." He slipped several cut pieces of leather in the shape of sole under the needle to demonstrate. "You folks plug up your ears 'cause this thing is damn near as old as I am and can holler just about as loud." With a flick of his wrist, he twisted the tension wheel and the needle began to rise and fall rapidly. The old equipment cracked like submachine gun fire, made even louder by the close quarters of the workshop. The guests were quick to follow Wylie's advice and plugged their ears. Lynn did the same. After what seemed like at least five minutes, the needle ceased its pumping, and all was quiet.

"I warned ya," Wylie said and the guests laughed, looked around for a few more minutes, then left. He winked at Lynn. "Runs 'em off every time. Be right back."

While Wylie checked his handwritten log, Lynn glanced around the workshop at the finished boots and those still in production. They were, quite simply, things of beauty. She had always thought a boot—the national footwear of Texas—was a boot, was a boot. Now, thanks to Serena's talent and flair for marketing, she knew differently. Each pair of boots was as individual as the person who wore them.

"Looks like they're finished, Miz Russell, but they're not here. Maybe up at the lodge. Want me to check?"

"That's all right, Wylie. I'll stop and check on my way out. Will you tell Cal and Serena I stopped by?"

"Sure thang."

With a smile and a wave, Lynn stepped out the back door and walked toward her truck. When she reached for the handle to unlock the door, she glanced down...

"Oh damn. My back tire is flat." She stepped back for a better look and discovered her front tire was flat as well. *Both?* "How can that be?" Had she driven over some broken glass or nails and not been aware of it?

On impulse, she walked around to the front of the truck and a soft gasp escaped her. Another few steps to the other side and...

"Oh my God. They're all flat!"

All four of the truck's tires were flatter than cold buckwheat pancakes.

"How in the world..."

Instinctively, she glanced up at the stand of live oaks, remembering her feeling that someone had been watching her. Fingers of fear clutched at her and panic rolled up from within her like a volcano about to erupt. *Get hold of yourself. Easy, easy.*

Lynn forced her fears to recede, forced the panic to give way to rational thinking. She stared at the deflated tires. "What in God's name did I drive over to puncture all four tires?"

She tried to think and for the life of her, couldn't recall anything that could account for flattening all her tires. She hadn't driven through anything or over anything. No glass, no nails. "How could this have happened?"

Wylie Crump stuck his head out the back door of the bootery. "You okay, Miz Russell? I never heard your truck start, so..." His eyes went wide. "Holy jumpin' Jehoshaphat! Would you look at that!"

"I—I...Wylie, I don't have any idea how...I can't even begin to imagine how this happened."

He walked up to the truck, hunkered down beside the left front wheel and began to run his hand over the tire tread. After a second he stopped, leaned closer to examine a spot. Then, without saying a word, he checked the left rear tire, then the remaining two. "Miz Russell," he said, turning to her with a perplexed frown on his face, "looks to me like somebody shot ever one of your tires."

"Shot?"

"Somebody took a gun and shot your tires smooth out. If you'd been movin', you'd had a wreck, sure enough. And it's a good thing you weren't settin' inside or you mighta been in a bucket fulla trouble. Coulda been real bad."

"But why would...who would do such a thing?"

He pushed his cowboy hat just far enough back to allow him to scratch his head, and for the Hill Country sunshine to emphasize the deep wrinkles in his weathered skin. "Beats me. Poachers maybe. Mr. Harris gets 'em occasionally, what with all them exotic animals around here."

"You think someone was aiming at an ostrich and hit my truck instead?" she said incredulously.

"Don't seem too logical, does it?"

"But I didn't hear any shots being fired."

"Musta happened while I was running the stitcher. Reckon I better fetch Mr. Harris."

"Wait," Lynn called out as he started to walk away. "I'll go with you." Suddenly the last thing she wanted was to be left alone.

WITHIN forty-five minutes Lynn found herself on her way home, courtesy of Scott and Val Harris.

"Lynn, I can't tell you how sorry I am that this happened to you."

"Scott, that's the third time you've apologized and it's not necessary."

"The hell it's not. You were on my property and you're out four tires. The Hole in the Wall carries insurance for just such a problem and I insist you allow me to take care of this."

"Don't be silly. It wasn't your fault."

"But we feel responsible," Val added.

Seated next to the passenger door with Val in the middle, Lynn had to lean forward to look at Scott. "But I can't—"

"No arguments. I'll have your truck back to you by tonight, good as new. Now, that's the end of it."

Val grinned. "He's cute when he's being masterful, isn't he?"

Lynn had to laugh. "Seriously," Val said, "the poachers were undoubtedly after some of our animals, and if they hadn't been, none of this would have happened to you. We wouldn't feel right *not* taking care of it."

When Lynn started to protest again, Scott held up his hand as if to silence her. "All right, all right," she finally agreed.

Val and Scott dropped her off at home, waiting until they were certain she was inside before driving off.

"Oh," Lynn said when she walked in and found Sam home.

"Hi. I thought I'd have a sandwich with my favorite wife, but she wasn't here." He noticed the flush on her cheeks and frowned. "You okay?"

"Fine," she replied a little breathlessly.

Sam glanced out the window. "Where's your truck?"

"Uh, well uh, there's a problem...."

"What kind of problem?"

"Well, you see—"

"You didn't have a wreck, did you?"

"No," she snapped. "Would you care if I had?"

Sam looked at his wife as if she had lost her mind. "What the hell kind of question is that?"

"A darn good one, if you ask me."

"I only thought that maybe...well, you looked so flustered...."

"You would too if all four of the tires on your vehicle were shot—"

"What do you mean, shot? Those were practically brand-new tires. Lynn, we've talked about this. You've got to take better care of that truck. We can't afford—"

"I said shot, S-H-O-T, as in bang, bang, you're dead." At that moment she could cheerfully have shot *him*. "I did not have a wreck. I went to La Herencia and while I was there somebody *shot*—"

she pointed her finger at him like a gun "—all four of my tires out. And, for your information, Scott's insurance will more than cover the cost of four new tires."

"Shot?" Sam said, her meaning finally coming through. "Are you all right?" He took a step toward her. "Are you hurt? The baby?"

"We're both fine," she assured him, satisfied that he had eventually asked the question she wanted to hear. "Just . . . just frustrated and worn-out."

Sam put his arms around her and pulled her close. "Poor baby." She laid her head on his chest and sighed. "Who in the world would do such a thing?"

"Scott and Val both think it was poachers."

"Poachers?"

"Hmm," she sighed again, feeling better the longer Sam held her. "Some folks don't like all those exotic animals. Scott said it had happened before."

"You sure you're okay?"

She nodded, her cheek brushing against his lightly starched collar.

"Well, that's all that matters." Sam kissed the top of her head and continued to hold her.

Lynn leaned into Sam's embrace, enjoying these brief moments of intimacy, and wishing they could last forever. For the moment she didn't want to think about being watched or shot at, or about anything but the feel of Sam's arms.

CHAPTER FOUR

"WELL, WELL," Sam announced, engrossed in his biweekly copy of the *Crystal Creek Record Chronicle.* "Looks like our little community had itself a burglary."

"A burglary?" Lynn set Sam's wheat toast and cereal in front of him.

"Manny Hernandez's office was vandalized night before last." He folded his copy of the newspaper and laid it beside his plate. "Not much taken, but a lot of weird stuff."

"Who would want to break into a vet's office? And what do you mean, weird stuff?" Although it was a school day, the girls had yet to make an appearance, and Lynn hoped they wouldn't for a few more minutes. This was the first quiet time she and Sam had had together in almost two weeks.

"No drugs were taken. No equipment. Only some frozen bull semen."

"Bull semen?"

Sam took a sip of coffee. "You heard correctly. I'm told some cattlemen consider semen from certain bulls to be as valuable as gold."

"Sure, but . . . stealing it?"

"Actually, I knew about it before now."

"Who told you?"

"Ten," Sam said, referring to his receptionist-technician, Tennie Williams. "And Rosa over at the café told her. It seems that Bubba Gibson told Rosa. And Bubba got the news from the sheriff. All of which probably took less than an hour with the way gossip travels in this town."

"Don't I know," Lynn mumbled, fully aware that since Thanksgiving her family had been the subject under discussion among many of Crystal Creek's residents.

"The paper indicates very little damage was done to the office, but the word is, some of Manny's equipment was destroyed and the place was generally trashed." Sam took a deep breath, his jaw tense. He didn't even want to think about what he would do under similar circumstances. At the moment he was counting every nickel and stretching every dollar as far as it would go. If it had been *his* office that had been vandalized, he suspected he might very possibly have had to close his doors. "I hope he had insurance up the wazoo."

Lynn cut him a glance. He sounded so cold, so bitter. "I'm sure he does. But we should be thankful Manny wasn't working late as he does so often. No telling what could have happened."

"Of course, I'm glad he wasn't there," he snapped.

"Well, don't bite my head off."

"I wasn't—"

"Good morning," Sandy and Allie said, one right after the other.

Sam offered his daughters a bright smile. "Good morning."

Lynn attempted to match her smile to Sam's. "What would you like for breakfast? There're some hot biscuits on the stove and some bacon draining on a paper towel."

Allie wrinkled her nose. "Too much fat for me. I'll just have cereal."

Her eyes sparkling in anticipation, Sandy headed for the food. "I'll eat hers."

Allie made an oinking sound.

"Don't start," Sam warned, then went back to reading his paper.

"Oh, by the way, have either of you girls seen my silver earrings?" Lynn asked. "You know, the ones with the black and turquoise stones that Serena brought back for me from her last trip to Colorado? I can't find them anywhere."

"I haven't seen them," Sandy said, taking her first bite of a hot, buttered biscuit.

"Allie?" Lynn asked when the other girl didn't reply.

The teenager's cereal-laden spoon stopped halfway to her mouth. "Same here. I haven't the vaguest idea where they could be."

Lynn glanced over at Sam's oldest daughter.

"Are you sure?"

Allie stopped eating. "Sure, I'm sure. What would I know about your lost earrings?"

A lot, Lynn thought. *Like, where they are.* There was no question in her mind that Allie was lying. She simply *knew* it. Maybe she was getting the hang of this motherhood thing after all. Hadn't she heard all her life that mothers always knew when their children weren't telling the truth? *I may not be her mother, but I'd bet my last dollar she's lying through her clean, white teeth.* "If you should run across them, either of you—" she turned to include Sandy in her gaze "—please let me know."

"Okay."

"Of course." Allie pushed her half-full cereal bowl away from her. "I'm stuffed," she announced, leaving the table. "Okay if I wait for you in the car, Daddy?"

"Sure, sweetheart."

Out of the corner of her eye, Lynn saw Allie give her one last look before she left the room.

"Sam—"

"Oh, honey, would you pick up the dry cleaning? I'm running out of clean shirts." He pushed his chair back from the table.

"Of course. Sam—"

"And you need to have your Suburban serviced."

"All right, but—"

"Promise?"

"Yes, I promise. Sam, I think we should talk about the girls."

"What about the girls?"

"Oh, you know, rules, and the consequences when they break them. That sort of thing."

Sam kissed her lightly on the lips. "You're sweet to worry, but I don't think we have to start locking them in their rooms just yet."

"Please don't make light of this, Sam. All children need boundaries. They need to know how far they can go and what will happen when they cross the line."

He grinned. "You've been reading those parenting books again. Good girl. You can pick up lots of tips for when the baby arrives." He kissed her again and headed for the door. "Gotta go. Don't forget about your truck. Love ya."

Lynn stared after him, feeling the need to throw a good, old-fashioned temper tantrum—until she realized that then she would be acting in a manner befitting the way her husband was treating her—like a child.

How dare he walk away from me like that! I'm his wife, not one of his kids! "You might be ten years older than me, Sam Russell, but that doesn't make you any smarter." She waved her fist in the air. "In fact, you're dumb as dirt," she shouted to the now-empty house.

That afternoon after Allie got home from school, Lynn's silver earrings mysteriously turned up in the pocket of one of her shirts, and Allie just happened to discover them while sorting the laundry.

IN THE DWINDLING TWILIGHT, Walt Taggart carefully eyed the man getting out of the custom-finished and immaculately clean pickup truck not thirty yards from where he had parked his own Scrambler. In his mid-thirties, dressed in Levi's and a bold-colored Western shirt that undoubtedly bore a label with the signature of a popular country and western singer, the man was the perfect example of a media-image cowboy.

Tag didn't like the look of him worth a damn. *Drugstore cowboy. Useless as tits on a boar.*

When the man saw the rifle resting in the crook of Tag's arm, he stopped, leaving about five yards between them. "Y-you Taggart?"

"Who's askin'?"

"A-a customer."

"Who sent ya?"

"Stillwell."

"Come ahead."

"I guess you're the careful sort," the man said.

"Bet on it. You got my money?"

"Yeah." The man pulled a handful of folded bills from his jeans pocket. "This is top-quality stuff, right?"

Tag eyed the wad of money and decided this joker was as green as the rest of the men in the syndicate—mostly doctors, lawyers and other yuppie

professionals—who fancied themselves as gentle-
men ranchers.

"Stillwell and my friends in the cattle syndicate
told me—"

"I ain't interested in your life history—" his gaze
raked the other man from the top of his well-blocked
Stetson to his fancy boots "—dude."

The customer nodded and counted out six one-
hundred-dollar bills. "Here you go." He held out the
crisp new money.

"You know, mister, I've seen some fools in my
time, but you take the cake."

"Excuse me?"

"It ain't what I'd call bright to try and cheat a man
when he's holdin' a gun."

"Cheat? What makes you think I'm trying to
cheat you?"

"The price is eight hundred, and unless I forgot
how to count, there's only six hundred in your
hand." Casually, Tag shifted the weight of the rifle
so that his fingers were poised, but not clutching, the
trigger. His knowledge of guns was second only to his
knowledge of horses.

The effect on the other man of that single movement was anything but casual. "Hey, hey." He held
up both hands in protest, his gaze fixed on the gun.
"They told me the price was six. I'm only the messenger."

Tag narrowed his gaze. "Well, I'm tellin' you that
eight hundred is the price. Take it or leave it."

"I'll take it," the man said without hesitation. In a flash, he fished two more bills out of the wad of hundreds still in his hand.

Tag took the money, stuffed it into his shirt pocket, then reached over into the bed of the Scrambler, opened a small ice chest and retrieved a vial of bull semen—all without altering his hold on the rifle. He handed the vial to its new owner.

The man looked at the small glass cylinder. "Is this it?"

He raised a bushy eyebrow. "Don't take much."

"Yeah. Uh, yeah. Guess you're right. Well," the customer said, uncertain how to end the transaction, "thanks."

Tag didn't answer, only watched the man back away, then turn and reach for the door of the chrome-fancied truck. Suddenly, for no reason other than he was itching to vent his rage and this jerk was a handy target, he decided the opportunity was too good to pass up. *What the hell. This son of a bitch is too dumb to live. But I'll have a little fun with him first.*

"Hold it...dude." Tag stepped away from his own vehicle, putting him at an angle, rather than in front of the other man.

The customer froze.

"I'm gonna do you a favor."

"A-a favor?"

"Yeah. I've decided you're too dumb to be runnin' around loose." With one hand he raised the rifle and pointed it at the dude's chest. "And you're sure as hell too stupid to be walkin' around with that kinda money. Let's have it," he said, motioning with his other hand.

"H-have what?"

"You're already buckin' for jackass of the year. Don't make it worse. Now pitch that fistful of bills over here before I decide to make that your epitaph."

"Look." The dude held up both hands. "This money doesn't belong to me. If I come back without it, my ass is grass. For cryin' out loud, I'm just a messenger—"

"Shut up and toss me the money or you're gonna be a dead messenger."

"Hey, listen—"

With an ever so slight adjustment in order to alter trajectory, Tag shifted the barrel of the rifle upward and fired. The shot sent the dude's hat flying off into the darkness. Then, in a flash, he tried to open the door to the truck in order to escape.

Tag put a shot into the truck about four inches above the handle.

The guy jumped as if he had been hit instead of his truck. "Don't—don't shoot," he begged, cramming his hands into his pocket. In a heartbeat he pulled out the money and threw it toward the back of the Scrambler.

Tag glanced over to where the knot of bills had rolled to a stop not three yards away, then glanced back at the dude. He swung the rifle into a dead-on position, but the other man was quicker than Tag expected. Seizing the split second of hesitation, he jumped inside the truck, slumped down in the seat, started the engine and shoved it into Reverse. Tires spun and gravel spewed as the truck shot backward down the road, only the very top of the dude's head visible as he made his hasty getaway. Fifteen seconds later the truck screeched to a halt, made a one-hundred-eighty-degree turn, then raced off into the night.

"Stupid jackass," Tag said as he checked the rifle, then climbed into his own vehicle and headed for his campsite by the Claro River. Now that he had a bankroll, he could step things up a bit, and the beauty of it was, no one was going to come looking for the money. How did one thief turn in another? *When you're dealin' with hot merchandise you gotta expect to get burned once in a while.*

Tag laughed out loud. "Now for the fun part. Your turn, Duchess."

"YOU GONNA BE all right here by yourself, Lynn?" Sandy scraped the remains of her meat loaf dinner into the garbage disposal.

"Of course," Lynn said as she loaded the dishwasher with dirty dishes. It was Friday and both of the girls were spending the night away from home: Sandy with a friend from the old neighborhood in Austin and Allie with her new best friend in the whole, wide world—or at least Crystal Creek. "Besides," she said, grinning, "if anybody tries to snatch me away in the night, they'll turn me loose when the sun comes up and they get a good look at me. Who would want to kidnap a short, fat, pregnant woman?"

Sandy giggled. "You're not as fat as some of the pictures of my mother."

Bent from the waist, holding a dinner plate in her hand, Lynn halted. "I'm not?"

"Daddy said she was huge with Allie and even huger—"

"Even larger," Lynn corrected.

"Yeah, even larger with me. We've got pictures somewhere."

Lynn straightened, massaging her back. "You don't say." She knew it sounded crazy, but Sandy's simple statement was the bright spot in an otherwise dismally gray day. And to think that there might actually be photographs to prove it was almost too much to hope for. She had, of course, seen snapshots of Sam's late wife, Marta, but those pictures had presented her as a tall, slender, dark-haired woman of delicate beauty—the antithesis of Lynn. To actually find one that showed the paragon of motherhood with tired eyes, swollen feet and something less than a sweet smile on her face was a rather delicious idea.

You should be ashamed of yourself, Lynn McKinney Russell. How can you be jealous of a dead woman?

Jealousy wasn't exactly the word for the emotion Lynn felt for Sam's first wife. Envy was a better word. She absolutely, positively envied the woman's obvious ability to manage a marriage, a home, children, and a thriving medical practice. *How did she do it? I can barely find the time to go grocery shopping and cook dinner.*

"Lynn?"

"What?" Lynn said, realizing Sandy had called her name for the second time.

"I'm done cleaning off the table." She tossed the sponge she had just used into the side of the sink opposite the garbage disposal.

"Thanks. Uh, do you have your overnight bag all packed?"

The eleven-year-old gave her new stepmother a look that could only be defined as pained. "You mean my duffel."

Realizing her terribly old-fashioned mistake, Lynn smiled. "Of course. Now, I know Susan's mother is picking you up at Dr. Bailey's after your cello lesson, but what time is she bringing you home tomorrow?"

"Gee, it's Saturday. Who knows?"

"Well, your dad and I would like to know. How about noon? That should give you plenty of time to sleep as late as you want."

"Okay, I guess. When's Allie have to be home?"

"The same time."

"I don't think she's going to like that," Sandy singsonged.

Too bad, Lynn thought. "Why not?"

"'Cause she and Mary June Wynn have got plans. I heard her talking on the phone."

Lynn suspected the eavesdropping had been deliberate, but didn't confront the issue. *Now what? Do I ask about the plans and run the risk of being labeled a snoop? Or tell Sandy she needs to learn to respect privacy if she ever hopes to have any for herself?*

"When I was little I used to love to eavesdrop on my brothers' telephone conversations, then tease them." Sandy's gaze darted to hers. "But when I got old enough to receive phone calls myself, they paid me back and I have to admit, it wasn't very much fun."

"I wasn't listening on purpose."

"Of course not. I know that you're mature enough to realize that *everyone* needs some privacy."

"She doesn't know the meaning of the word."

Lynn and Sandy glanced up to find Allie standing in the kitchen doorway.

"Yes, I do," Sandy insisted.

"You little narc."

"Am not."

"Girls," Lynn began, trying to intercede.

"Are so. Narc, narc, narc. That's all you are."

"I am *not*." Sandy stomped her foot.

"Girls!" When quiet once again settled in the room, Lynn turned to the younger sister. "Sandy, go upstairs and make sure you didn't leave any lights on in your room."

"O-kay."

"And Allie—"

"Where's Daddy? Isn't he going to take me to Mary June's house, or am I going to have to walk?" The put-upon expression on her face was a perfect match for the one Sandy had worn earlier.

"No, you won't have to walk. Walking isn't safe even in a town like Crystal Creek. And no, your father won't be driving you. He's working late. I'll drop you off at your girlfriend's house when I take Sandy to her lesson."

"But that's not for another half hour."

"So?"

"So, everybody will..."

"Everybody what?"

"Oh...oh, nothing." Allie turned and went upstairs.

Thirty minutes later, Lynn pulled her Suburban to a stop in front of Mary June Wynn's house and Allie scrambled out as fast as she could. As was the usual game plan whenever there was a sleep-over, Mary June's mother had been contacted. Lynn had verified that the Wynns planned to play cards at their next-door neighbor's house for a couple of hours and the girls would be supervised. Had it not been for the fact that she had talked to Mrs. Wynn, Lynn might have wondered at Allie's eagerness. But all appeared to be in order, and she left feeling comfortable with the arrangements.

An hour and forty-five minutes later she had dropped Sandy at Dr. Bailey's in Austin, made a brief stop at the supermarket and returned home. With a deep sigh of relief, she kicked off her shoes, grabbed the mystery novel she had started the week before and prepared to take Cynthia's advice and indulge herself. Uninterrupted reading time was practically a thing of the past since her wedding, and she suspected, once the baby arrived, she would have even less. Tonight she intended to take full advantage of her solitude. With a tape of Christmas carols playing softly in the background, she settled down to enjoy her novel.

Lynn had no idea how long she had been reading when she heard the noise. It sounded like someone was in the garage. *No, that's crazy,* she thought. But crazy or not, the noise did sound like someone or something had moved the galvanized bucket she used when mopping floors. She usually left the bucket at the bottom and just to the left of the garage steps. The sound—a scraping, metal-scooting-over-concrete kind of noise—was too raspy to be the wind and too loud to be coming from outside the house.

Lynn went back to her novel, but the noise came again.

"Oh-h-h-h, I'll bet it's that possum I saw the other day," she thought, frustrated at the interruption. "Little varmint, probably came into the garage looking for food and accidentally got closed inside." She decided to ignore it.

After several unsuccessful moments of trying to climb back into the story on the pages, she gave up and decided to chase out the trespassing possum. Knowing the winter night could sometimes turn chilly, she slipped into a lightweight cardigan, then marched straight to the broom closet, selected her weapon—a serviceable broom with good, sturdy, old-fashioned straw bristles—and prepared to engage the enemy.

"All right, you little varmint," she announced, determined to be victorious. "Prepare to meet your maker—" She opened the back door, stepped onto the garage landing... and found herself in complete darkness.

She reached for the wall switch, flipped it once. Twice. Nothing happened. "Great. The bulb is out. Now I've got to go find a flash—" A noise, this one sounding like the wind blowing over dry leaves, brought her up short. The sound was close by. But in which direction? She couldn't be sure. Then it stopped.

"Damn," Lynn muttered, and went to fetch a flashlight. Twenty seconds later she was standing in almost the exact same spot...and she heard the noise again. This time it sounded as if it was coming from the area around the bottom of the steps. She flicked on the flashlight, aimed the beam downward . . .

And almost screamed.

Not two steps away from where she stood was a copperhead snake, approximately five feet long.

"Oh, my God," she gasped, staring at the highly venomous snake caught in the glaring beam of light. She swallowed hard, feeling as if she were frozen to the spot, while at the same time a remote part of her brain kept screaming, unheeded, for her legs to move, move—

The copperhead began to slither toward her, and the message from brain to muscle finally connected. Lynn jumped backward into the kitchen and slammed the door.

Her pulse hammering in her throat, Lynn made it to one of the kitchen chairs before she started to cry. And shake. And cry harder.

She had lived in the Hill Country all her life and on the fingers of one hand could count the number of times she had actually seen a live snake. And she had *never* come face to face with a copperhead! But her great-grandfather, Hank, had. Lynn remembered being no more than five, maybe six, when her father had brought Hank in off the range, his leg already badly swollen from a copperhead bite. She also remembered how her great-grandfather's leg had continued to swell to the point that Dr. Purdy had even talked about taking "drastic measures." At that young age Lynn had no idea what such measures could mean. She only knew the look on her mother's and father's faces had been more frightening than anything she had ever known.

"I need to call Sam," she whispered, her voice as shaky as her hands. But when she tried to stand, she found her legs were also trembling. "Just...take it...easy," she told herself. "Take a deep breath." She did. "Now another. And another." Finally, she was steady enough to walk the several feet to the phone and dial Sam's number at the Crystal Creek office.

"Dr. Russell," he answered immediately.

"Sam?" Her voice was still paper thin.

"Lynn? Honey, is that you?"

The sound of his voice was the most wonderful thing she had ever heard. "I—I—I..." She took another deep breath and tried not to stutter. "I...found a...s-s-snake in the garage."

"A snake! Are you all right?"

"I'm fine. Fine."

"It didn't bite—"

"N-no. But i-it's still out there."

Sam's sigh of relief sang through the telephone wires. "Okay. Just don't go back in the garage—

"Don't worry, I won't."

"I'll be there in five minutes."

"Hurry," was her only reply.

Sam took only enough time to call Wayne Jackson, the sheriff of Claro County, tell him the problem and ask him to send one of his officers to the house, double quick. The uniformed officer showed up at almost the same time as Sam pulled up in front of his house, slammed on the brakes and raced inside. Lynn was still sitting in the kitchen chair, but the instant he came through the door, she jumped up, hurried to him and threw her arms around his neck in a fierce embrace.

"I've never been so clear-to-the-bone scared in all my life."

"You sure you're all right?" He pulled back enough to look into her eyes. She nodded.

"Dr. Russell?" the officer said from the open front door.

Lynn looked around just as Sam said, "Come on in." Then to her he explained, "I called the sheriff because I didn't know what people did in cases like this." He tried to lighten the mood with a grin. "We city boys don't have much experience in this area."

The officer, a new recruit and not anyone Lynn recognized, tipped his hat, but didn't remove it. In his right hand he held a long metal wand with a braided wire loop at one end and a cord running from the loop down the wand. A heavy cotton duck drawstring hung from his belt. "Ma'am. If you could show me the last location of the snake?"

She licked her lips. "In the garage." She pointed to the door. "On the steps. And the light bulb is burned out," she added quickly.

Lynn and Sam waited while the policeman, using a flashlight with a beam strong enough for a searchlight, checked out the garage. "Found him," they heard several moments later. "Doctor, could you hit the automatic garage door opener?"

Sam walked to the door, reached around and touched a small transmitter mounted on the other side of the wall switch. Instantly, the big hinged door began to grind upward.

Lynn walked up behind Sam in time to see the officer carry their unwanted visitor off in the drawstring bag. Her whole body slumped forward in relief. "Thank God."

Sam turned and gathered her in his arms. "You okay, now?" She nodded. "The officer motioned for me to meet him out front. Probably has to make some kind of report." He kissed the top of her head. "I'll be right back. Why don't you go on up to bed? And I'll be there as quick as I can."

"Hurry," she said once again.

After what seemed like an hour but was in fact only minutes, Sam closed the door to their bedroom behind him and came to her.

He sat down beside her on the bed. "You sure you're okay?"

"A little shaky, but I'm fine."

His voice was whisper-soft as he reached out and stroked her cheek. "I don't even want to think about what could have happened."

"Me either," she murmured, reveling in his caress.

He held her sweet face in his hands and stared into her eyes. "If you had taken two more steps in the darkness..." His voice trailed off and he shook his head as if to dispel the image of what might have been. He gathered her in his arms and held her tight.

"Oh, Sam," she whispered, kissing his neck, his jaw.

He turned his head and found her lips moist and waiting.

His original intent had been only to comfort, to reassure, but as usual, he couldn't kiss her without wanting more. He couldn't touch her without needing more.

Delicious sensations wound through Lynn. The familiar melting in her middle. The aching in her breasts that always made her want to feel Sam's mouth there. The wonderful exhilaration, anticipation.

As he deepened the kiss, his hands moved over her shoulders and down her arms, then cupped her breasts.

"Ahh." She arched her back, taking her mouth from his.

"Tender?"

"A little."

"I'm sorry. I'll stop—"

"No, don't. Actually... it feels kind of... good."

"You sure I'm not hurting you?" He gently caressed her.

"Positive."

"Here?" he asked, stroking the soft fullness in ever shortening circles toward her nipple.

"Yes." She sighed.

"And here?" He teased her nipples until she again arched her back. Only this time she put her hands at the back of his neck and urged his head down.

He moved his mouth from side to side over each nipple, loving the soft little sounds she made, the almost urgent shifting of her legs against his. His hands slid over her belly and he felt his child move beneath his hands.

"Is it okay? Maybe we shouldn't—"

"Yes, we should." She unbuttoned his shirt and pushed it from his shoulders and down his arms.

"But what if I hurt you?"

"You won't." She reached for his belt. "And Dr. Nate said we've got a little more time yet."

Sam pulled back just long enough to step out of his jeans. "Then I guess we better make every minute count."

Lynn forgot about her anxieties, about the near miss with a poisonous snake. The only thing she remembered for the rest of the night was how right it felt to be in his arms. How wonderfully right it felt to love and be loved by Sam. For this brief time they were free of the thousand and one little things that seemed to form an ever-widening wedge between them during the daylight hours.

CHAPTER FIVE

THE FOLLOWING MORNING Lynn woke up and gazed over at Sam sleeping peacefully beside her.

We touch each other and our emotions automatically kick in, take us to such wonderful intimacy, she thought, remembering the night past. *I wish we could feel that closeness somewhere other than the night.*

But outside the bedroom reality seemed to separate them. For Lynn, part of that reality was trying to live up to the memory of Marta Russell, and as far as she could see, progress was painstakingly slow.

"Oh, stop dwelling on that, for heaven's sake," she said out loud.

"What?" Sam said, stretching as he came slowly awake. "What did you say, sweetheart?"

"Uh, I said, 'Are you going to sleep all day, for heaven's sake?' "

"Hmmm, wouldn't that be a treat. Just you and me in a big ol' pile of bare arms and legs..."

Even though he continued to speak, inside Lynn's head his voice faded away, and all she heard were the words "you and me in a big ol' pile," repeated over and over. But the voice wasn't Sam's. She was remembering the sound of Walt Taggart's voice as he had spoken almost the exact same words. A cold chill skated down her spine, and she shook off a shiver.

"Obviously you don't care for the idea."

"What?" she asked, finally realizing he was talking to her.

"I said something about just the two of us spending the day together. Maybe a movie or a picnic. No kids, no phones, no interruptions...but I guess not."

"No, Sam, I didn't mean...I wasn't listening. My mind was somewhere else."

"Seems to be happening a lot lately." For a moment, she thought she saw genuine disappointment in his eyes, heard it in his voice, but then it was gone. "But," he said in a rather forced, bright tone, "that's probably way too much activity for a woman in your condition. You should probably rest and reserve your strength."

"No, you don't understand."

"It's okay. And you really should take better care of yourself."

"Good Lord, I'm pregnant, I'm not dying...." Her eyes widened in horror as she realized that what she said *had* to have recalled memories of Marta's death. "Oh, Sam, I didn't mean... that just slipped out... I'm so sorry."

"I know." He smiled, but she could see the hurt in his eyes. "It happens. No big deal." Now his smile seemed a little too bright, too fixed. He threw back the covers, got out of bed and slipped into his robe.

"Listen, why don't you just relax and I'll put on the coffee. How about some pancakes and bacon?"

"No thanks," she whispered.

"I'll give a yell when the coffee's ready."

She nodded and he went downstairs.

"Great. Wonderful. Way to spoil the mood." Lynn fell back on the bed and called herself several kinds of fool for her slip of the tongue. "Why didn't you just broadside the man with a two-by-four and be done with it?" Feeling embarrassed and guilty, she dressed and went downstairs, intending to make it up to her husband by cooking the best country breakfast he had ever eaten. But by the time she came downstairs, he was on the phone with a patient.

"I see. Well, of course, Mrs. Browning, I'll be happy to take a look at it right away." He glanced at Lynn as she entered the kitchen and motioned to the pot of freshly brewed coffee. "Sure. Give me fifteen minutes and I'll meet you at my office. No problem." He hung up. "As you probably heard, that was a patient."

"I figured as much."

"She broke her crown—"

"And Jill came tumbling after," Lynn finished, trying to lighten the tension between them.

Sam grinned. "That's cute." Despite the grin, she doubted he thought it humorous. "I hate to cut into our Saturday time, but I really do have to take care of this."

"Of course." She sipped her coffee. "Go. I'll be fine. Besides, the girls will be home in a couple of hours."

"I doubt Mrs. Browning will take that long," Sam said, then added, "but you never can tell."

"No, you never can." She wondered if he would stretch the time to the limit because it would mean less time he would have to spend with her.

He returned to their bedroom and in a few moments came back downstairs, dressed and with his car keys in his hand. "When I get back, remind me to replace that bulb in the garage."

"Hmm," Lynn said, sipping her coffee. "We don't want any more visits like the one we got last night from our nasty little friend. But I can do it."

"No," he insisted. "I don't want you climbing on a ladder in your condition."

"But that's silly. I can—"

He held up his hand to silence her. "I'll take care of it." He walked over and briefly kissed her on the lips. "I'll call you and let you know when I'll be home."

"Fine." She closed the door behind him and went to the window. *I'm not helpless, for crying out loud. I'm surprised he didn't pat me on the head. O-o-oh, sometimes I could just...* She was torn between indignation and pain, between longing for Sam's attention and disappointment over the kind of attention she received. Her hands resting on the windowsill, she watched him drive off until his car disappeared from sight. Until she felt the first tear splash onto her hands.

Lynn had no idea how long she stood at the window and cried. It seemed that lately crying was the thing she did best, and today didn't appear to be any exception. Finally, she dried her eyes, deciding she was sick and tired of feeling like poor pitiful Pearl. She had plenty to do around the house to keep her busy.

Starting with replacing the burned out light bulb in the garage.

Armed with an I'll-show-him attitude and a new bulb tucked into the pocket of her shirt, she hauled out the sturdy wooden four-step ladder Sam kept handy. As she put her foot on the first rung, she glanced toward the light fixture.

The bulb wasn't just burned out; it was completely broken with only the filament remaining. "That's strange." She looked at the floor of the garage. No glass. Not a fragment. "That's *really* strange. How do you break a light bulb and not wind up with broken glass everywhere?" She reached up and touched the filament and discovered the bulb was loose in the socket, almost as if someone had been in the process of unscrewing it when it broke in his hand. Almost as if someone had deliberately meant to destroy the bulb without anyone knowing about it. Almost as if someone had caught the glass in his hand and carried it away...

"And that's exactly what you're doing, Miss Wild Imagination. Getting carried away." Lynn shook her head as if to clear away the disturbing thought, then finished installing the new light bulb.

True to Lynn's prediction, Allie and Sandy arrived home shortly. Sandy hit the door gushing about some video game her girlfriend had, then headed straight for the refrigerator. Like most growing girls, she consumed enough food to feed a football team, and burned the calories off the way a steam engine burns coal. Fifteen minutes later, Allie walked through the door accompanied by Mrs. Wynn, and right away, Lynn could tell something was wrong.

"Uh, listen, Lynn," Darlene Wynn began. "We had a little, uh, situation at my place last night."

"Situation?"

"I told you Earl and I would be playin' canasta last night for a couple of hours, didn't I?"

"At your next door neighbor's."

"Right. Well, it seems during those two hours Mary June, Allie and another one of their girl friends decided to invite company over to the house. *Male* company."

Lynn turned to Allie. "Is this true?"

There was just enough fear mixed with the teenager's rebellion to make her aware she was in real trouble. "Yes ma'am."

"I see." Truly shocked, Lynn wasn't quite sure how to respond.

"Of course, Mary June is as much to blame as the other two girls. More, because it's her house and she knows how her daddy and I feel about such behavior. I don't know what I'm gonna do with that girl."

"Darlene, I don't quite know what to say. I'm sorry if it's caused you any embarrassment—"

"I'm not embarrassed. I'm mad as hell and I grounded Mary June for a week."

"You have every right to be upset. I don't blame you." When Darlene didn't leave right away, it became clear that she was waiting to speak to Lynn privately. "All right, Allie, why don't you wait for me in your room?"

"Yes ma'am."

When she had gone, Darlene stepped closer. "I didn't wanna say anything in front of Allie, but Earl really gave those boys what for. He told them Mary June and her friends were decent girls and he wasn't gonna put up with any shenanigans. He also told them he intended to call their parents and they better not come sniffin' around again."

"I'm sure he handled it very well, Darlene."

"Well, I've raised four girls and take it from me, they can be sneaky little devils. When they hit the boy crazy stage—and Mary June is showin' all the signs—they go a little nuts. Too bad parents can't keep them locked up between the ages of thirteen and eighteen until they get a little sense."

At the moment, Darlene's solution sounded infinitely reasonable to Lynn. It wasn't, of course, but confining Allie to her room was certainly within the realm of possibility.

"Thanks again, for bringing Allie home and for taking care of the situation. And thank Earl for me, too."

"Sure thing, honey. And don't get your tail over the dashboard about this. They're just bein' teenagers—Lord help us—and this probably won't be the last time." Darlene Wynn walked to the front door and Lynn followed. "Gimme a call when you and Sam figure out how you're gonna handle Allie's punishment, will ya? I don't want Mary June tormentin' me with stuff like 'nobody else got grounded' or 'everybody's free but me.'"

"Yes, of course. I'll let you know."

"And chin up, sugar." She patted Lynn's stomach. "You got years before this one needs a short leash."

After Darlene left, Lynn thought again about calling Sam, but decided against it. Even if he was through with Mrs. Browning's crown, there was no point telling him this kind of news over the phone. When she told him, she wanted him to be able to deal with the situation immediately. And if she was honest with herself, she wanted to see his reaction.

Not that she wanted to cause him any pain—and this surely would—but she needed to see if his overprotective attitude toward both of his girls would cloud his judgment. Sam was not a disciplinarian and Lynn had come to realize he was anything but strict where Allie and Sandy were concerned. Discipline must have been the province of the late Marta Russell, as well. *Add some more sparkle to the woman's halo.*

At any rate, this problem was not going to go away. Lynn knew all too well the churning emotions a young girl could experience, particularly after she'd lost her mother. She had been not much older than Allie when her own mother died, and she had dealt her father a great deal of misery afterward.

Looking back now, Lynn could honestly say that she might have gone on grieving, torturing herself and everyone else in the family, if J.T. hadn't decided enough was enough. Her father might not have understood the tender heart of a young girl, but he knew that even grief was no excuse for disrespect and lack of consideration. For months after her mother's death, Lynn had been a sullen, unresponsive, spoiled brat, taking advantage of the fact that she was the only daughter. Finally, her daddy had stalked into her room and told her he was sick and tired of the whole family having to tiptoe around her like she was some princess. He told her that just because her mother was gone didn't mean she held sole grieving rights and it was time she looked around and took note of how much the rest of the family was hurting. If it hadn't been for that angry, but overwhelmingly honest appraisal of her behavior, she might have continued to hoard her grief until she couldn't express it, keep it bottled up so long it was detrimental to her own future.

Lynn knew Allie was hurting, but she also knew that sometimes leaving someone alone to her grief—even out of love—was the wrong strategy. She knew how that kind of pain could fester, breeding anger and resentment against those who loved you the most. She didn't want that for Allie or for Sam.

An hour later Sam walked in to find Lynn and Sandy eating lunch and wearing two of the longest faces he had ever seen. "What's going on?" He glanced into the living room, where Allie usually spent time on the phone. "Where's Allie?"

"Upstairs in her room," Lynn replied.

"Can she come down now, Daddy? Lynn said she had to stay there until you got home."

Sam looked from his daughter to his wife, who was refusing to look him in the eye. Something *was* going on. "I think maybe we better wait until I find out what's going on here."

"Sandy, would you give your dad and me a few minutes to talk alone?" Lynn asked. The girl shrugged her narrow shoulders, then picked up her sandwich and soda and left the room.

"All right, now. Just exactly what—"

"Would you like a cup of coffee?" Lynn tried to keep her voice calm, but her insides were fluttering.

"No, I don't want coffee. I want to know what the hell is going on around here!"

"You don't have to yell."

"Lynn, just tell me."

"All right. I'll give it to you straight. It seems Allie and a couple of her girlfriends invited some young men over to visit last night, only they forgot to ask the Wynns' permission. Or ours either, for that matter."

"What!"

"And they might have gotten away with it, if Darlene Wynn hadn't walked back in unexpectedly and interrupted the little get-together."

Stunned, Sam couldn't believe his ears. *Allie? It can't be. She's never done anything like this in her life.* "Well, why in the hell weren't the Wynns keeping an eye on them?" he blurted, finding it easier to place blame than deal with reality. "They had no business leaving children alone in a house."

"Sam, we talked about this when Allie asked our permission to spend the night. The Wynns told us they were going to be next door playing cards for a couple of hours, and you agreed it was fine."

"Well, I never thought anything like this would happen." Then, as if an explanation had just popped into his head, a hope gleamed in his eyes. "Are we sure Allie was even a party to all of this? Maybe she didn't even participate. I mean, in the back of my mind I knew she was approaching the age where she would start thinking about boys, but she really hasn't shown any signs—"

"Sam, would you listen to yourself?"

"What do you mean?"

It was pitiful, but understandable, that intellectually, he wanted to keep the girls confined to their childhood, but surely he couldn't look away from the facts when they had practically slapped him in the face.

"'Not a party to all this,' 'approaching the age to start thinking about boys,' 'showing no signs.' Open your eyes, sweetheart! Allie is thirteen—"

"She's only twelve."

Lynn sighed. "In a couple of days she'll be thirteen. Officially a teenager, whether you like it or not. Whether you accept it or not."

"What does that mean?"

"It means that if you want to keep her a child forever, you can do it in your heart, but not in your head. She's filling out her sweaters, she's already gotten her period. You can't—"

His eyes went wide. "She what?"

Oh dear, Lynn thought. She had assumed he was at least aware of *that*. In fact, judging from Allie's knowledge and the way she had stepped effortlessly into the next phase of growing up, Lynn had assumed that father and daughter had discussed the subject thoroughly.

"She's not the little girl you're keeping so lovingly pictured in your mind, Sam."

"The hell she's not," he mumbled under his breath.

"You can't give her a swat on the bottom and not take her to the latest Disney movie this time." Lynn paused. "I think," she said, trying to keep her voice calm, "that it would be a good idea if we grounded her."

Suddenly, all of this was too much for him to comprehend, and he lashed out at the most convenient person.

"And what makes you such an authority on raising kids? You're not her mother!"

Shocked and hurt, Lynn fought back tears. They stared at each other for long seconds, each trying to deal with hurtful words and wounded hearts. Finally, Lynn said softly, "No, I'm not her mother, but it hasn't been that long since I was a motherless teenager, very much like Allie. And I think I know how she feels and maybe even what she needs right now."

Sam couldn't believe he had spoken to Lynn as he had, but he couldn't seem to get far enough past his shock about Allie to apologize. "She needs *me,*" he said, the rage slowly subsiding. "She needs her father." He turned and went upstairs, leaving Lynn to gape after him. Leaving Lynn to cry alone.

ALONG ABOUT SUNDOWN Tag sauntered into the dingy bar looking for a cold longneck and some warm flesh. Like most of the drinking establishments on Oak Springs Road in east Austin, this one—an old standby for Tag over the past year or so—was smoke-filled, poorly lit and populated by men and women looking for love in all the wrong places.

He'd headed into the city with an itch desperately in need of a good hard scratch. The kind of scratching he couldn't get in Crystal Creek. Besides, he was still keeping to himself and couldn't afford for anyone to see him hanging around. It might spoil his plans.

"Hey there, darlin'." A petite woman with short curly blond hair sidled up alongside Tag. She had on a tight blue dress made of some knit fabric that held on for dear life to every curve of her body.

"Hey there, yourself."

"I seen you in here before, haven't I?"

"Maybe."

"Yeah, I think I have. I'm in here a couple times a week."

He looked the woman up and down and decided she might make one hell of a scratcher. "That a fact."

"It's a fact, sugar." She climbed onto the bar stool next to his. "My name's Maedell, but you can call me Mae."

"And you can call me lucky...'cause I ran into you."

She laughed. "Now, ain't you the sweet-talker, Lucky."

"How 'bout a drink?"

"Well, I guess one little drink won't hurt. We could just sit here and get to know each other." She put her hand on his thigh, rubbing back and forth ever so slightly.

"Yeah," Tag said, almost drooling. "I think we oughta get to know each other real good."

Two hours and countless beers later, Mae was unlocking the front door to her duplex with Tag at her elbow. "Shh. I got a nosy neighbor, so we gotta hold it down."

Tag adjusted the crotch of his jeans. "Girl, right now it'd take both of us to hold it down."

Mae giggled. "Oh, Lucky, you're so funny."

"Damn straight."

The door swung open and they both staggered inside. Mae bumped into the sofa and giggled again. Then she flicked on a small reading lamp beside the sofa. "I'll turn on some more lights."

"No need." He grabbed her and gave her a slobbery kiss. She didn't seem to mind. In fact, she kissed him back.

"Slow down, darlin'," she gasped. "We got all night."

"The sooner we get to it, the sooner I'm gonna be one satisfied cowboy," he said, giving her breasts an indiscriminate squeeze.

"Well, 'scuse me for livin'," she said, her words slurred from the beer. "Who says you get your jollies first?"

"Ain't that just like a damn woman." He pressed her back against the arm of the sofa, pulling her dress up as they went. "Always thinkin' you come first."

"Hey, cowboy." She tried to shove him away, but her aim was as unsteady as her gait. "Not so rough."

"Don't kid me. I know your kind. You like it rough." Tag kissed her again, harder. This time he bit the corner of her mouth.

"Hey, don't get carried away."

"Shut up." He pulled her up so that she stood between the sofa and a coffee table. "Take off the dress."

"Maybe I'm not ready to—"

"I said take it off." Tag grabbed her wrist and gave it a hard twist.

"Ouch. Hold your horses. I'll take it off." With her arms crossed, she grasped the hem of the knit dress and began to pull it up.

"Make it snappy."

Mae whipped the dress off and over her head. "There. Satisfied?"

Tag laughed, his hot-eyed gaze traveling over Mae's seminude body. "In a minute, bitch. In a minute."

"Take it easy with the name-call—"

Without warning, he pushed her to her knees in front of him, then grabbed a handful of her short, blond curls and yanked her head back. He leaned down until his face was mere inches from hers, his fetid breath making her stomach roil. "Listen, bitch,

I'll call you whatever I want to, whenever I want to. And I'll *do* whatever I want. You got that?"

Some scrap of healthy fear finally penetrated Mae's beer-soaked brain, because she suddenly realized this man she had invited into her home was dangerous. Shocked and now frightened, she blinked, tears welling up in her eyes. "S-sure. Wh-whatever you s-say, sugar." She started to get up. "No need to—"

"Stay where you are."

"But—"

"Beg me," he said coldly, reaching to undo his belt. "Beg me for it."

Mae lifted her gaze to his and knew then she had underestimated the gravity of her situation. She had to get away from this maniac before he hurt her badly.

"You deaf, bitch?"

Haltingly, Mae shook her head.

"Then do it."

"Please," she whispered, her mind frantically seeking a means of escape.

"Louder." He grabbed her throat, forcing her head back again.

Mae seized what might possibly be her only opportunity and used the force of his grasp as an excuse to fall backward. Now she was on the floor at his feet.

"Don't piss me off. You ain't callin' the shots, I am." Before she could scramble free, he fell on her, shoved his knee between her legs and pried them apart. "And what I want, I take."

"You son of a bitch," she screamed. She reached across to the coffee table, now only inches from her, and picked up a ceramic ashtray. With "Lucky" sprawled on top of her, her aim was something less than perfect, but what Mae lacked in skill she made up for with determination. She swung the ashtray as hard as she could at his head.

Tag saw the movement out of the corner of his eye just as he turned his head. The edge of the ashtray caught him on his cheek, then went flying across the floor.

The same cheek Lynn Russell had used for target practice.

Instantly, roaring like a wounded grizzly and holding his face, he shoved himself away from his attacker. "You stupid bitch," he bellowed. "I oughta kill you."

"Get outta here," Mae yelled. "Get outta here or I'm gonna call the cops."

Tag came toward her, a murderous glint in his eyes. He shoved her against the wall. Hard. "You shouldn't've done that. No woman's gonna make a fool outta me and live to tell about it." Blinded by rage, Tag suddenly saw not Maedell, but Lynn Russell.

Mae saw the soul-black hatred in her attacker's eyes and knew he meant to kill her. Desperate to save her life, she shoved herself away from the wall and ran for the door.

Grabbing a handful of her short, curly hair, he yanked her back and around to face him. "I'm gonna make you sorry, Duchess. So sorry."

CHAPTER SIX

SAM WASN'T ASLEEP when the phone rang. Nonetheless, its jangling in the stillness at three o'clock in the morning propelled him bolt upright in bed.

"Hello," he croaked into the receiver. "What? When?"

By now, Lynn was awake, half-sitting, and listening.

"How can you be sure? Yeah." Sam raked a hand through his hair. "Yeah, sure. I'll be right there."

"What is it?" she asked when he hung up. "What's happened?"

He swung his feet onto the floor, propped his elbows on his knees and raked both hands through his hair. "I can't believe this."

"Believe what? Sam, you're scaring me."

"That was Wayne Jackson on the phone. Somebody broke into the Crystal Creek office tonight."

Lynn's hand flew to her mouth. "Oh, no! What happened?"

"They're not sure, but it looks like maybe the thief was after drugs. They said..." Sam swallowed hard, his heart beating so loud in his ears it sounded like a runaway herd of wild mustangs.

Don't panic. Maybe it's not as bad as you think.

But he didn't believe himself. He tried to keep the terror out of his voice, tried to keep the turmoil from overtaking him. "They said the place was pretty torn up." He reached for the jeans lying on top of the chest at the foot of the bed and stepped into them, then yanked on a T-shirt. "I've got to get down there and see what's been taken."

Lynn got out of bed and came to him, thoughts of the argument of that afternoon completely put aside. "Oh, sweetheart." She put her arms around him and held him close. "You've worked so hard on that office and I know how important it is to you. I'm so sorry."

Sam held her, needing her comfort, needing her understanding. "It's . . ." He swallowed hard. "It's probably not as bad as I'm imagining." *Please, God, don't let it be.*

"Is there anything I can do?"

He leaned back far enough to look into her eyes. "You can kiss me."

She smiled, and he noticed there were tears in her eyes. "I love you," she whispered and kissed him.

Sam had never needed a kiss more in his life. She felt so warm and sweet in his arms, for a second or two he forgot about the call and gave himself over to the simple pleasure of kissing his wife. But the moment the kiss ended, reality came crashing back. He rested his forehead against hers. "I'll call you as soon as I know how bad—"

"Don't take time to call. Just come home. I'll be waiting up for you."

"No, you should try and go back to—"

"Sam." She frowned at him. "How could you even *think* that I could close my eyes for two seconds until you come back?"

"I just don't want you—" he patted her rounded belly "—and Baby to worry."

She covered his hand with hers. "We'll be just fine. And we'll be waiting right here until you get home."

"You told me yourself that Dr. Purdy said to avoid stress and I—"

"Sam, this is crazy," Lynn said, becoming slightly irritated at his insistent solicitation.

"What?" He blinked, truly surprised by her comment.

"Why are we arguing about the loss of a few minutes of sleep when you should already be at your office?"

"Oh. Well..."

"Please." She put a hand on his shoulder and gave it a gentle pat. "Go. Wayne Jackson is waiting for you and I'll be fine."

"Well...all right." He kissed her cheek, then left.

From the bedroom window Lynn watched him drive off. "Sam, Sam," she whispered. "I wish you would treat me like you did when we first met. I'm not a child and I don't need a nursemaid. I need a husband."

Hearing her words out loud, she was suddenly ashamed of herself. Here she was thinking about herself when Sam was about to deal with God-knew-what kind of damage. Forty winks and a little self-pity were nothing compared to what he might find when he arrived at the office.

When he'd opened the Crystal Creek office, he'd had high hopes that eventually it might become his primary office and the one in Austin only part-time. She knew the expense had been great, but Sam had told her the payoff would be worth it. Thank goodness, they had insurance.

SAM GOT TO THE OFFICE in less than five minutes and found Wayne Jackson and his deputy waiting.

"Sorry to have to call with such bad news, Sam."

They shook hands. "Yeah."

"We need you to check things out, see what's been taken. My guess is drugs, but you never can tell about the criminal types."

"All right." Sam gathered himself together and stepped inside.

And his heart sank.

The entire office was a shambles. File cabinets were overturned, instrument drawers emptied and supplies scattered over the floor. But worst of all, his brand-new, high-tech, state-of-the-art and unreasonably expensive dental chair lay overturned on its side. Even the table-top Christmas tree was on the floor, its ornaments broken.

"Damn, Doc. This place is really a mess," the sheriff commented.

"Yeah" was all Sam could say. Deep down inside he felt like doubling up his fists and railing at the heavens that life was unfair. But instead, he stood in the center of the wreckage and simply stared around him.

When Sam remained unmoving for several moments, Wayne said, "Better check your drug cabinet, Doc."

Sam nodded.

The cabinet containing the entire supply of drugs, narcotic and nonnarcotic, prescription and nonprescription, was still locked. Sam unlocked it and examined the shelves. Everything was there. Absolutely nothing was missing.

"I don't get this. It appears nothing was taken."

Wayne Jackson looked up from making notes. "What do you mean, appears?"

"Well, without an inventory, I can't be certain, but it doesn't even look as if anything has been moved around or rearranged. Whoever did this—" he gestured to the vandalism with a sweep of his hand "—wasn't after drugs."

"I'm surprised. Anything else he could have been after? You keep any money in here, Doc?"

Sam almost laughed. "If only you knew how ironic that question was, Sheriff. No. No money."

Wayne studied Sam, his cop's brain assessing the man and the situation, while his civilian side denied the possibility of any wrongdoing. He had gotten to know Sam since he had married the little McKinney, and he liked the man. Liked him enough that he would hate like hell to have to arrest him.

"Why don't you take a good look-see, and I'll meet you outside by your truck. We'll talk."

Sam nodded again, then began to roam through the debris. Fifteen minutes later he had seen all he wanted to see and had determined nothing was missing.

"I don't understand," he said, joining Jackson outside. "Why would anybody break in and just destroy my office?"

"Can't answer that. Yet."

The way the big law enforcement officer said the word caught Sam's attention. "You have any idea who might be responsible?"

"Not sure. Could have been tanked-up kids. Austin's been havin' a bit of trouble with gangs. But the fact that two medical offices have been broken into in the past three days and no drugs were taken makes me wonder."

"You think the same person that broke into Manny Hernandez's office did this?"

"Like I said, not sure. Can I ask you some questions, Sam?" The sheriff flipped to a clean page in his notebook. "And I'll need the name of your insurance company."

When the dentist didn't answer right away, Wayne stopped writing and glanced up. "Sam? You *do* have insurance, don't you?"

Sam stared in through the shattered plate-glass window that had once borne the words, Samuel D. Russell, D.D.S. There was a desperation in his eyes that Jackson knew came only from losing something you'd worked hard for, or someone you'd loved beyond all else. And since, as far as he knew, Sam Russell and the little McKinney were still practically newlyweds and about to be parents, Wayne figured the loss was money.

Aw, hell. Don't tell me he doesn't have insurance. At the same time, Wayne half hoped it was the truth. Every instinct he had was telling him the vandalism was deliberate and *not* the work of liquored-up teenagers. He was going to have to ask Sam Russell some very tough and very personal questions. It was his job. But, damn, it was hard when he was a friend.

"Sam?" No response. "Hey, Sam." Wayne touched his arm.

"What? Oh, sorry. What were you saying?"

"How about sitting in my truck while we finish this report."

"Sure," Sam said. They walked to the truck and climbed in the front seat.

"I've got to ask you some questions, Sam. Hope you know it's nothing personal. I have to conduct an investigation. Just doin' my job."

"Of course."

"How long's the office been open?"

"Couple of months."

"Any problems before?"

"No. But you know all this."

"And you do have insurance?"

Again Sam didn't answer, and the look of desperation returned to his eyes.

"I don't like this part of my job, but I have to ask. You doin' okay financially, Sam?"

It suddenly dawned on Sam that Wayne was trying, without being insulting, to see if Sam had a reason to vandalize his own office. He could lie to Wayne, and maybe in another place, another circumstance, he would. But there was something about being here in the middle of the night, just the two of them, cloaked by darkness, that made Sam feel as though he could confide in Wayne without fear of condemnation.

He heaved a giant sigh of relief. As crazy as the situation was, he was glad to be able to tell someone the truth. "I've got insurance on the chair and some of the other equipment, but I'm not fully covered. Wayne, I'm not going to break even, much less make any money." Sam rubbed his forehead. "I almost laughed out loud when you asked if there was any money in the office. I just wish to hell there had been."

"You're wedged in pretty tight, huh?"

Sam's gaze met Wayne's. "If it gets any tighter, I won't be able to breathe."

About that time the deputy walked up to the truck and handed Wayne the report he had just finished. "Thanks. I'll take it from here. You can go on back to the station." The deputy nodded and left.

"What now?" Sam asked.

"Paperwork." Wayne Jackson shook his head. "Damn paperwork's gonna be the death of me." He made a couple more notes, then closed the notebook. "You wanna go on home?" Something told him the last place Sam wanted to be was home. Sure enough, Sam shook his head.

Wayne reached under the front seat and pulled out a huge thermos. "Cup of coffee?"

"Won't Jessie be waiting up for you?"

Wayne filled the lid to the thermos and handed it to Sam. "She's in Dallas recording a new song, and I hate that house when she's not there." He reached across, popped the glove compartment open, withdrew a cup that looked as if it had once resided at the Longhorn Coffee Shop and poured a cup for himself. "I got nothin' but time to kill," he said, hoping his friend got the message.

Sam did. And Lord, but he was grateful. "I may have to sell Lynn's horse." For a moment, it was deathly quiet inside the truck. "Did you hear—"

"Yeah. It's gonna break her heart."

"Don't you think I know that?" Sam said, self-disgust lacing his voice. "Don't you think that's been on my mind day and night?"

"How'd it happen? I thought folks went to the dentist even in a slumping economy." Wayne held his breath for fear his friend might say women, or gambling. The gambling he could deal with, but Sam cheating on the little McKinney was something he wasn't sure he could handle.

"Actually, the business is doing all right. For now, anyway. No, it's just that I'm stretched to the limit. You see, my ace in the hole, so to speak, has always been a two-hundred-acre section of land over in Louisiana that my aunt left me. I always had that in case times ever got tough. But when I met Lynn and she almost lost Lightning . . ."

"You sold the land to bail her out and now you got no backup."

"Yeah. I've had to update my equipment just to stay current and keep my patient load full. Dentistry has become dependent on technology over the past ten years, and if you want the business you've got to keep up. That means upgrading your equipment regularly."

"And I reckon that stuff ain't cheap."

"You said a mouthful. Then there's all of the expense of feed, vet bills and insurance for Lightning. It mounts up."

"I suppose you've tried the bank."

"Make that banks. No dice, although I can't say as I blame them. I've taken on a new home and opened a small, but new, part-time office, and I probably look like the worst risk since Nixon."

"But the Austin practice is still okay?"

"Thank God. I don't know what I'd do if it wasn't. Still..."

"Push has come to shove and the horse may have to go."

"Yeah. I've stalled about as long as I can. I've been hoping a decent-sized loan would come through, but now with the vandalism..." His voice trailed off.

"Sorry you and Lynn got more trouble."

"I haven't told her," Sam admitted. "I couldn't. Not with the baby coming and having to be a mother to the girls and taking care of the house. She's got enough to worry about. I didn't want to make things worse."

Unaccustomed to and more than slightly uncomfortable with hearing such a confession, Wayne said, "Look, Sam, maybe you should be talking to her instead of me."

"Sorry. I didn't mean to bend your ear, but I'm just grateful to be able to finally talk to somebody about all this. Thanks for listening."

Wayne shrugged. "No sweat."

"And I know you're right. I need to talk to Lynn, but she's not used to facing this kind of trouble. Sometimes, I look at her and think that, in some ways, she's as young and innocent as my daughters. I don't want any of them ever to suffer on my account."

"No man worth his salt does. But I think you're selling your wife short. I've known her a good deal longer than you have and I can tell you she's a lot stronger than she looks. She survived her mother's death and she built a dream outta nothin' and made it a reality. I don't call those the traits of a weak woman."

"I suppose not."

"Maybe she's keyed up because of the baby. Everything will probably be all right once the baby comes."

"Yeah, probably."

Sam was a proud man and Wayne could see that he thought he was doing the right thing. A little grin lifted the corner of Wayne's mouth. Jessie had taught him that sometimes doing the right thing could cause a heap of trouble, especially where love was involved. "I do know that tryin' to keep someone you love safe from all the bad things in the world is impossible. Sometimes you got to step back and give 'em room to breathe."

"Right now, *I'd* settle for just that—a little breathing room."

"Hang in there," Wayne said. "And keep me posted."

The two men shook hands and parted.

Wayne Jackson watched Sam drive off and sincerely hoped the act of vandalism on the dentist's office was nothing more than exactly what it appeared to be. But having a vet's office and a dentist's office vandalized in a matter of days struck the sheriff of Claro County as anything but coincidental. He'd bet his new pair of La Herencia boots that they were connected. As in committed by the same culprit. It was time he did some checking around town. Asked a few questions. Put a few pieces of the puzzle together. And if his hunch was right, maybe he could catch the nasty two-legged varmint who had targeted Crystal Creek.

ON THE DRIVE HOME Sam felt that, after talking to Wayne, at least a few tons of worry had been lifted from his shoulders. But a few thousand pounds were a drop in the bucket compared to what still remained. And now, he could add reconstructing his office to the list.

Lynn was in the kitchen when he walked in the door. "Is it..." She had been about to ask if the damage was bad until she saw the—"defeated" was the first word that came to her mind—expression on his face. "How bad is it?" she said, quickly revising her question as she held out a cup of freshly brewed coffee to him.

Sam glanced at her and immediately his expression lightened. He shook his head at the offered cup. "You shouldn't be drinking coffee this late. You should be upstairs in bed."

Frustrated, Lynn was tempted to make a sarcastic reply. Something to the effect that she couldn't go to sleep until he tucked her in and made sure she had her teddy bear. Instead, she smiled sweetly and walked over to give him a kiss. "It's decaf. And we've already had this argument, remember? Now, tell me what happened and how extensive the damage is."

Sam changed his mind about the coffee and took a deep breath. "There's not much to tell, except that someone or several someones broke into the clinic and sort of—" he searched for a word that would downplay the extent of the damage without being a lie "—disrupted everything."

"Were they looking for drugs?"

"Apparently not. Nothing was taken."

"Nothing? That's surprising."

"Yeah. Wayne Jackson said the same thing."

"So it was just ... vandalism?"

"Yeah."

"Just pure meanness."

"Looks that way. Teenagers probably."

Lynn sat her coffee cup on the kitchen table with enough force to make the dark liquid slosh over the rim and splash onto the wooden surface. "That burns me up. Some of these kids today need a serious lesson in how to respect other people's property. Probably some jocks with too much beer under their belts. Does Wayne have any idea who might be responsible?"

"Not a clue."

"And knowing the old boys-will-be-boys kind of attitude that flourishes around here, even if he finds out, probably nothing will ever come of it."

"Sweetheart, don't get yourself wound up. The damage is..." Again he sought for a way to avoid a lie without telling the whole truth. "The damage is not nearly as bad as it could have been." A half truth, but he could live with it. "Our insurance will take care of it." *Then hike our premiums completely out of sight,* he could have added.

"I don't know how you can be so calm about this!"

He rubbed the bridge of his nose between his thumb and index finger. "I'm not calm. I'm exhausted and so are you."

"I'm mad."

He took her by the hand and led her toward the stairs, reaching to turn off the light as he went. "All right, my little spitfire, but you'll have to finish being mad in the morning. Right now I'm going to put you and Baby to bed."

The previously unvoiced teddy bear crack was on the tip of her tongue until she glanced up and saw the tired expression on Sam's face a second before he flicked off the lights. He was right and he *was* tired. They could talk about this tomorrow. In the darkness she found his hand and held it.

"DADDY, ARE YOU GOING to work today?" Sandy asked the next morning, after Sam had told both of the girls about the events of last night.

"I'm afraid so. I have a lot to do now."

"But you said your office was trashed."

Over the rim of his Sunday edition of the *Austin American Statesman,* Sam peered at his daughter. "Well, not trashed exactly. There are some papers strewn about and drawers emptied, but I wouldn't say trashed. It'll be business as usual next week. Monday morning." *I hope,* he thought, going back to his reading.

"Your dad refused my offer to help clean up the mess, so I'm going out to the ranch right after church to help with preparations for the Christmas party. But I'll be back in plenty of time to take both of you to the mall shopping," Lynn announced to the girls.

Sam's head snapped up from the paper. "Shopping? For what?"

"Don't you remember? Amanda Walker and Brock Monroe are getting married tomorrow. Although why anyone would want to have a wedding on the twenty-second of December is beyond me."

"What does that have to do with shopping?"

"We're all invited. Allie and Sandy both need new dresses and—"

"We can't afford it," Sam said flatly. All three females stared at him. "Don't look at me like that. There's been entirely too much shopping going on around here lately."

"Daddy, it's Christmas," Sandy reminded him.

"Well," he said, shifting uncomfortably in his chair. "All the more reason not to go. I'm sure all of you have something suitable to wear in those bulging closets of yours. Just because it's an event doesn't mean you have to have a new dress." He returned his attention to his newspaper.

Allie and Sandy glanced from their father to Lynn, both obviously surprised at Sam's abrupt dismissal of the subject. Lynn was just as surprised. As far as she knew they weren't rolling in money, but neither were they one step away from welfare. She wasn't a spendthrift and Sam knew it. He had never objected to money spent on clothing before.

"I suppose we could make do with what we've got."

"Good," Sam said, without interrupting his reading. Again, both of the girls exchanged looks.

"Sandy, be sure you lay out your green velveteen and I'll take it to the cleaners."

"Okay."

"And Allie, if you need something cleaned, just put it with Sandy's dress."

The teenager's response was a sullen look and a quick nod. Arms crossed over her chest, Allie was definitely pouting over the incident with Mary June Wynn. Sam had taken away her telephone privileges for three days and disallowed any visits with the Wynn girl for the same amount of time. Hardly a stinging reprimand as far as Lynn was concerned, but then, it was more than she expected. Particularly after the harsh words between her and Sam.

"Would both of you finish getting ready for church?" The girls did as Lynn requested, but Allie in particular departed in her own sweet time.

Once they were gone, Lynn sat down at the table, intending to try, at least, to see if something was bothering him. "Sam..."

"You know, it's getting so that you can't pick up a newspaper or turn on television anymore without seeing violence graphically detailed. They found a woman beaten to death late last night. Somewhere in Austin on the east side. The paper says the body was almost unrecognizable. What kind of man would do a thing like that?"

"A sick one. Sam, I think we should talk—"

"Yeah, that's all the politicians do is talk about crime and violence, but nothing is ever done about it. The prisons get too full, so they turn a bunch of murderers and rapists loose. And the next thing you know, some poor woman is dead."

"I know. It's a shame, but—"

"Good Lord." He pointed to the clock over the refrigerator. "Look at the time. If we don't hurry, we'll be late for service." He grabbed her hand and pulled her with him up the stairs. "You light a fire under the girls while I hop in the shower."

Once again, Lynn thought, he had cut her off as if her concerns were unimportant. How much longer could this go on?

"I DON'T KNOW how much longer this can go on," Lynn said to Cynthia four hours later. She had just finished relating the events of the morning, plus the incident with Allie, to her stepmother.

"Until you make him listen to you, I suppose."

"That's the problem. He won't listen long enough to even hear that he's not listening."

They were unwinding artificial holly garlands to be used as decorations for the McKinneys' annual Christmas Eve open house. "How many more of these do we have to do?" Lynn asked, glancing around at the seemingly endless ropes of greenery that snaked around the McKinney living room floor like gigantic fuzzy green worms.

"We're almost done, but if you're tired, go ahead and stop."

"No." Lynn sighed. "Better this than going home to face the gruesome threesome."

Cynthia couldn't help but laugh. "I'm sorry, I'm not laughing at you—"

"I know, I know. I shouldn't exaggerate, but sometimes that's exactly how I think of Sam and the girls."

Cynthia's laughter subsided. "Are you aware that you've stopped calling them Sam's girls and are now referring to them as *the* girls?"

"You think that's progress?"

"Absolutely. And one of these days, I think you'll even refer to them as *our* girls."

"Boy, you really are optimistic."

"No. More realistic. I know that you're committed to Sam and to those kids. And if there's one thing a McKinney doesn't walk away from, it's a commitment."

Lynn sighed. "I don't know. It seems Cal and Serena—and you and Daddy, of course—are the only McKinneys seriously working at their commitments these days."

Cynthia glanced up from her untangling. "You're talking about Ruth and Tyler, aren't you?"

"Have you heard from either one of them? I thought one of us might at least get a Christmas card or something."

"As a matter of fact your father talked to Tyler a couple of nights ago."

"And?" Lynn asked hopefully.

"Tyler called about the business."

"No mention of what was going on between him and Ruth?"

"Just that they were talking things over and that he didn't know for sure when they would be back."

"They? At least that sounds encouraging."

"J.T. would never let on to anyone but me, but he's worried sick about them."

Lynn nodded. "I could see it in his eyes when he hugged me earlier. He looked sort of angry and lost all at the same time."

Cynthia debated whether to confide in Lynn, then decided that if sharing trouble was supposed to bring a family closer, this was a good place to start. "He blames himself," she said calmly.

"For Ruth and Tyler's breakup?" Lynn was genuinely shocked.

"Yes. At least, in part."

"But why? Lord knows, Tyler is as hardheaded as they come. That's not Daddy's fault, although they *are* an awful lot alike sometimes."

Cynthia looked directly at Lynn. "He doesn't think he has set a very good example for any of his children."

"But that's crazy..." Her gaze met Cynthia's. "Oh," she said, getting the point. "I see. He's worried about me, too."

"And Sam."

"Well, tell him not to worry."

"Telling a parent not to worry is like trying to stop the sun from rising every morning. You'll learn for yourself soon enough. You did say you were concerned about Allie, didn't you?"

Lynn opened a rectangular box of candles and began counting red and white tapers, all but ignoring the question because she could easily see where Cynthia was headed.

"Well, aren't you?"

She shrugged her shoulders. "I suppose."

"Doesn't that tell you something? Like maybe you already think of Sam *and* the girls as your family?"

"Maybe. I don't know. Right now, I'm not sure of anything."

At that moment, Jennifer's baby-sitter, Lisa Croft, walked into the room with her little charge in her arms. All of Cynthia's attention went immediately to Jennifer. Lynn watched her stepmother quite literally light up at the mere sight of her daughter.

"There she is," Cynthia cooed, the artificial greenery completely forgotten. "Did Mommy's big girl have a good nap?" The baby wiggled up and down within Lisa's hold as her mother approached, then stretched out her little arms and nearly dove into Cynthia's embrace. "Whoa, girl," said Cynthia. Now safe and exactly where she wanted to be, Jennifer grinned happily. Cynthia lifted one of the baby's hands and waved it. "Say hello to Lynn."

"Hi, sweet girl." Lynn kissed Jennifer's cheek and was rewarded with a whiff of powder and baby sweetness.

"Lettie Mae wanted me to find out if you were staying for supper," Lisa asked Lynn.

"No, thanks." Lynn glanced at her watch. "I had no idea it was so late. I better hit the road. I've got a starving family of my own to feed." She bade them both goodbye and headed for home.

The road from the Double C back into Crystal Creek was, for the most part, long, straight and dusty. There was only one curve of any consequence and Lynn had driven the road so many times she felt she could probably negotiate it in her sleep. Cal had done exactly that once or twice, and the result had been a nasty bump on the head and new paint and bodywork on his truck. Lynn, on the other hand, prided herself on the fact that, unlike both her brothers, she had a spotless driving record. Not even a parking ticket.

But tonight, as she approached the curve, her mind was on the things Cynthia had said.

Was it possible to make Sam listen to her? *Maybe I'm not trying hard enough.* Was she feeling closer to Allie and Sandy than she'd admitted to herself? *Maybe I'm expecting too much, too soon.* And what about her father? She'd had no idea he was so worried about all of them. *Maybe for the first time in my life, I'm beginning to understand, to see things from his—*

Lynn was so deep in thought, she was on top of the curve before she realized she was going entirely too fast. She tapped her brake pedal. Once. Twice.

And nothing happened.

She hit it again, harder, only this time the pedal went all the way to the floor and stayed.

My brakes are gone!

Almost at the same moment she realized that she had no brakes, the Suburban headed into the curve on a straight line. Lynn panicked, yanking the steering wheel hard to the right. She avoided the curve, but her overcompensation at the wheel sent her flying off the road into a two-foot bar ditch.

She screamed, instinctively wrapping both her arms over her belly as the truck pitched and rocked. Her head banged against the door. Then suddenly, the truck tilted at a crazy angle, plowed into the side of the ditch and smashed into the exposed edge of a huge concrete drainpipe. Thankfully, the ditch had slowed the Suburban's speed and the impact was jarring but not injurious.

Her breathing labored, Lynn glanced down at her stomach. *Dear God, please don't let my baby be hurt.* Almost as if her unborn child had heard her prayer, he kicked. "Oh, thank you," she whispered, her voice cracking with emotion. She wanted to laugh and cry at the same time. "Thank you, thank you, thank you."

Gradually, Lynn realized she was not yet out of the woods. The edge of the drainpipe was embedded into the hood of her truck, and the truck was virtually resting on its side. Her head was throbbing, but she remembered enough drivers' education training to know she should get out of the vehicle in case of an explosion or fire from leaking gas. The question was, how?

She considered the problem for a moment, surveying the damage. The lid to the console between the two front seats was ajar, its contents—more than a dozen country and western cassette tapes—strewn over the seats and floor. And along with the tapes, one forgotten item.

The mobile phone Sam had insisted on purchasing because they were both on the road between Austin and Crystal Creek, and Crystal Creek and the Double C almost every day. She had used it only

once or twice, and most of the time forgot she even
had it. With trembling hands she picked up the
phone.

"All right," she said, breathlessly trying to remember how it worked. She punched the button
marked POWER and was rewarded with a dial tone.
Automatically, she started to dial her home number.

No. she told herself. *You were right the first time.
Get out of the car. Then call.* She set the phone aside,
then carefully unfastened her seat belt. Her body slid
against her door. Grabbing the steering wheel with
both hands, she turned as best she could, so as not to
fall out and land on her butt in the dirt as soon as the
door opened. Clutching the steering wheel with one
hand, she unlocked, then tried to open the door. Her
efforts netted her a six-inch crack before the door
refused to go farther. "Damn."

One way or another she had to get out, but crawl-
ing out the back was out of the question. She would
never be able to get her considerable bulk over three
bench seats. No, the door was still her best chance,
and as far as Lynn could see, there was only one way
to handle the situation. She drew her knees up as far
as she could and kicked. The crack widened another
few inches. Another kick, a few more inches. Until,
finally, the opening was wide enough for her to slide
out of the seat. Her feet hit the dirt with a thud and
her knees almost buckled. Lynn hadn't realized until that moment how deep-down, gut-level scared she

was. She grabbed the mobile phone, staggered up and over the other side of the bar ditch and gracelessly but gratefully plopped down on the side of the road. She dialed the Double C's phone number.

CHAPTER SEVEN

SAM HAD NO IDEA how many traffic violations he committed when he raced toward the Double C as if the devil himself were right behind. He prayed Lynn was all right. He prayed the baby was all right.

She *had* sounded all right when she called.

Thank God, I had enough sense to get that portable phone.

But what if she had been hurt and was still in too much shock to know it?

Take it easy, Sam. Take it easy. She told you she wasn't bleeding. No broken bones. And the baby was still kicking like a soccer player.

Maybe the baby being that active wasn't a good sign. Maybe the wreck had done something—jiggled him around, or something.

He couldn't stop his mind from conjuring up scenario after scenario, none of them good. And he wouldn't be able to stop until he determined for himself that his wife and unborn child were unhurt.

Sam whipped his sedan through the gate and straight up to the front door of the main house. In less time than it took to sneeze, he was out of the car and reaching for the front doorknob. Lettie Mae opened the door before he made contact.

"She's in the parlor," the cook informed him. "And she's—

Sam shot past her without hearing a word and dashed into the parlor.

Lynn was lying on the antique sofa, covered by an afghan, with Cynthia and J.T. on either side of her. Sam couldn't get across the floor quickly enough.

"Are you all right?" He knelt beside the sofa and captured her hand.

"I'm fine. A little bit of a headache," Lynn assured him, pushing herself up to a sitting position. "Really, I'm fine."

"But don't you think you should see a doctor?"

"Daddy has already called Nate Purdy. He didn't think he needed to see me, but if I felt *I* needed to see him, then he could have met me in the emergency room."

"The emergency—"

Lynn touched his face. "Nate was just finishing a house call on a visitor at the Hole in the Wall. Daddy called him and he was here in five minutes. He checked me out, and I'm okay. He says I'll probably be a little stiff and sore tomorrow, and wind up with some prizewinning bruises, but otherwise, your son and I are both fine."

Now that he could see for himself that she did indeed appear to be perfectly fine, Sam started to shake. He sat beside her and held her hand, not trusting his trembling arms to support her. "Good Lord, you scared me half to death." He ran his other hand through his hair. "You sure you're all right?"

"She was damned lucky," J.T. said, coming to stand beside his wife. He slipped an arm around her waist.

"Very lucky," Cynthia agreed.

"And thank goodness you bought that portable phone, Sam. No tellin' how long she might have sat out there in that bar ditch before you realized she had been gone too long." J.T. looked at his daughter, and emotion threatened to overwhelm him. "Yeah," he said, his voice hoarse, "I'd say you were damned lucky, little girl."

"I'm sorry, Sam. I know I scared you. You too, Daddy."

"Well, the important thing is that you're here now, safe and sound." Cynthia glanced up at her husband, and with a slight nod of her head, indicated that they should leave Sam and Lynn alone. "We'll be in the kitchen if you need us," she said, taking J.T. by the hand and leading him out of the room.

Sam finally gathered Lynn close, as if hugging her and touching her confirmed the fact that she had survived without a scrape. "I could wring your neck for scaring me like that."

He always sounded as if he wanted to do precisely that. "It wasn't exactly my idea of fun, either."

"What happened? How did you end up in a bar ditch?"

"My brakes failed."

"What? How could that be? You've never had any problems before."

"I know, but—"

"How fast were you driving?"

"Actually, going *into* the curve, probably faster than I should have been," she admitted.

The admission hit Sam like a bucketful of ice water right in the face. All the fear, anxiety and anger rolling around inside him over the near miss snapped back in a whiplash of emotion. He started to tremble again, and didn't know whether to kiss her or shake her until her teeth rattled in her head.

"But then I—"

"Dammit it, Lynn!" he exploded, emotion rushing out of him. "I told you a week ago to have your truck serviced. If you had done what I told you to, none of this would have happened. You don't know what you've put me through in the past half hour."

His outburst so shocked her that she didn't notice he was still trembling with fear. She completely missed the pain of regret in his eyes, the agony etched across his face. All she heard was criticism, and it pitched her into a swirl of emotions: disappointment, hurt pride and anger—mostly anger, because it was easier to deal with at the moment and a convenient way to mask her pain.

She couldn't believe her ears. He was actually berating her for not servicing the damned truck! "I'm sorry," she said calmly, coldly, despite her anger. "I was under the mistaken opinion that I was the victim, not you."

Sam's head snapped up. "Oh, sweetheart, forgive me. I didn't mean for it to sound like I blame you."

"That's exactly what it sounded like."

"No, no. It's just...I was so scared. And it's...you know how it is. Like when one of your kids gets temporarily lost, and then you find them. You don't know what to do first—hug them or scold them."

"No, I don't know," she said pointedly. "You're acting as if you think I'm some teenager who's been out for a joyride and dented the fender to the family car."

"I don't think that."

"Then stop treating me like an irresponsible child."

"I wasn't—"

"The hell you weren't."

Sam stared at her, wondering what had happened to the sweet woman he married. "You've got to be a bundle of nerves. And I think right now you're overreacting."

"And I think right now you're being a jerk, so that makes us even."

Cynthia and J.T. picked that moment to rejoin them. "Better now, punkin'?" J.T. asked.

"Yes." She cut Sam a hard look. "Thanks for everything, Cynthia, but I think it's time I went home." She started to rise from the sofa. Sam quickly came to her aid.

"Careful, punkin'," J.T. warned when Lynn swayed slightly.

She pulled her arm free of Sam's assistance. "Don't worry, Daddy. I'm stronger than I look."

J.T. smiled down at her. "Just don't be afraid to ask for help if you need it." Then he turned to Sam. "I had one of the hands take a tractor down and pull Lynn's truck outta the ditch. She didn't know if you might want it hauled off to the dealership where you bought it or to some body shop, so we stuck it out behind the stables. It's there whenever you're ready to call a wrecker."

"Thanks," Sam said and followed in Lynn's wake.

Their arms around each other, Cynthia and J.T. walked out to see them off. When they were gone, J.T. turned to his wife and asked, "How long has it been since I told you I love you?"

"As a matter of fact, you said so just yesterday, but it's certainly worth repeating."

"I do love you. More than you'll ever know."

Knowing how hard this kind of intimacy was for him, Cynthia looked into his eyes and smiled. These moments, each a treasure to be stored in her heart, were becoming less strained, more frequent. "And I love you. Just the way you are."

"Warts and all?"

"Warts and all." She kissed him gently on the lips.

There, in front of any of the ranch hands who might happen by, or anybody else in the world who might care to look, he kissed her back. Long, hard and thoroughly.

TAG TOSSED DOWN the last swallow of his last long-neck, then threw the beer bottle as hard as he could. It hit a boulder on the opposite side of his campfire, showering the rock with shards of amber glass.

His trip into Austin hadn't scratched his itch one bit. If anything, the itch was worse than before.

That bitch last night pissed me off. She shouldn'ta done that. But I showed her. His right fist hit the center of his left palm. The smacking sound of the blow drifted over the campfire, then fell silent in the blackness of the night. *She won't cross me no more. I showed her real good.*

But it wasn't enough.

He'd known the minute his fist hit Mae's face the first time that it wasn't enough. *She* wasn't enough. Or the right one. And every time he hit her, it wasn't Mae's face he saw, or her voice he heard begging him to stop. It was Lynn Russell's face he saw, her voice he heard.

Tag stared into the campfire, watching the flames leap and dance, choreographed by the light wind. As he watched the flames, he became mesmerized, almost as if his mind were free from conscious thought, and he was able to visualize his greatest fantasy.

It was then the idea came to him. It was perfect. The perfect revenge. He needed the real thing, and by God, he would have it.

Have her.

That's what I need. Her. Right here in front of me, so's I can show her like I showed the rest of 'em. And that's what I'll do. Bring her here. Right here. And when I get her here, she'll be sorry. I'll make her sorry.

Suddenly, the idea of kidnapping Lynn Russell, bringing her to his campsite, and extracting his revenge was so sweet, Tag actually licked his lips in anticipation.

BY THE NEXT DAY, "a little" was no longer Lynn's description of how stiff and sore she was. She felt as if she creaked when she walked, which she tried not to do unless it was necessary.

Allie and Sandy had been much more upset over the situation than she had anticipated. In fact, both girls had cried when Sam told them the details of the accident. To herself, Lynn admitted to feeling guilty about expecting so much less from them. The admission, and their solicitous attention, took a bit of the sting out of Sam's reaction. She hadn't forgiven him; in fact, she realized, she didn't *want* to forgive him.

"Here you go, sweetheart," Sam said, carrying a cup of steaming hot coffee and some toast into the living room. Lynn was ensconced on the sofa, complete with extra pillows, comforter, cordless phone, remote control for the TV and enough novels, how-to-parent and baby-care books to open a used-book store.

"Thanks."

"Sure you don't want a couple of scrambled eggs?"

She shook her head. "This is fine."

"And are you certain you don't need me to rearrange some of my appointments so I can stay with you?"

"No," she said, so quickly there was no way he could not get the message that she didn't want him to stay. "I'm perfectly fine. Besides, the girls are here."

"That's my point. When they wake up, someone needs to fix their breakfast and you're certainly in no shape—"

"They *can* do for themselves, Sam. They're not helpless."

"No," he said, shrugging. "I suppose you're right."

"Go on and go. I'm fine. And Cal said he'd probably drop by sometime before noon."

"Then how about I fix you a sandwich before I go so you won't have to worry about lunch? Or I could bring you something from the Longhorn."

"No, thanks. Don't bother."

"Okay." He sighed. His wife was giving him a well-deserved cold shoulder. "Well, then . . . I guess there's not much more I can do."

"Thanks. You've done enough."

The double entendre wasn't lost on Sam. If anything, it hit him squarely in the heart. He wasn't proud of the way he had behaved about the accident.

He squatted beside the sofa, balancing on the balls of his feet. "Lynn, I'd like to talk to you."

"About what?"

Clearly, she didn't intend to cut him any slack. "About yesterday—"

"It's getting late." She glanced at her watch. "This can wait until later."

He wanted to yell, *No. It can't wait, dammit.* But he didn't, because he knew in his heart of hearts that he was guilty of not listening to her yesterday.

"All right," Sam said, resigned to the fact that she wasn't ready to listen to him. He leaned over and kissed her on the forehead, only because he couldn't face kissing her on the lips and getting no response. "I'll call you later."

Lynn heard the kitchen door close, heard Sam turn the lock behind him. Then she started to cry.

Three hours later, Cal arrived and found her, puffy-eyed and depressed.

"Hey, Skunk. How's it going?"

"Fine," Lynn said. "If you can stand the gloom and doom, orchestrated to the tune of 'Winter Wonderland.'"

From the den, situated at the other end of the house, cello music drifted in. "Sandy is practicing her Christmas piece," Lynn informed her brother.

"Where's Allie?" Cal followed Lynn into the living room, where she promptly reclaimed her place on the sofa.

"In her room, getting ready for her field trip to the planetarium this afternoon, I suppose."

"Field trip? Thought school was out for the holidays."

"This has all been planned for months. Seems this is the only time you can see a certain star or something." She shrugged. "It's a class project, but if it was up to me, she wouldn't be going."

"She giving you and Sam trouble?"

"Heavens no. Why, she's a perfect angel... according to *her father.*"

"I see."

"I doubt it."

"Hey." He held up both of his hands as if to ward off her next attack. "I just came by to see how you were doing after going three rounds with that bar ditch yesterday." He eyed her carefully. "Looks like a couple of bruises, but you'll live," he teased.

"Your bedside manner stinks."

Cal grinned. "But you have to admit I'm cute."

"Only if you brought me chocolate."

Still grinning, Cal pulled a candy bar from his shirt pocket. "Behold, a cowboy bearing gifts."

"Want some?" she asked when he handed her the chocolate.

"Nope."

"Good." Lynn unwrapped the candy and took a bite. "I was watching Oprah. Today's topic is race car drivers and the women who love them but can't live with them ... or something like that."

"Sounds ... fasinating," Cal commented dryly.

"No, it doesn't." Lynn hit the button on the remote and the television screen went dark. "But I'm bored. If I'm lucky, maybe some talk show host will want to interview me on the subject of women who love their husbands but would like to strangle them."

"Yeah, we're a sorry lot."

"Don't patronize me."

"Would I do a thing like that? What does *patronize* mean anyway?"

Lynn couldn't help but smile. "You're hopeless."

"Yeah, but I'm—"

"Cute," she finished for him.

"Seriously," he said, taking the chair across from her, "I was worried about you after yesterday." He didn't add that he had stopped by the ranch and Cynthia had dropped a few subtle hints that maybe his little sister could use some cheering up. He also didn't add that Lettie Mae had put in her two cents' worth and had not been so subtle.

"I'm fine."

"Oh sure, you're just dandy. Probably sore from head to toe and, judging from what you just said, sore *at* your husband. Come on, Skunk, tell big brother. Sam fail to compliment your meat loaf or something?"

"Drop dead," Lynn said, her voice suddenly raspy with emotion, her eyes filled with tears.

Cal was instantly contrite. "Hey, I was only teasin'. Is something *seriously* wrong?" He moved to sit beside her on the couch.

She shook her head. Cal's good-natured ribbing was easy enough to handle, but she wasn't up to genuine brotherly concern at the moment. "Don't pay any attention to me. My hormones are going berserk."

"Thank goodness. For a minute there, I was afraid we were about to share some emotional bonding or something."

"You really are hopeless."

"So Serena tells me."

"How is she?" Lynn sniffed, wiping her nose.

"Vicious. She asked me to get her some panty hose at the drugstore, since I was coming into town. It seems every pair she owns has a run and—" he raised his voice to mimic a female "—she simply can't go bare-legged to one of the biggest weddings this year."

"Wedding?"

"Sure. Brock and—"

"Amanda. Oh Lord, I'd forgotten that the wedding is tonight. I...I think I'll skip it."

"Why?"

"I probably won't feel like going." Absently, Lynn picked at a fuzz ball on the afghan. "Anyway, I'm not in the mood to listen to 'Oh, Promise Me' and a lot of mushy sentimentality."

"Bullsh—"

"Cal!" Lynn shot him a warning look. "There's an eleven-year-old with big ears at home."

"You and Sam had a fight, didn't you?"

She didn't meet his gaze. "What makes you say that?"

"I'm psychic?"

"Oh, yeah, right." She paused for a second, then added, "Who told you?"

"I got an earful from Lettie Mae this morning."

"Oh. Well, then, you know Sam was pretty upset about the wrecked car."

The way she said the words *wrecked car* told him her feelings were a little wrecked as well. "And not as upset about you. Is that it?"

She shrugged.

"The way I heard it he was shaking like a leaf and pale as a ghost when he got to the ranch."

"And yelling," she added, glancing down at her hands folded in her lap.

"Some people do that when they're afraid."

With a heavy sigh Lynn looked up at her brother. "I keep disappointing him, Cal."

"Aw, hell. If Serena got blue every time I disappointed her, we'd never have made it past the first six months of our marriage. It goes with the territory."

"His first wife was perfect."

"Sugar, nobody's perfect."

"She was."

"Says who?"

"Says..." She stopped short of saying Sam, because in truth he had never really voiced his disappointment. But he hadn't needed to. She heard it and felt it in a thousand little ways. "Says my instincts."

"Didn't you just say something about hormones going berserk? Maybe your feminine intuition is on the blink."

Something else was now clear. Cal didn't understand a thing she was trying to tell him and she was wasting her breath. "Well, it's working well enough to tell me that if you forget those panty hose, Serena will intuitively kill you."

He grinned. "Bull—"

"Watch it."

"Bull's-eye."

Now it was her turn to grin. "Scram."

"Yes'm. I really am glad you're all right, Skunk." He leaned over and kissed her on the cheek. "See ya," he said and left.

Twenty minutes later, Cynthia arrived with lunch.

"So, how do you feel?"

"Better," Lynn said honestly.

"Good. You know, you gave us quite a scare last night. Poor Sam was frantic when he arrived at the ranch. I've never seen so much sheer terror in a man's eyes or so much pure, sweet relief in them when he realized you were all right."

"He seemed more worried about the truck."

"I'm not surprised. For the most part, I don't think men have the faintest idea what it means to express their feelings. In fact, I'm sure most of them don't even recognize feelings when they feel them."

"Makes communication slightly difficult," Lynn commented, a little bite to her words.

"Sometimes you have to dig out their emotions like a miner looking for the mother lode, and it's not always easy. But then, nobody said it would be."

"No," Lynn said thoughtfully. "I guess they didn't."

After a very pleasant lunch, Cynthia left for home, Sandy went next door to play with a friend and Allie left for her field trip.

Alone in the house, Lynn decided to pamper herself. She took a nice long soak in the tub, then relaxed with a short nap. By the time she woke up and thought about dinner, Sam called and she graciously accepted his offer to bring home fried chicken from the Longhorn.

Sandy came home. Sam arrived with the chicken. But it was getting late and Allie hadn't returned.

"What time did she say they would be back?" Sam asked, piling chicken pieces onto a platter.

"About five."

Sam glanced at his watch. "It's five-thirty."

"Well, there were several cars. A number of parents volunteered to chaperon. Maybe whoever she rode with had to stop for gas or something. I'm sure she'll be here shortly."

"They assigned cars to everyone, and she had to ride in the same car with Billy Thompson." Sandy poked her finger toward her open mouth. "Gag."

"Sounds like a fate worse than death," Sam teased.

"Don't you remember when sitting next to a girl *was* a fate worse than death?"

With her back to him, Lynn was dishing up the mashed potatoes that had accompanied the chicken. He couldn't tell by the sound of her voice if she was still upset with him.

"Well, uh, I guess I was abnormal then, because I always thought girls were pretty neat."

She turned to hand him the bowl of steaming potatoes and, to his surprise, she was smiling. "Spoken like a true chauvinist. Are you taking notes, Sandy?"

"I think boys are silly," the girl informed them.

"You'll get over it—"

"You won't for long—"

They spoke simultaneously, then stopped, looked at each other and laughed.

At the sound of her laughter, Sam's smile flowed into a full-fledged grin. He loved when she laughed so freely, so naturally. But most of all he loved that she enjoyed laughing and did it often. Marta had always had a beautiful smile, but he couldn't remember her laughing out loud very often. She had been serene and polite, but she didn't possess the exuberance that Lynn did.

Lynn laughed again and he realized that last night he had come close to never hearing her laughter again. Too close. He still didn't know what was troubling her, but at least she seemed more herself today than she had in weeks.

"One of these days you'll change your mind about boys," Sam said, gazing at his wife.

It felt good to laugh like this, Lynn thought, feeling closer to Sam than she had in a long time. "Or some boy will come along to change it for you." Lynn's words were for Sandy, but her loving gaze was for her husband.

"Yuck."

Lynn laughed. "Here." She handed the girl a plate of food. "Until you decide boys are worth the time of day, you'll need to keep your strength up."

Sam glanced at his watch again, and his grin slowly faded. "I can't imagine what's keeping Allie."

"She's just running late. C'mon, let's go ahead and eat," Lynn urged. "I'll save her a plate."

Half an hour later dinner was over, Sandy was dressing for the wedding and Sam and Lynn were both getting more nervous by the minute, but trying not to let each other see it.

"I think I'll take a quick shower," Sam announced, with a show of confidence he didn't really feel. His daughter had never before been this late without calling, and even though his head told him there was probably no cause for concern, the dread in his heart was another matter. "When Allie gets home, better hurry her along or we'll be late."

Lynn nodded. "Where the hell are you, Allie?" she whispered to herself as soon as Sam left the room. "You've got your whole family worried."

Half the people in Crystal Creek had been invited to the wedding of Amanda Walker and Brock Monroe, including many of the parents of the kids on the field trip. Lynn began to wonder if anyone else was late. On a hunch, she made three calls to the parents of girls she knew were in Allie's class.

All three girls had returned home more than an hour ago.

Lynn could hear the water running in the upstairs bathroom and debated whether or not to interrupt Sam. *Let the man at least finish his shower. Besides, this news doesn't necessarily mean something bad has happened to Allie.* In fact, Lynn had a hunch that young Miss Russell was just fine.

Before Lynn heard Sam turn off the shower, Allie sailed through the door as if she were right on time.

"Where have you been?" Lynn asked, careful to keep the anger churning inside her out of her voice.

"We went to the planetarium—"

"Everyone else has been home for some time."

Allie's eyes widened. "Who told you that? They just dropped me—"

Quickly, Lynn moved to the kitchen window, lifted a curtain and looked out into the gathering dusk in time to see a pickup driving off. The truck looked suspiciously like the one driven by the fourteen-year-old boy Sandy had identified as Ronald.

"They? Who is *they?*"

"You know, the people I rode with."

"No, that's just the problem, Allie. I don't know the name of the people . . . or person, who brought you home. I thought we reached an understanding the other day when—"

"Hi, sweetie." Sam walked into the room and put his arm around Allie. "Glad you're home. We were getting worried about you."

"I'm fine, Daddy. We just ran a little late."

"And speaking of running late, you better scoot upstairs and get ready. We don't want to walk into the church in the middle of the I-do's."

Allie rose up on tiptoe and kissed his cheek. "Okay, Daddy, I'll hurry." And she left the room without so much as a glance in Lynn's direction.

Lynn opened her mouth to make a comment, then closed it. Now was not the time to tell Sam she thought his daughter was lying through her pretty white teeth about where she had been, and with whom. Later. She would talk to him later.

CHAPTER EIGHT

THE FIRST BAPTIST CHURCH of Crystal Creek looked like a Christmas fairyland, all decked out in greenery, off-white and deep-wine-colored poinsettias, candles and even some gold tinsel. It was no secret that Amanda Walker had exquisite taste and a pipeline to practically every good deal from Texas to New York. And it had paid off handsomely, because the wedding decorations were nothing short of breathtaking. Six candelabras, each perched atop imposing standards, formed a wide semicircle behind a tall latticework arch draped with antique ivory lace that was tied with bows and adorned by several pairs of artificial white doves. All that was covered with greenery and poinsettia blossoms. A wide ivory satin runner traveled from the bottom step of the pulpit platform, down the long aisle separating the rows of pews.

The setting was perfect. The effect was dazzling and humbling, all at the same time.

Lynn knew from talking to Cynthia that Amanda wanted the ceremony to be traditional from beginning to end, because she fully intended to have a very traditional marriage—faithful and loving. Lynn could identify with those sentiments because they were exactly the same things she had wanted when she married Sam. Now, here she was, standing next to him, carrying his child and feeling more unsure of herself than she ever had in her life. Not wanting to dwell on her unhappiness, Lynn sighed and glanced around the church.

"Looks like practically the whole town is here," Sam said.

"Looks like it," Lynn replied.

Cal and Serena, Cynthia and J.T. were sitting two pews down with Ken and Nora Slattery to their right. She could see her aunt, Carolyn, and Vernon Trent at the end of the same pew she occupied, and glancing over her left shoulder she noticed Bubba Gibson with his daughter, Sara, and Warren Trent. Soon to be wed themselves, Sara and Warren had eyes for only each other. On the other side of the wide isle were Manny Hernandez with Sheriff Jackson and his wife, Jessica, and Scott and Val Harris. She also noticed Eva Blake and her daughter, Margaret Langley, and made a mental note to ask Margaret how her husband was recuperating after his recent stay in the hospital.

Lynn's gaze wandered over the guests until she caught a glimpse of a stately-looking woman with silver hair. This was undoubtedly Brock Monroe's Aunt Millie, about whom she had heard from Serena. Lynn stared, then blinked, almost as if she couldn't believe her eyes.

"Sam," she whispered, tugging on his sleeve. "Do you see the woman with the silver hair sitting down front?"

"Where?"

"There." She pointed. "Second pew from the front."

Sam tilted his head to see around the guests in front of him. "What about her?"

"Am I losing my mind or is that who...or should I say, *what* I think it is, sitting next to her?"

Sam looked again. "It looks like... Well, that can't be... If I didn't know better, I'd swear..."

"You'd swear what?" Lynn urged.

"I'd swear that was a dog sitting next to her."

From the pew behind Lynn and Sam, Rose Purdy leaned forward and whispered, "It is. That's that mutt Brock and Amanda are so fond of. Alvin. He's the one that found that scientist and Marjorie Perez's friend... What was her name? Nell or something like that."

"Shush," Nate warned his wife.

"Oh, shush yourself." She waved aside the warning. "They said if it wasn't for Alvin they wouldn't be together and *insisted* he be at the wedding. Have you ever heard such—"

"I said shush!" Dr. Purdy grabbed his wife's arm and urged her to sit back.

Grinning, Sam glanced at Lynn. "I guess the whole town *is* here."

At that moment, the music that had been softly playing in the background segued into the bridal processional, signaling the wedding was beginning.

Reverend Howard Blake took his place at the center of the arch, followed by Brock and his attendants. Then came Amanda's attendants: Tracey Hernandez, Mary Gibson and Beverly Townsend. All three women looked stunning in full-length gowns of forest-green velveteen. But Lynn had to admit that she couldn't ever remember seeing Mary Gibson look so lovely. Considering the difference in their ages and background, Mary and Amanda's friendship might have seemed strange, but Lynn knew from Beverly that the two had formed a special relationship.

As the attendants took their places, the strains of the bridal march filled the church, and the congregation turned for their first look at the bride.

Amanda was breathtaking in a gown of ivory satin and lace, accentuated with seed pearls and delicate whispers of ribbons. But it was the smile on her beautiful face that made her truly a joy to behold.

Sam watched Amanda come down the aisle almost as if she were floating on air. She was quite lovely. *But not as beautiful as Lynn was on our wedding day.*

He vividly remembered his first glimpse of his bride. He'd almost stopped breathing, she was so stunning. And the thought that in a few moments from then she would be his wife was even more stunning. He remembered, too, the feeling of contentment and joy he had felt. He wanted that feeling again.

Reverend Blake began: "Dearly beloved, we are gathered here in the sight of God and in the face of this company to join together Brock and Amanda in holy matrimony...."

As he listened to the words, Sam's need to feel close to Lynn was so powerful that he reached over and gently took her hand.

And at the touch of Sam's hand on hers, Lynn's heart leapt. She glanced up and was instantly disappointed to find his gaze straight ahead instead of on her. Listening to the words of the marriage covenant, she wondered if Sam remembered how it had been between them at first. Did he remember how much in love they had been?

"Will you love her, comfort her, honor and keep her, in sickness and in health..." The reverend went on. "And forsaking all others, give yourself to her, so long as you both shall live?"

The words made her question Sam's true feelings. *Have you forsaken all others, Sam?* Lynn wondered. *Will I ever be equal to Marta in your eyes?*

With her other hand, Lynn reached across her belly and covered Sam's hand holding hers. Her fingertips touched the underside of her wedding ring, and he gave her hand a little squeeze. While the rest of the congregation watched Amanda and Brock lighting the unity candle, Lynn looked at her husband and wondered how she could bear to continue living in another woman's shadow. While the rest of the congregation listened to Howard Blake's prayer and benediction, Lynn heard her heart crying out, desperate to hold on to Sam's love.

THE CHURCH'S Fellowship Hall, where the reception was being held, was as dazzlingly decorated as the sanctuary had been. And as crowded.

Cynthia and J.T., with Jennifer in her father's arms, materialized out of the crowd and walked over to Lynn.

"Where's my son-in-law?" J.T. asked, looking around and hoping he wasn't posing the wrong question.

"He's getting me some cake." Lynn patted her stomach. "As if I needed it."

"Cake sounds like a good idea," Cynthia said, turning to J.T. "Why don't you and Jennifer bring me some?"

"I thought you were avoiding sweets like the plague. Not that you need to," he added hastily.

"I'll share it with you." She smiled at him.

"Darlin', when you look at me like that, you can ask for anything."

"I'll remember that when we get home."

J.T. grinned, then hitched his daughter higher in his arms and headed for the cake and punch.

"I think half the town showed up," Cynthia said.

"Including Alvin."

"Alvin? You mean that mutt that found those two kids in that cave a while back?"

"The one and only." Lynn shrugged. "Go figure. I saw him sitting in one of the pews with the woman I assumed was Brock's aunt, and then Rose Purdy told me that Amanda and Brock insisted he be at the wedding."

"You're not serious? A dog? At a wedding?"

Lynn raised her right hand. "Swear to God. Right there in church. I never would have believed it, if I hadn't seen it with my own eyes." She glanced across the room at the guests streaming into the reception hall. "Turn around and see for yourself."

Cynthia turned, and sure enough, there, next to the Purdys, was Millicent Monroe, holding a small, ragged, mongrel dog in her arms. The group headed toward them. "Oh my Lord."

Lynn giggled.

"Cynthia, I don't believe you've met my old friend, Millie Monroe," said Nate.

"Nice to meet you, Millie. And may I introduce J.T.'s oldest daughter, Lynn Russell."

"Delighted to meet you both."

"Thank you," Lynn said, still grinning. "Lovely wedding, wasn't it?"

"Gorgeous. Absolutely gorgeous. But then Amanda does everything so well."

"Are you going to be in town long?" Cynthia inquired.

"I'll be around for a few days while Amanda and Brock take a short honeymoon. They're going to New Orleans, you know. It's my wedding gift to them, and I'm going to take care of Alvin while they're gone. He's quite the hero, you know."

"Yes, we all heard about the rescue." Lynn eyed the mutt and almost laughed out loud. Someone, presumably Millie Monroe, had tied a forest-green velvet ribbon around the dog's scruffy neck. Lynn had never seen anything that looked more ridiculous in her life, and she had a suspicion Alvin shared her opinion.

"And to think that I hardly liked him at all the first time I saw him," Millie remarked.

"Hard to imagine," Lynn commented with a smile.

Alvin yawned as if he were completely bored with the entire conversation. He tried unsuccessfully to scratch while being held and started to squirm.

Thankfully, Amanda and Brock came into the room just then. Brock waved and Millie waved back, lifting Alvin's paw in greeting as well.

Cynthia looked at Lynn and rolled her eyes.

Soon after, Millie excused herself, claiming Brock and Amanda would want to say goodbye to Alvin.

Cynthia and Lynn were still laughing when J.T. and Jennifer returned with Sam and the requested plates of cake. Wayne and Jessica Jackson were close behind.

"Wasn't the wedding gorgeous?" Jessie said. "And that dress! My Lord, it looked like it cost a fortune."

"Knowing Amanda, she probably knew someone, who knew someone, who knew someone who got her a great deal," Cynthia said.

Jessie lifted her glass of punch in salute. "We should all be so lucky."

"Talk about lucky... heard you had a run-in with a bar ditch," Wayne said to Lynn.

Sam put his arm around her. "Scared the hell outta me, I don't mind telling you."

Wayne frowned, his gaze roving over Lynn as if he were checking her for any sign of injuries. "You okay?"

"I'm fine. A little sore, but otherwise, good as new."

"Y'all have had some bad luck lately. First that snake—"

"What snake?" Cynthia asked, wide-eyed. "I thought Sam's office was bad enough, but Lynn, you never mentioned anything about a snake."

"I'll tell you about it later," she insisted.

"Yeah, your office got hit, Sam. And now this wreck. If I didn't know better," Wayne remarked, "I'd say someone had it in for you guys."

"Naw." Sam dismissed the idea. "Snakes pop up every now and again. You said so yourself. The vandalism was probably due to teenagers. And as for the wreck...I've been so preoccupied lately that I haven't taken care of any of our vehicles like I should have." He looked into Lynn's upturned face. "Fact of the matter is, I've let a lot of things slip that need attention."

Lynn blinked, her eyes moist with tears. In his own way, Sam was apologizing for his behavior last night. She wanted to throw her arms around his neck, but she simply smiled at him.

"And what about getting all four of your tires shot out from under you?"

"What?" J.T. exclaimed. "Where? When?"

"The Hole in the Wall." Sam hurried to explain. "Scott and Val Harris think it was poachers. They've had some trouble before. I'm sure you know, Wayne."

J.T. was obviously worried. "Why didn't you say something, Lynn?"

"Because it was all taken care of. No harm done."

Jennifer McKinney was growing restless in her father's arms and started to fret. "I think," her mother said, patting the child's back, "that we'd better get home and put this one to bed." She turned to Lynn. "I'll call you tomorrow."

"Yeah. I think Lynn's been on her feet long enough. Maybe we'll call it a night too," Sam added.

WAYNE WAS GLAD to note things looked okay between Sam and Lynn as they strolled off together.

Maybe Sam had decided to discuss his problem with his wife after all. But Wayne hadn't been at all pleased when he heard the news of Lynn's wreck. And regardless of the fact that Sam dismissed the series of unusual events as coincidence, Wayne was beginning to wonder if possibly Providence had had some help. The odds that such a string of misfortunes could occur to the same people within a week were a hundred to one. Maybe even a thousand to one.

Wayne Jackson wasn't a betting man. But he did rely on a hunch once in a while. Like now.

Ken and Nora Slattery were standing across the room enjoying the festivities. Wayne grabbed Jessie's hand and pulled her along with him. "Hey, Ken. How's it goin'?"

"Wayne, Jessica. Goin' good. How 'bout yourself?"

"Can't complain."

Nora engaged Jessie in conversation about her trip to Dallas, giving Wayne the opportunity he was looking for.

"You hear that the little McKinney wound up in a bar ditch last night?"

"Yeah," Ken confirmed. "Brakes went out. 'Bout scared us all outta ten years' growth, I don't mind tellin' you. Her Suburban was messed up pretty bad in front, but they hauled it off to Elton's Texaco. I hear his new mechanic is a whiz."

"Elton's, you say?"

"How come you're so interested in Sam and Lynn all of a sudden?"

Wayne shook his head. "Just curious. Seems they've had a lot of crap happen to them lately. Know any reason why they'd be singled out?"

Ken Slattery cocked his head to one side and looked at the sheriff, a man he'd been acquainted with long enough to know that he wasn't given to idle curiosity. "Can't think of a one. Far as I know, neither of them got any enemies. Sam's easygoin' and Lynn wouldn't hurt a fly." Then Ken frowned, as if he were remembering something.

"What?"

"Nothin', except..."

"Except what?"

"The only time I've ever known Lynn to cross swords with anyone was just about a week ago."

"What happened?"

"She had to fire that hand we took on a couple of months ago to help train Lightning until after the baby comes. He and Lynn never did exactly hit it off, and she caught him whippin' the horse. Fella named Walt Taggart. Fired him on the spot."

"What kinda man is this Taggart?"

"Saddle bum mostly. Real good with horses, but a real ass when it comes to people."

Wayne thought for a moment. "Know where he went?"

"Naw. He's a drifter. They roll in, work till they get a few coins in their jeans, then drift on."

"Seen him around since he left the Double C?"

"You know," Ken said, "you're soundin' an awful lot like a cop."

Wayne gave him a deceptively easy grin. "Sorry. Force of habit."

"Hey, you two look way too serious," Jessie said, moving close to her husband. "Commiserating about the demise of Brock's bachelorhood?"

"Not me." Ken held Nora's hand. "Don't ever let anybody tell you being footloose and fancy-free is better than hog-tied and homebound."

"Hog-tied!" Nora exclaimed good-naturedly.

"Did I say hog-tied, darlin'? I meant hog heaven."

"That's better."

"Great save," Jessica commented, and they all laughed.

But long after Wayne and Jessica had said their goodbyes to Ken and Nora, Brock and Amanda and several other guests, Wayne's conversation with Ken stayed on his mind. Long enough that he decided to find out more about the man called Walt Taggart.

THE PHONE WAS RINGING when Sam, Lynn, Allie and Sandy walked in the back door.

"I'll get it," Allie yelled and raced for the phone. But Sandy beat her to it.

"It's for you, Daddy," she said a second later.

Without paying much attention to Sam's conversation, Lynn shooed the girls toward the stairs.

"Okay, ladies, upstairs and out of those good clothes."

"Thank you for calling," she heard Sam say, before he stopped them with "I want to talk to you."

All three females turned around. "No, Sandy, you can go on to bed. Allie, you stay." Deciding she, too, had been dismissed, Lynn turned to leave. "Don't go, honey. I think you should hear this, too."

Sam looked directly at his daughter. "That was your social studies teacher, Mrs. Greenway. She's been calling all evening to make sure you got home all right. She said you had her drop you off at the school parking lot this afternoon because we were coming to pick you up and do some Christmas shopping."

Allie looked stunned, but didn't say a word.

"Want to tell me what this is all about?"

"I don't know, Daddy. She must have me mixed up with one of the other girls."

Lynn couldn't believe her ears. The girl was lying again. And Sam looked as if he was on the verge of believing her.

"Mrs. Greenway didn't sound confused at all. In fact, she was very sure it was you."

Allie just shook her head.

"Now, I'll ask you straight out, Allie. Did you ride home with Mrs. Greenway?"

"Who else would I have ridden with?" Allie asked, maintaining her innocence.

"Maybe Lynn can shed some light on this question."

Lynn's head snapped up. "Me?"

"You were here in the kitchen when Allie came home, weren't you?"

"Well . . . yes."

"Did you happen to notice who brought her home?"

Truth or consequences time, Lynn thought. She didn't want to get Allie into trouble, but she would not lie to Sam. "I didn't see exactly who was driving," she said, hoping that much of the truth would suffice. It didn't.

"Was it a car?"

Lynn looked directly into Allie's eyes and hoped and prayed that she wasn't causing more trouble for all of them. "No. It was a pickup with a young man at the wheel." She put her hand on his shoulder when she saw the muscle in his jaw tighten. "Sam. It's late. Maybe tonight is not a good time to deal—"

"No. I think now *is* the right time to deal with this." Pulling a chair away from the kitchen table, he turned to a wide-eyed Allie. "Take a seat, young lady. You and I are going to have a serious discussion about lying."

Before Allie sat down, she gave Lynn a dirty look.

"Sam—" Lynn tried again.

"Why don't you go on. I'll be up in just a minute."

"If you want me to stay . . ."

He shook his head. "Allie and I need to work this out, just the two of us. Besides, I can see that you're beat."

"Are you sure?"

"Positive." He kissed her on the cheek.

Exhausted, Lynn climbed the stairs. *Just the two of us,* Sam had said, excluding her again.

TWENTY MINUTES after Lynn went upstairs, Allie followed and slammed the door to her room behind her. As Sam secured the house for the night and turned out the lights, he thought about everything that had happened that night.

Discovering that Allie had lied to him was devastating. Besides his uppermost desire that his children be safe and happy, he wanted them to be good people, honest caring people. And in his heart, he felt Allie was an honest caring person. But it was a parent's duty to reinforce those traits by setting boundaries and establishing guidelines. Marta had been big on boundaries and guidelines, and he had always depended on her for that. Now, the job was his. And if he was honest with himself, he had to admit that lately, he had not done his job.

Lynn had tried to talk about rules and he had dismissed her. *But she was right. If I had listened to her, Allie and I might have avoided a confrontation tonight.* As things stood now, Allie had been grounded: no calls, no TV, no visitors, no nothing for a week. The only exception would be Christmas with the McKinneys. *If she wants to be treated like a grown-up, then she will damn well have to start acting like one.*

"Well, I did it," he said, closing their bedroom door behind him. "I grounded Allie for lying. Needless to say, she's not very happy with me at the moment, but I think she'll live." He walked toward her side of the bed where she lay half on her side, a book in her hand. "Sweetheart, I want to thank you for—"

Sam realized she hadn't responded to a word he'd said. "Sweetheart." He leaned close to her face and discovered she was sound asleep. He smiled and pushed a wayward wisp of bangs from her forehead. Whatever he had to say could wait until tomorrow. Everything except one thing. "I love you," he whispered and kissed her good-night.

THE MORNING AFTER Brock and Amanda's wedding, Wayne Jackson made a visit to Elton's Texaco station and garage.

"How's it goin', Elton?" he asked casually.

"Fine as wine, sheriff." The long-time owner of the station, a lanky man named Elton Fugate, wiped his hands on a grease rag and shook hands. "Whatcha up to?"

"My ears in paperwork."

Elton laughed. "Yeah, I guess lawmen got their share just like the rest of us."

"And then some," Wayne said. "I hear you're workin' on Lynn Russell's Suburban."

"That's a fact."

"How's it comin'?"

"Okay. I got to order a new bumper and grille, not to mention new tubing for the brake fluid lines."

"I take it there was a leak in one of the lines."

"Well..." With one hand Elton shoved his baseball cap back and scratched his head. The movement exposed a hairline that had progressed well beyond receding. "Funny you should mention a leak. Fact is, looked to me like somebody cut 'em plumb in two."

"The backup line, too?"

"Yeah. Both the primary *and* secondary lines from the master cylinder to the slave cylinder were cut. No wonder that pedal went to the floorboard and stayed there. She didn't have a drop of brake fluid left."

"You sure?"

Elton raised his right hand. "Swear to God. I'm dyin' if I'm lyin'."

"Have you told the Russells any of this?"

"I was just fixin' to call them when you drove up."

"Do me a favor and don't mention anything about the lines being cut."

"Don't know, Sheriff. Seems kinda dishonest to me."

"Trust me, Elton. For the time being, it's better that they don't know. And you don't have to worry.

I'll take full responsibility for making sure they know the truth eventually."

"All right, if you're sure."

"Thanks," Wayne said, eager to get to his office. Suddenly he wanted to know *everything* about Walt Taggart. If his hunch was right, everything would probably include a rap sheet as long as his arm.

CHAPTER NINE

THE AIR WAS CRISP, with just the hint of a chill as Tag slung the braided leather strips and canvas tarp into the back of his Jeep Scrambler. He checked his hip pocket for the bandanna he'd stuffed in there earlier. He had everything he needed. And he'd gone over the plans in his head a hundred times.

He had watched her long enough to know her schedule, at least what little of a schedule she had. Most mornings she went to the Double C, and she always went alone. Perfect. So far, the only thing he hadn't figured into his original plan was the fact that those two brats were out of school for Christmas holidays. But luckily, they didn't go to the ranch with her.

At first he had decided to try and run her off the road as she drove to the ranch; then he changed his mind. What if she got hurt or killed? Even though she had lucked out after he cut her brake lines, how lucky could one person be? No, he wanted her alive and alert for what he had in mind. Then he decided to try and take her at the stables, but quickly threw out that idea. Too risky. Too many people might recognize him. Finally, he decided to take her before she left to go to the ranch. He'd time it just right; right after the husband left for work and before the brats woke up. Brats always slept late.

So, he had it all worked out. He'd pick the lock to the door on the side of the garage, wait for her until she came out to leave . . . then grab her. He'd even planned to park his Jeep a couple of blocks away and walk, so none of the neighbors would notice a strange vehicle and maybe call the cops. Once they got to his truck, he'd ditch her car and light out.

Foolproof, Tag thought, as he poured river water on the campfire. No one knew he was still in Crystal Creek, much less right under the McKinneys' noses. And he didn't plan to keep Lynn Russell long enough for them to find him. Just long enough to get his revenge.

Tag turned up the collar of his denim jacket against the nip in the December air. *So now it's just gonna be you and me, Duchess. Now you're gonna learn some respect. And when I'm through with you, nobody's gonna want ya.*

He climbed into his truck, started the engine and headed toward Crystal Creek.

"SO HOW LONG are you gonna be grounded?" Sandy asked her big sister.

"Probably forever, if they have their way. Now I can't go shopping at the mall today with Mary June."

"Was Daddy mad?"

Allie looked across the table at her sister and didn't have the nerve to admit she had lied. She shrugged. "I told him not to have a cow, but he got so bent outta shape. Just because I rode home with Ronald."

"He'd really freak if he knew you saw Ronald almost every day after school."

Allie glared at Sandy. "You promised you wouldn't tell."

"I didn't tell. If I'd told, Daddy *would* have grounded you forever."

"Well...you better not. Besides, I haven't seen Ronald *every* day."

"Only because we're outta school for Christmas holidays."

Allie wrinkled her nose. "You think you're so smart."

"Smarter than you."

"Fat chance."

"I'm smart enough not to get grounded."

"O-o-oh!" Allie gritted her teeth. "You make me so mad."

"You're mad at Daddy, and you just wanna take it out on me. No way, José. Just go be mad at somebody else."

Frustrated and angry, Allie needed a scapegoat. "Daddy was never like this when we lived in Austin. And he was never like this before he married Lynn."

"I like Lynn. She's neat. She does neat stuff like Mom used to do."

"She's not our mother!" Allie jumped up from the table. "Our mother's dead. Lynn will never take her place. Never!"

Sandy started to cry. "You don't have to say it like that. I know Mom's dead, but I miss her."

"You think I don't? My whole life got screwed up when she died. Now Daddy has Lynn and he doesn't care about us anymore."

"He does, too."

"No, he doesn't. And neither does Lynn. At first, she took us to the ranch and shopping. But that was just to impress Daddy. Now she's got him. What does she care if we don't get to go anywhere or do anything? And in a little while her and Daddy will have a new kid. Then they *really* won't care about us. Well, I got news for them. If they think I'm gonna baby-sit their brat, they can just forget it."

She threw her spoon at the half-empty bowl of cereal. "I hate my life!" The spoon ricocheted off the rim, flew across the table and landed on the floor. Allie ignored it, turned to stomp out of the room and . . . found her father and Lynn standing in the doorway.

The silence in the room was deafening.

Allie's eyes widened and her mouth dropped open as if she intended to speak, but then closed. Her gaze darted between her father and Lynn, trying to read past the stunned expressions on their faces. She had done it now. She would have to do some tall talking to get out of this one.

Sam stared at his oldest child as if she were a stranger. Indeed, the things he had just heard her say were every bit as shocking as if they *had* been uttered by a complete stranger. A hostile stranger.

"Daddy, I didn't mean—"

Sam held up his hand to cut her off. "Allison, turn around. Walk back over there and pick up that spoon. And your cereal bowl. Then put them in the sink," he said calmly. Too calmly. "Then I want you to go to your room and stay there until I tell you that you can come out."

"But, Daddy—"

"At this very moment I am angrier at you than I think I've ever been in your life. Angry enough that I don't want to talk to you until I calm down." He pointed to the stairs. "Go."

Reluctantly, Allie headed for the stairs.

"And Allison..."

"Yes, sir?" she replied without turning around.

"If I hear one mumbling complaint, one temper tantrum stomp as you leave, I'll add another week to your punishment."

"Yes, sir."

When she had gone, Sam turned to Lynn, expecting to find not only shock, but condemnation in her expression. What he found were tears. "I'm...I'm so sorry you had to hear all that."

"And I'm sorry *you* had to hear it." Lynn's heart went out to him. Never had she seen so much pain in his eyes, so much disappointment and regret. The only comforting thing she could think to say was lame at best. "I know every parent wants his child to be perfect, but none of us ever is. Allie is at an angry age. It's only natural that once in a while that anger explodes."

Sam couldn't believe what he was hearing. "How can you stand there and defend her after everything she just said?"

"I'm not defending. I'm explaining. Her manners were atrocious, but we have to look past the words to the underlying cause. Obviously, she needs more of our understanding, not less."

Sandy was still sitting at the table, quietly taking everything in. "Daddy?"

They both looked up as if just remembering she was there. "What is it, sugar?"

"I'm not mad at you. Or you." She looked at Lynn.

Sam went to her and kissed her on the cheek. "Thanks, sweetie." He thought for a moment, then asked, "But do you...have you ever felt the way Allie does?"

Thoughtfully, Sandy looked over at Lynn. "I'm glad about the baby. And Allie was, too. At first."

"I know," Lynn said.

"But those stupid girls she runs around with all act so stuck-up, and Allie thinks she has to act the same way. All they do is talk about boys and clothes and lipstick and stuff."

Lynn had to smile. Sandy had just covered the three most important topics in the universe as far as a teenage girl was concerned. And she would probably be shocked if Lynn predicted that one day, Sandy herself would be totally engrossed in those same subjects. Instead, she simply replied, "That's natural for girls her age."

"Well, I don't like it."

Sam appeared to be as hell-bent on taking a hard-line stand as he had previously been about taking no stand at all. There had to be a middle ground they could all live with.

"I'm not suggesting Allie shouldn't be punished. But Sam, I can remember lots of times when I had some downright vicious thoughts about my brothers and my parents. I don't believe she actually hates her life. Or us, for that matter. Well, you, anyway."

"I won't have her talking about you the way she just did," Sam insisted.

Lynn nodded. "I agree. The way she blew up was not the best way for her to handle her anger. But as her parents we need to provide her with a way."

"You mean . . . a shrink?"

She could see the hesitation in his eyes and knew she would have to proceed gently or he might misunderstand. "You told me once that you had considered the idea of all three of you seeing a counselor after Marta died."

"Yes, but things settled down after a while and I didn't feel it was necessary."

"Settled down?"

"Not so painful. Not so—" Sam searched for the word he wanted and when he couldn't find it, settled for "—traumatic."

"Yet you and the girls never talk about Marta, or how you felt about her. I never hear you reminisce about any of the good times, and I know that there must have been a lot of them over the years."

"Of course."

It was obvious that Sam was uncomfortable discussing this topic, and poor Sandy was still at the table, quietly observing. Lynn knew she could relieve the tension in the room by simply changing the subject. But she had a feeling that a great deal of what was happening in the present was being influenced by what had happened in the past. Specifically, Marta Russell's untimely and unexpected death. She also had a feeling that until Sam, Allie and Sandy were able to deal with the pain and anger over her death, it would continue to cause problems in the home. And in their marriage.

"But you don't *talk* about her, Sam."

"Of course I do. I told you all about Marta before we got married."

"No. You told me that she died. You told me that you missed her and the girls missed her. All of that is a given. What you didn't tell me was how you felt, how you grieved. Sam, how can your daughters ever feel free to talk about her if you don't?''

"And I will...sometime. But not now. We had our whole day planned to go Christmas shopping. Sandy has her party at Professor Bailey's and—''

"When is sometime, Sam?''

He was desperately trying to avoid dealing with this issue he obviously wanted to keep buried. Suddenly, Lynn knew that dealing with this was more than important, it was imperative.

"How did we get from talking about Allie's behavior to discussing...'' He turned to Sandy, who was riveted on their conversation. "Sweetie, I think you should get ready. We're going to leave in a little while.''

Sandy glanced from Lynn to her father. She didn't really want to leave. She wanted to hear how the conversation ended. And she wanted to tell her daddy that sometimes *she* would like to talk about her mother, but was afraid to because she knew how much it hurt him. She wanted to say these things, but instead she merely said, "Yes, Daddy,'' and left the room.

"Lynn—''

"Sam,'' she interrupted him. "I know you feel this isn't a good time to talk about all of this, and maybe you're right.''

"Thank you.''

"But...I think it's *very* important.'' She gently stroked her belly. "We are going to have a new life to care for soon and I want this child to feel loved, to be part of a family. I don't want any of our children to feel alone, or as if they had to get mad for us to pay attention to them."

He came to her and put his arm around her. "Sweetheart, this baby will be loved and I promise you none of our children will feel alone."

"Sam," she murmured, touching his cheek, "I want you to promise me that we will talk about this again. It's important."

"Lynn, I—"

"Promise me."

Sam gazed into her eyes and saw that this topic was something she wouldn't forget. Whether he promised or not, she would bring it up again. But a secret dread tugged at his heart. He didn't want to relive all the pain and anguish that had accompanied Marta's death. He had worked hard to put it as far back in his memory as possible. What good could be gained from dredging it up now? He sighed. But Lynn wasn't going to let it go. He could see the determination in her beautiful eyes.

"All right," he finally said. "I promise."

She rose on tiptoe and kissed him. "Thank you."

"Now, can we go ahead with our day as we planned? Tomorrow is Christmas Eve, and I'm ashamed to admit that I've done almost no shopping whatsoever."

"Things have changed since we made our plans. Are you willing to leave Allie alone in the house while we're gone?"

"Damn. I didn't think about that."

"I have an idea. Let me call Cynthia and see if she could use an extra pair of hands to help her get ready for tomorrow. As a matter of fact, how would you feel if the girls spent the night at the ranch? It would give them some time away from us and—"

"It would give us a chance to be alone," he finished.

"Exactly."

A wide grin split his face. "Great idea. I'll go make sure Sandy is ready."

When Lynn telephoned the ranch, Cynthia answered. "Hello."

"Good morning. Did I catch you at a bad time?"

"Not unless you consider oatmeal as a hair mousse a bad time."

"Excuse me?"

"My daughter just decided to wear her breakfast instead of eating it," Cynthia said, suddenly not at all upset over such event. "Good thing we buy the large economy size of baby shampoo."

"Uh, I'm glad to hear you're in a good mood, because I have a favor to ask."

"Ask away."

"Would it be possible for Allie to come out to the ranch today while Sam and I drive into Austin to do some last-minute shopping? I thought maybe she could help you with tomorrow's preparations."

"You thought right. I would love for the girls to help. As a matter of fact, there are at least a million things I need help with."

"Just Allie. We have to drop Sandy off at Professor Bailey's in Austin."

"That's fine. I'm thrilled that Allie wants to come."

"Well, to be honest, it wasn't her idea. We had a little confrontation of sorts here last night and Sam grounded her."

"I see. Anything serious?"

"Nothing life-threatening, but we really didn't want to leave her in the house all day by herself. We haven't actually given her a choice."

"Does she even have one?"

"Well, she could go with us, but—"

"But you and Sam wanted to spend the day by yourselves."

"It *would* be nice."

"Then, go for it. I guarantee you, if you give Allie a choice between coming here and trudging after her parents, the ranch will win hands down."

Lynn laughed. "You're probably right."

"I'll even go you one better," Cynthia said. "I have to drive into town anyway to go to the dime store, so I'll save you a trip out and pick up Allie."

"That's too much—"

"Nonsense. No point in making the drive out here. This will save you time."

Lynn thought for a moment, then agreed. "Thanks. And on the outside chance that she decides to 'trudge along,' we'll call you back and let you know."

The arrangements set, Lynn was relieved. She even felt a sudden surge of genuine Christmas spirit, something that had been sorely lacking. Tomorrow was Christmas Eve and her whole family would be together. Almost her whole family, she reminded herself. Tyler and Ruth were still in California, and since only J.T. had talked to Tyler since they left, no one knew if they would be home for Christmas or not. She prayed they had worked out their problems by now and that they would be back with the family soon. True, the McKinney Christmas Eve get-together wouldn't be the same without them, but Lynn was determined to make this the best Christmas ever.

When Sam returned a few minutes later, both the girls were with him. Lynn straightened her shoulders in preparation to face Allie. She had made up her mind not to shy away from what had happened earlier. It was important for Allie to see and understand that Lynn was not going to be intimidated, but neither was she going to condemn.

"Did you call Cynthia?" Sam asked hopefully.

"Everything is all set. Cynthia is even going to pick Allie up, which will help because we're running late to Sandy's party. I told her we were leaving now and she said she would be here in about twenty minutes. Thanks for agreeing to help out at the ranch," Lynn said to Allie.

"Daddy told me I had to go."

Lynn surprised everyone by saying, "No, you don't. But since your father and I aren't comfortable leaving you in the house by yourself, you only have one other choice. You can come with us."

Sam almost blurted out his objection until he caught the flash of a warning in Lynn's eyes.

"Cynthia hoped you would want to come to the ranch. I agreed, but said we would call her back if not. You make the choice," Lynn said patiently.

A sullen Allie glanced from one to the other. "The ranch."

The other three Russells all heaved a sigh of relief.

Within minutes Sam, Lynn and Sandy were headed out the back door to leave. Almost to the door, Lynn stopped unexpectedly and turned back to Allie.

"Allie, be sure and lock the door behind us."

"I know what to do."

"Yes, but..." She shivered as a strange feeling came over her. A feeling that she needed to be certain Allie was safe. The sensation was so powerful, she was compelled to walk over to the girl to satisfy a need to be close to her. Every instinct cried out for Lynn to take her in her arms, a gesture she knew would be flatly refused. So she compromised by sweeping a wave of dark hair back from Allie's shoulder.

The gesture startled Allie so much that the affection in it didn't even register until it was gone. "Just…don't let anyone in but Cynthia," Lynn said.

"Yes, ma'am." The girl pronounced the two words distinctly and more than a little coldly.

Her father cut her a warning glance and said, "We'll call you as soon as we get home." He hustled Lynn and Sandy out the door, closed it and listened for the click of the lock behind him.

Allie waited until they had driven completely out of sight before she went to the phone and dialed the Double C. Again, Cynthia answered.

"Hi, Cynthia, this is Allie."

"Hi. I hear you're going to be my lifesaver today."

"Gee, I'm sorry, but I decided to go shopping with Daddy and Lynn."

About which they're thrilled, no doubt, thought Cynthia. "I'm sorry, too. Sure you won't change your mind?"

"I'm sure."

"Well, all right then. See you tomorrow."

"Yeah. See ya." The instant Allie hung up, she dialed Mary June's number.

"You're gonna die when I tell you what happened," Allie informed her friend.

"What? What?"

"I'm grounded."

"You've got to be kidding."

"I swear."

"So you can't go. You're not going! Allie Russell, you can't do this to me. I'll just die if I have to meet Ronald's friend all by myself. I'll just die. This is the worst day of my life. What am I going to do?"

"No, I'm going, only..."

"Only what?"

"You can't tell anybody. It has to be a secret because Daddy and Lynn think I'm going out to the Double C."

"But my Mom'll know."

"We'll tell her they let me go so I could buy a present for Sandy. Parents are suckers for that kinda stuff. Besides, she doesn't know I'm grounded."

"What if she wants to come in and talk to your parents?"

"Take a lot of time getting ready, so all she'll have time for is to honk. She always pulls up in front, so she won't notice the car is gone."

"Cool. But what are you gonna tell your folks when they get back and find you at home? They'll freak. Maybe we better forget it."

"No! Ronald's probably halfway to the mall by now. No, we're going."

"You're gonna be in worse trouble."

"I don't care. Besides, Daddy's never done anything like grounding me before. I'll just tell Lynn I'm re-e-eal sorry. Tomorrow is Christmas. They can't stay mad at me on Christmas."

"Yeah. You're right. Cool."

"Okay, see ya." Allie hung up the phone and started upstairs, but she heard a noise at the back of the house. For a moment she thought her dad and Lynn had come back. She rushed to the kitchen, lifted a corner of the curtain for a peek and held her breath. Her heart pounding, she heaved a sigh of relief. There was no one outside. No cars. Nothing. She decided the noise must have been a dog, and went to her room to finish getting ready. After all, she wanted to look her best for Ronald.

SOMETHING WASN'T RIGHT. Tag could feel it. Her Suburban was still in the garage, yet it didn't look like anyone was home. He ground his teeth. *Where the hell was she?*

He stood in a vee formed by one side of the Russell garage and the back of the house, close enough to the house that he couldn't be seen if anyone looked out the kitchen window.

What was he gonna do?

He had to make a decision and act on it. Soon the neighborhood would be up and moving and he might be seen.

Gotta walk away and wait for another time, or...

Restless as spit on a hot griddle, he finally let his impatience win out. Tag walked around to the back door, pulled the bandanna out of his pocket and wadded it up into his palm, ready to shove it in Lynn Russell's mouth the instant she opened the door.

ALLIE HAD barely finished getting ready and was on her way downstairs when she heard the knock at the back door. It was probably that dorky little friend of Sandy's from next door, she thought. She pushed aside the curtain and peeked out.

Tag grinned and tipped his hat.

Recognizing the Double C ranch hand, Allie opened the door. "Hi," she said.

"Mornin', missy."

"Did Cynthia send you?"

"Uh, you mean, Miz McKinney?"

"I told her I wasn't coming."

"Actually, I'm lookin' for Miz Russell. It's uh, about her horse."

"Lightning? Has something happened to him?"

"Yeah, kinda. Is she home?"

"They went Christmas shopping."

"They?"

"Her and my daddy."

Tag glanced over the girl's shoulder and decided she was probably telling the truth, since no adult had come to see who was at the door. *Accounts for her truck still bein' in the garage. Now what?*

"Is Lightning sick?" Allie asked, genuinely concerned.

"Kinda. You know when they're comin' back?"

"They're gonna be gone all day, I think. You want me to call the vet or something?"

"Uh, no, that's okay." Tag started to walk away, then stopped. Damn, but he had screwed the whole thing up. Now the brat would probably be able to describe him well enough to put the duchess on guard. His impatience had cost him his revenge. *Probably never get another chance.*

Then suddenly, Tag saw an opportunity he hadn't even known existed. In a heartbeat he made a decision. "Hold it a second," he said as Allie was closing the door. "Can I come in and leave her a note?"

Allie hesitated. "I'm not supposed to let strangers in the house."

Tag grinned his most charming smile. "Hey, I'm not a stranger."

"Well, I guess it'll be all right."

"It'll be perfect," Walt Taggart said as he stepped inside and closed the door behind him.

THE MALL IN AUSTIN was jam-packed with last-minute Christmas shoppers. After almost an hour of shopping, Sam and Lynn had barely made a dent in their list. Part of the problem was Lynn's distraction. She couldn't seem to get Allie out of her thoughts.

"You want to stop for a while?" Sam asked. "Maybe get a cup of coffee?"

"No, I'm fine. Besides, if I have coffee, I'll just have to hunt down the nearest ladies' room. Who have we got left to buy for?"

Sam pulled the list out of his shirt pocket. "Half of the civilized world."

"Don't get cute. You think we should get something for Tyler and Ruth?"

"Are they coming home?"

Lynn shook her head. "Nobody's heard from them. Let's put them at the bottom of the list for now."

Sam arched an eyebrow at his wife. "He's your brother. It's up to you."

"Okay, bottom of the list and we'll see how much time we have left after all of this." She waved the paper in the air.

"Seriously, I think we should keep our spending down as much as possible."

"Absolutely. I think whatever we get for my family should be tokens, so we can concentrate on Sandy and Allie. I want to make this especially nice for them."

"You already have."

"I'm not so sure they would agree with you."

"Give them time," Sam said, taking the list from her and tucking it back into his pocket. They continued on to the next store, one known for catering to "in" clothes for students. Sam was standing patiently watching Lynn browse through some jackets she thought Sandy might like, when suddenly she became very still.

A feeling of coldness washed over her, holding her in an icy grip. Dread, thick and hard, settled around her heart, and she had a sense that something terrible was about to happen.

"What? Is it the baby?" Sam said, concerned.

She shook her head. "N-no. He's fine. But..."

"But what? Lynn, you're scaring me."

She reached for his hand, holding it tightly.

"Sweetheart, your hand is like ice."

That's what I feel. Ice. Cold, ugly, frightening—

"Sam, would you think I'm crazy if I said we should call Allie?"

He pulled back to look at her. "Why on earth would you want to do that?"

"I don't know. It's just that I feel—"

"If you're about to say guilty, don't. Everything you said this morning was right. In fact, you've been right about a lot of things. Besides, if we call, she'll just think we're checking up on her."

Everything he said made sense, but Lynn couldn't quite shake the feeling of dread, of impending danger.

"C'mon," Sam insisted, pulling her along with him. "Let's go find a table in the cafeteria and have a nice quiet, early lunch before it's too crowded."

"Sounds lovely," she told him, a hint of hesitation still lingering. *You're being silly. Maybe Sam's right. You're feeling guilty.* Why else would Allie have stayed on her mind ever since they'd left Crystal Creek?

CHAPTER TEN

THE DAY HAD BEEN more than Lynn had hoped for. She and Sam had talked; they'd gotten back into the rhythm of dialogue with each other, expressing opinions, sharing thoughts and ideas. Their subjects ranged from the mundane and fanciful, such as hemlines in women's wear and the lifestyles of people who shop at specialty coffee stores to the serious: they talked about the baby and all their hopes for him. They laughed and joked and walked hand in hand. But the most important thing was that they *talked.* By the end of the shopping trip she was physically worn-out, but mentally and emotionally she had never felt better. And she felt closer to Sam than she had in months. Totally exhausted, but pleased with the day, she fell asleep on the way back to Crystal Creek.

"Daddy?" Sandy whispered from the back seat.

"Yes, sugar." Sam kept his own voice low and even so as not to wake Lynn.

She leaned as far forward as her seat belt would allow. "Are you and Lynn still mad at each other?"

"Sandy, we're not mad at each other. You have to understand. Married people don't always agree. And sometimes when they disagree, they talk loud, even yell. It's not a good way to settle differences, but sometimes it happens. That doesn't mean they don't love each other."

"Do you love Lynn?"

He glanced in the rearview mirror just long enough to make eye contact with his daughter. "Yes, Sandy. I love Lynn very much. I can't imagine what my life would be like without her."

She waited for another second or two of eye contact and smiled. "Me, too, Daddy."

Well, one down and one to go. Now all he had to do was get Allie to come around, and maybe they could really begin to be a family. That is, as soon as he kept his promise to Lynn and talked about Marta.

Briefly, he glanced at Lynn again. If their outing today had done nothing else, it had proved how good they were together. He couldn't remember the last time he had felt so relaxed. And considering their present financial problems and the fact that they were actually spending money, the day should have been more, not less, stressful. But spending time with Lynn, talking, sharing, even laughing, had made him recognize all the reasons he had fallen in love with her. And for the first time, he realized how different those reasons were from the motivations that had prompted his love for Marta. He realized how dif-

208 SOMEWHERE OTHER THAN THE NIGHT

ferent this marriage was from his first. How different he had become.

He began to see that perhaps he had placed some unfair expectations on Lynn. And on himself.

THE MESSAGE LIGHT on the answering machine was blinking when Sam, Lynn and Sandy walked in the back door. Sam hit the retrieval button. After the computerized voice announced that they had two messages, Mary June Wynn's recorded voice came on.

"Allie Russell, you are a traitor. We honked and honked and honked. My mother was foaming at the mouth, she was so mad. She wouldn't let me come in and get you. And we had to go without you! You ruined the whole thing. I will never, never, *never* trust you as long as I live."

"My heavens," Lynn said, at the finish of the message. "What was all that about?"

"Beats me."

The next message was from Wayne Jackson, asking Sam to call him.

"Probably about the vandalism," Sam said, only half-listening.

"Why would Mary June think Allie was going somewhere with her? And what does she mean, 'ruined the whole thing'?"

"I don't have the vaguest idea." Sam stared at the machine as if he expected Mary June's voice to come back on and provide the answers.

"Maybe we should—"

"Maybe we should—" They had spoken simultaneously.

"Call Cynthia?" Lynn asked.

Sam nodded.

J.T. answered on the second ring. "McKinney."

"Hi, Dad, how are you?"

"Fine, punkin'. How are you and that almost grandchild of mine doin'?"

"We're both doing fine. Dad, can I speak to Allie?"

"Allie?"

The instant J.T. responded, Lynn knew something was wrong. "She was out there to help Cynthia get ready for tomorrow. Sam and I were shopping most of the day—"

"Hold on a minute, Lynn. I think you better talk to Cynthia."

Standing beside her, Sam whispered, "What did he say?"

She looked up at him, unable to hide her concern. "He went to get Cynthia."

A second later, Cynthia came on the line. "Lynn? Your father said something about Allie?"

"She spent the day with you, didn't she?"

There was a pause. "No," Cynthia said, trying to keep the surprise out of her voice. "She called after I talked to you and said she had decided to go shopping. I tried to change her mind, but she said no."

"What is it?" Sam demanded, seeing the expression on Lynn's face. He reached out and took the receiver from her hand. "Cynthia, this is Sam."

Evidently Cynthia repeated what she had told Lynn, because Sam's expression mirrored Lynn's. "What time did she call?" he asked. Then, "And that's all she said?" And finally, "Nothing else? You're sure?" Lynn saw tension tighten the muscles in his neck.

"All right. Yes, we'll call you as soon as she comes home," Sam said and hung up.

"Where could she be?"

"I don't kn—"

"Mary June's!" Lynn said. "That has to be where she is. She must have heard the message and gone to talk to her."

"But she was grounded. She knew she couldn't—"

"Sam, my love," she said, reaching for the phone, a spark of hope in her eyes. "I hate to break this to you, but it's possible that Allie completely ignored your punishment." After a second, she said, "Hello, Darlene, this is Lynn Russell. Is Allie at your house?"

In the next second, the spark of hoped died. "Has Mary June seen her, or talked to her?" Lynn looked up at Sam. "The mall?" she said quizzically. "And she didn't come to the door or call Mary June later? Sure, I'll hold on."

Lynn put her hand over the mouthpiece. "Darlene said the girls had plans to go to the mall today, but when they came by to pick Allie up, she wasn't here.''

"Ask her—"

"Yes, Darlene, I'm still here. What *boy?* And this was all preplanned? Yes, Darlene, please. And ask her if she can remember anything Allie might have said about this boy, or where they might go. Absolutely. Anything, no matter how insignificant it sounds. Thanks, bye."

"Well," Lynn said, turning to an anxious Sam. "It seems that Allie and Mary June not only planned to go to the mall today, but they planned to meet a couple of boys there as well."

"Boys?" Sam frowned. "Who?"

"*A* boy. Darlene said she would get as much information out of Mary June as she could, and call us back."

"Well, maybe I need to go over there and talk to—"

"His name's Ronald."

Sam and Lynn both spun about at the sound of Sandy's voice. "What?"

"His name's Ronald. He's Allie's boyfriend."

Lynn gasped. "That boy in the pickup."

Sam's head snapped up. "You knew about him?"

"No. I mean, yes…in a way. Last week Allie rode home from school with a kid named Ronald. We talked about it and she promised me it wouldn't happen again."

"I can't believe you didn't tell me. Why didn't you tell me, for God's sake? Who is this kid? Where does he live?"

The phone rang, and Sam fairly pounced on it. "Hello," he barked into the receiver. "Mrs. Wynn, yes." A pause followed. "And that's all she told you. You're sure? No, I'm not insinuating she's lying...." Sam shook his head as if to clear it. "No. Of course not, it's just that we're so worried— Yes. And tell Mary June thanks."

"Sam?"

"The boy's name is Ronald Bodecker. He lives on West Street and he's fifteen. That's all Mary June knows."

Lynn reached under the counter where the phone was sitting and pulled out the Crystal Creek telephone directory. Slowly, she ran her index finger down a column of names. "Bodecker on West Street ... got it!"

Sam talked to Mr. Bodecker, then Ronald, then Mr. Bodecker again. Lynn was able to pick up the gist of the conversation from listening to Sam. And the news wasn't hopeful.

While she listened, she kept remembering the sensation of coldness she'd experienced when they were shopping that morning. She also remembered the almost overpowering urge to call and make sure Allie was all right. *If only I had. Maybe Allie would be home right now.*

"So, we're back to square one. Nobody seems to have any idea where she might be."

"Then we have to start calling all of her friends, even the ones in Austin."

Sam brightened somewhat at the mention of Allie's Austin friends. "Of course. Maybe some of them have talked to her. Or maybe she went to see one of them."

Lynn doubted very much that that was the case, but she didn't have the heart to put a damper on his hopes so quickly. However, after six or eight phone calls with no results, she couldn't ignore the growing sense of dread.

Sam rubbed the knots of tension along the back of his neck. "Do you think she could be doing this to get back at me for grounding her? Deliberately hiding out until she thinks I've suffered enough?"

Lynn wished with all her heart that she could truthfully say that he was right, but she couldn't. In fact, she was beginning to suspect the situation was much more serious than any of them had thought at first. "No," she said honestly. "And Sam, I don't want to upset you further, or make it seem like I'm giving up, but..."

"But what?"

"I think we should call Wayne Jackson."

Sam stared at her, knowing the suggestion was valid, yet fighting it because somehow it did imply that they were giving up, that there was no more that *they* could do. That the situation was serious enough to warrant making it official.

"Daddy?" Sandy came to him and he held her. "Is Allie going to be okay?"

"Of course she is, sugar. Of course she is." His gaze met Lynn's and she thought she saw tears in his eyes. "We're going to find her. We just need some help to do it, so we're going to call Sheriff Jackson."

WAYNE JACKSON ARRIVED in less than ten minutes. "You folks doin' okay?" he asked as soon as he walked in the door.

"We'll be fine as soon as Allie is home safe and sound," Sam replied.

"How long has she been gone, do you think?"

When Sam thought back, counting the hours since they had left for Austin and the time Darlene Wynn said she came by...

"My God," he said. "Seven hours. She's been missing for seven hours!"

Wayne put a hand on his shoulder. "We'll find her."

"But she's just a kid! It's so dark outside—"

"Sam, we'll find her. You hear me?" He looked at Lynn. "What I need from both of you is the hardest thing for you to do. I need for you to try and stay calm and give me every piece of information you've got, no matter how small. Sometimes a little thing can make a big difference. In the meantime,

I've got my deputy canvassing the neighborhood asking questions.''

For the next twenty minutes Wayne questioned Sam, Lynn and Sandy, having them relate practically everything that had happened in the past twenty-four hours.

"Has she ever done anything like this before?" Wayne asked.

"Never."

"But, Lynn, you said she rode home with this—" He flipped a page back in his palm-sized notebook "—Bodecker boy one day last week. That wasn't her usual behavior, was it?"

"No, but—"

"Yes, it was." Sandy's softly spoken statement got the immediate attention of all three adults.

The little girl was sitting at one end of the sofa, next to Sam. Wayne squatted beside her, balancing on the balls of his feet. "You think it was more than once, Sandy?"

She glanced at her father. "I promised not to tell. You won't ground her for longer if I tell, will you, Daddy?"

Sam had to fight to keep the emotion out of his voice. "No, baby, I won't. You tell the sheriff everything you know, okay?"

"Okay." She looked back at the broad-shouldered lawman.

"Was it more than once, Sandy?"

"Yessir. They met every afternoon after school. Ronald was always trying to get Allie to ride with him."

"And did she?"

"Just twice. The time Lynn saw her and one other time before that."

"Sandy," Wayne asked, keeping his voice as gentle and even as possible because the child was obviously frightened, "think very hard. Is there anything else that you can tell us that might help us find Allie? Maybe some favorite or secret place where she liked to go and be alone?"

Sandy shook her head.

"How about some place she wanted to go, or dreamed about going?"

The girl thought for a moment, then said, "Disney World."

Wayne barely controlled a grin. "Any place else?"

Sandy shook her head again just as there was a knock on the door. Wayne Jackson stood up quickly. "I'll get that. It's probably my deputy."

True to the prediction, the deputy stepped inside the kitchen and began talking to Jackson in a low voice.

Lynn and Sam had followed Wayne and now Lynn reached for Sam's hand.

"Can you hear what they're saying?"

"No." Sam held on tightly to her hand.

Neither of them ~~voiced the~~ question that was uppermost in their minds. *Was there news, and was the news good or bad?*

A frown on his forehead, Wayne came over to them. "We've got a woman one block over who said she saw a strange man in the neighborhood this morning."

"What do you mean, strange?"

"She said she'd never seen him around here before. One of the two reasons she remembered him so well is because he walked right past her house while she was out ~~looking~~ for her cat. According to her, the guy was short, maybe five foot nine or ten. Not skinny, but wiry, like he worked for a living. She described him as just a cowboy, dressed in jeans, boots, a faded, dark blue plaid shirt, down vest and cowboy hat."

"You said there were two reasons. What's the other?"

"She said he was wearing chaps. Those stovepipe kind that zip down the outside of your leg. She thought it was odd."

Suddenly Lynn's heartbeat kicked into double time and her mouth went dry. *It couldn't be. It wasn't possible. Oh, please, dear God, it can't be.* "Wh-what did you say?"

"She thought a guy in chaps looked odd," Wayne repeated.

Lynn swallowed hard. "Did he...did she say what kind of hair he had?"

"Do you know this guy?" Sam said.

"I'm not sure. Please, Wayne, did she tell the deputy what kind of hair he had? Was it dark and curly?"

Wayne glanced over at the deputy, who then looked over his notes. After a second, the deputy lifted his gaze from the page and nodded to the sheriff.

At the nod, Lynn felt her knees turn to rubber. Eyes closed, she swayed ever so slightly, and instantly Sam's arm was around her waist.

"Sweetheart, what is it?" He helped her across the kitchen to a chair, then pulled up one beside her for himself.

"Lynn?" At the no-nonsense tone of Wayne Jackson's deep voice, her eyes snapped open. "You got some idea who this guy is?"

"I—I . . . think so." She took a deep, steadying breath. "From the description, it could be a man by the name of Taggart. Walt Taggart. He always wore a pair of stovepipe chaps."

Sam looked puzzled. "Isn't that the ranch hand helping you train Lightning?"

"Not anymore," Jackson said calmly, and without surprise. "You fired him, didn't you?"

Lynn's gaze went to the sheriff. "H-how did you know?"

"Ken Slattery mentioned it at the reception last night."

"Why didn't you tell me that you'd fired him?" Sam asked.

"It wasn't all that important—"

Wayne began scribbling in his little notebook. "Why'd you fire him?"

"He'd been mistreating Lightning. I suspected it had been going on for some time, but I couldn't prove it. Then one day I walked in and found him with a riding crop raised to Lightning. I told him to get off the Double C."

"And did he?"

Lynn glanced away. "Not immediately."

"Taggart came on to you, didn't he?"

Sam's head snapped up. "Just what the hell are you saying?"

Ignoring Sam, Wayne continued. "And you had to defend yourself, didn't you?"

Lynn paused for a moment before answering. "Yes, but it wasn't anything. He'd been drinking, I think."

"What?" Sam glanced from Wayne to Lynn. "Why didn't you tell me?"

"Because it was no big deal. Ken showed up about the time Taggart became obnoxious, and that was the end of it."

"I'm not so sure," the big sheriff said.

"Look," Sam said, shaking his head in confusion. "This is all sounding a little too weird."

"Makes perfect sense when you add it to everything else that's been happening to you two lately."

Wayne held up his big hand, fingers wide and began to count off. "First there was the snake. In December, when snakes in general, copperheads in particular, are scarce. Then the break-in at your office, Doc. Then there's the business with Lynn's brakes."

"What are you talking about?"

"I talked to Elton over at the garage. Both of the brake lines in Lynn's Suburban were deliberately cut."

Sam and Lynn looked at the sheriff as if he had just announced Martians had landed. "If you don't believe me, you can call Elton yourself," Wayne assured them.

"But that would mean..." Sam's mind jumped to the logical conclusion, but he couldn't bring himself to voice the thought.

"Yeah ... I know. The funny thing is, I was just about to pick up the phone and dial your number when you called. After what Ken said, and after talking to Elton, I sorta put two and two together and decided to run a check on this Taggart fella."

"And?" Sam felt Lynn's fingers curl over his.

Wayne hesitated long enough for both Sam and Lynn to dread what he was about to say. "The guy's bad news. Real bad news. I'm sorry. He's served time in Huntsville for assault and battery, and he's wanted for questioning in several..." He almost went ahead and said "murders", but changed his mind. Sam and Lynn were upset enough without having all the nasty details, no matter how truthful, dangled in front of them, "counties," he added. When neither of them pushed for him to define the statement, Wayne was relieved.

"So," Sam said, more than slightly stunned by all that had happened in the past hour, "what do we do now?"

"With your permission, I'd like to call in the FBI."

"But I thought that you would—"

"Claro County doesn't have the manpower or the equipment for an all-out search. They're better equipped to handle a..." Again, he hesitated to use the word that accurately described what he believed to be the situation. But try as he might, Wayne couldn't come up with anything other than the truth. "Kidnapping. They're better equipped to handle a kidnapping. I believe that Walt Taggart has kidnapped your daughter."

By now Lynn was crying; fat teardrops rolled down her cheeks and were plopping onto her protruding stomach. "Oh, Allie, Allie."

Sam tried to swallow the knot of fear lodged in his throat and couldn't.

"I know it's hard to think of anything in the situation even coming close to being good, but we've got one thing in our favor."

"What?" Sam jumped at even a faint ray of hope.

"I don't think he'll hurt Allie because he's after bigger fish."

"Money?"

Wayne shook his head and gazed down at Lynn. Damn, he could see that she was hanging on by a thread. A slender thread. This wasn't the best timing, but they needed to be prepared. "I think Taggart took Allie as second choice. I think he came for you, Lynn."

CHAPTER ELEVEN

"SHUT UP your goddamn whinin', brat." Tag picked up a half-dollar-size rock and threw it across the campfire. It struck Allie Russell on the leg, and she whimpered. "I'm sick of that goddamn whinin', you hear me? One more time, and it won't be a rock you have to worry about."

Above the bandanna covering her mouth, Allie's eyes went wide and she stopped whimpering. She also stopped straining against the leather strips binding her hands and feet.

"That's better." Tag reached into the cooler positioned beside him, pulled out another beer and opened it. "Want a brewski?" He grinned, holding the bottle up. "Naw, you're probably holdin' out for wine or champagne. Like the duchess. But, 'course you're not here, are you, Duchess? Lousy timing, huh? Went to get a woman and had to settle for a little girl."

Allie stared at him, terrified and confused. What was he talking about, and where were they? she wondered. She couldn't begin to identify her surroundings and had no idea how she had gotten here.

But she could remember very well the moment she had turned her back on Tag, the moment the nightmare began. Before she knew what was happening, he had her in a choke hold, cramming the bandanna in her mouth so she couldn't scream. Then he had shoved her down on the kitchen floor, forcing her to lie on her stomach. He tied both her hands and feet behind her, then put another bandanna across her mouth to make sure she didn't spit out the first one. Despite the gag, Allie cried the whole time.

And then he left her there.

Allie had been so horrified, so traumatized, that for a few moments she didn't even realize he was gone.

At first she had been so relieved and so happy, she sobbed hysterically. All she had to do—she assured herself—was stay calm until her family came back. But her euphoria was short-lived because in a matter of minutes, Tag returned. He blindfolded her, practically dragged her through the kitchen, out through the garage and into what felt like the back of a pickup. Then he had thrown something over her, and sometime later had pulled her out of the truck, dumped her on the ground and yanked off the blindfold.

Now, the only thing she knew for certain was that the man across the blazing fire was drunk. He'd had at least eight beers since he had brought her to this...place. And even though she couldn't be sure exactly when that was, it had been long enough for him to get slobbery, stumbling drunk.

"Yeah, like mother, like daughter. 'Scuse me. Stepmother. The wicked stepmother, right, kid? Yeah, right." He took a long pull on the beer. "Well, here's to you, little duchess, 'cause you're gonna help me get back at the big bitch duchess for what she done to me." Tag rubbed the still healing wound on his cheek. "Gonna make her pay." Tag looked at his watch. "Startin' now," he said, getting to his feet.

Propped against a rock, Allie watched as Tag started in her direction, and for one heart-stopping moment she thought he was coming for her. She wanted to scream for him to get away, stay away. She twisted against her restraints, then... at the last minute, he veered off to her left, and a second later she heard the sound of him relieving himself somewhere behind her. She squeezed her eyes shut as if she could shut out the sound.

"Whatsa matter?" Tag walked back into view in the process of zipping his pants. "Too crude for ya? Yeah," he said, disgust ringing clear in his voice. "You're kin to the duchess, all right."

He leaned down, and Allie shut her eyes again, fearing the worst. Tag just laughed, his foul breath moving over her face, but he didn't touch her. Instead, he tested the security of the bandanna and her bonds. Then he went to the back of his truck, retrieved a multicolored horse blanket and tossed it over her body.

"So's you don't catch a chill and die on me while I'm gone." When Tag saw the shock in her eyes, he laughed again. "Oh," he said in mock sympathy. "You gonna miss ol' Tag? Now, ain't that sweet."

This time when he hunkered down beside her, Allie didn't think her luck would hold twice. Sure enough, Tag flipped the blanket back and stared down at her. At thirteen, Allie's figure was far from in full bloom, but neither was it still in the budding stage. Her breasts were small, but the oversize cotton knit sweater did little to hide their nicely rounded shape. Her hips flared becomingly from her narrow waist, and the leggings she wore defined slender legs.

At his leisure, Tag let his greedy gaze roam her body, lingering on first one spot, then another. "Yeah, maybe you'd like to show me just how sweet you can be."

Allie closed her eyes and silently screamed. Then she prayed. And prayed, and...

"Better yet, why don't we wait till I bring the duchess back here? Then we'll give her a real show. Right before I kill her." He tossed the blanket back over her. "Now, don't you run off till I get back." Tag threw back his head and laughed, the sound shooting off into the darkness. He walked to his truck, got in and drove away.

Allie waited for the sound of the truck's engine to fade into silence before she opened her eyes again.

At first, the quiet was welcome solitude. But gradually, Allie began to realize that she was alone, in the middle of nowhere, bound and gagged, with no sign of any other life.

In the distance a coyote howled.

Shivers skated down Allie's spine and she wondered how far away the coyote was. And what about other animals? she wondered. Could they smell her? Hear her? Fear crowded her mind. What if there was a pack of coyotes, hunting for food? Or what if there were other night creatures even closer? Like tarantulas? Or snakes? What if a snake slithered out of the darkness? She was helpless. She wouldn't be able to do anything but watch it crawl closer and closer....

No!, she screamed in her mind. The fear was biting into her sanity like the imagined snake biting into her flesh. She *had* to stop, she told herself. She had keep her mind clear and steady.

Then she looked at the campfire, remembering that animals and insects usually avoided fire in any form. If she could just get closer. She thought about rolling, then changed her mind. What if she went too far and rolled into the flames? No, she decided, better to take it slow and easy. So, she did precisely that, slowly and painstakingly wiggling and scooting her way across a six- to eight-foot stretch of dirt and rocks. By the time she worked her way to within a foot of the fire ring, she was exhausted, scratched and scraped, but feeling a lot safer.

Allie relaxed, her cheek pressed to the dirt and grit, and waited until her breathing calmed and her heart rate slowed. Now what? she wondered. Would he

come back in a few minutes? What if he didn't?
What if he had left her out here to die? Again, the
fear closed in on her. And again, she fought to stay
clearheaded.

Silently, she recited the Lord's Prayer. Twice. And
it helped her to calm down. Then she began asking
herself questions about what had happened and why.
Tag had mentioned going for a woman and having to
settle for a girl. Had he meant Lynn? Had he intended to kidnap Lynn and decided to take her instead? But why Lynn? Why did he say he was going
to kill her? What did he have against her? She'd
never hurt a fly, as far as Allie knew. And what did
he mean when he said he was going to bring Lynn
back here?

Allie knew that by now her father must have called
the cops. Maybe even the FBI. Tag wouldn't try and
go back to the house, would he? Suddenly, the
thought that Tag might do just that terrified Allie
more than the thought of coyotes. What if Tag was
going back to kill them! Her father. Sandy. Lynn...
and the baby.

She started to cry again. Her whole family. What
if she lost her whole family? The concept was almost too much for her already tortured mind to
handle. What if she never saw them again?

Her dad. She loved him so much. If she ever got
out of this, she would never disobey him again.
Never think he was an old fogy. Never give him a
reason to ground her. Never.

Sandy. She loved her sister. If she ever got home, she would never call her a smart-mouth again. And she would let Sandy play with her lipstick and perfume as much as she wanted.

And Lynn. She'd been terrible to Lynn. And all because she didn't want to share her father. Lynn had never done anything but be nice from the minute she came into their lives. And she didn't treat her like a kid. Not the way some adults did.

At that moment, Allie would have traded all the outings to the mall, all the stolen afternoons with Ronald for just one glimpse of her family.

Except Lynn, she thought. She hoped she wouldn't see Lynn because that would mean that Tag had taken her, too. And he would kill her. Not for one moment did Allie doubt that Tag meant his threat. If he could, he would kidnap Lynn and he would kill her.

LYNN WAS SURVIVING on nerves alone and Sam wasn't much better. Cynthia and Lynn's father had arrived, bringing with them a horde of volunteers from the ranch, as well as Cal and Serena. Carolyn and Vernon were on their way, along with Scott and Val Harris and as many of the Hole in the Wall staff as they could spare. The street in front of the Russell house was bumper-to-bumper cars and pickups waiting to drive the searchers, and her kitchen was full of men waiting for the search to begin. Wayne Jackson was still there and a team of FBI special agents was on its way from the San Antonio office because the Austin office was not only too small, but at the moment, understaffed.

"I made some sandwiches and a pot of coffee for the men. Would you like something?" Cynthia asked, placing a hand on Lynn's shoulder.

Lynn shook her head.

"How about some tea? It's no trouble at all to—"

"No, thanks."

"Honey, listen to me." Cynthia sat down beside her on the sofa. "You've got to keep up your strength. For the baby's sake and for Sam's sake. If he knows you're taking good care of yourself, that's one less thing for him to worry about."

"What are they doing?" Lynn asked, motioning toward the kitchen.

"Mostly just waiting for the FBI, and trying to figure who's going to search in what area."

"Where's Sandy?"

"Serena's with her. The last time I looked in, she had Sandy on her lap, sitting in that big old wicker rocker, reading her a story."

"I need to go see how she's doing." Lynn started to rise, but Cynthia stopped her.

"You need to sit right here and relax for a minute."

"How can I relax when Allie is out there with that...that..." Lynn couldn't think of a name terrible enough for Walt Taggart and what he'd done.

"It makes me sick to my stomach to think that man walked around the Double C for almost three months, and none of us had any idea what kind of person he was. Is," she corrected herself.

"You couldn't have known."

"You did. Ken said you had asked for someone else to help with Lightning from the very first. Instinctively, you must have..." Cynthia's slender shoulders lifted in a shrug. "I don't know, picked up some negative vibrations, or something. We'd all be better off if we had listened to you."

"It was just a *feeling* I had about him. Every time he was near me, I wanted to get far away."

"Well, from now on we'll pay more attention to those feelings of yours."

"You would think I had learned a lesson after I fired Tag, but I didn't. I had another one of those strange feelings this morning while Sam and I were shopping, and I put it off as guilt."

"What kind of feeling?"

"While we were shopping, I had an overwhelming urge to call and make sure Allie was okay. But after the big confrontation we'd had and Sam grounding her before we drove into Austin, I dismissed it as guilt. If I had just followed my instincts, she would be home right now, safe and sound."

"Lynn, you can't blame yourself for what's happened—"

"Can't I? Look at the facts, Cynthia. *I* was the one who fired Taggart. *I* am the one he wants revenge against. It should be me out there instead of Allie. If anything happens to her, I'll never forgive myself. And I certainly don't think Sam will, either."

"Is this a private pity party or can anyone join?"

Both women looked up and found Cal leaning against the doorway.

"Calvin," Cynthia scolded.

"How 'bout it, Skunk?"

Lynn managed a weak smile for her brother and for just a moment, her spirits felt lighter. "Since when have you ever needed an engraved invitation to butt into somebody else's business?"

Cynthia heaved a sigh of relief when she realized Cal was trying to help, not hinder. She got up from the sofa and motioned for him to take her place.

"Well." He pushed himself away from the door. "How the hell do you expect me to be head honcho around here if I don't know what everybody's up to? Scoot over," he said and promptly flopped down beside her, stretching his long legs out in front of him.

"How does Serena put up with you?"

He grinned. "She's a sex fiend and I'm the only one that can satisfy her."

In spite of herself, Lynn laughed.

Cal reached up and gently touched her cheek. "That's better. You draggin' a long face around ain't gonna help nobody. Now, let's get down to business. I heard what you told Cynthia about this mess being your fault. And you know what I say to that—"

"Don't," Lynn said, knowing his liberal use of four-letter words.

"Hogwash." At the surprised look in her eyes, Cal added, "See, you don't know me as well as you think you do. Besides—" he patted her belly "—with all these little rug rats comin' along, I'm tryin' to clean up my act."

"Looks like fatherhood is already having a positive effect on you."

"It was either that, or Serena was gonna pin my ears back."

"Now the truth comes out."

"And speaking of truth, who the hell said that you had to shoulder all the blame for what's happened to Allie?"

"Cal, you heard what I said. It *is* the truth. If I hadn't fired Taggart, none of this would have happened."

"Oh, so you were just supposed to let the man paw you, or worse, is that it? Cut the crap, Sis. You know as well as I do that you can't be responsible for other people's actions. You didn't force the guy to drink on the job. You didn't ask the man to be all over you like a cold sweat. And you sure as hell didn't put the idea of kidnapping in his twisted little mind."

"Still, if only—"

"If only nothing. I'm not gonna sit here and listen to you beat yourself up over something that's not your fault."

"You don't know the whole story, Cal."

"Oh, I don't? Okay, I got a few minutes to kill. Lay it on me."

"You don't know how much tension there's been in the house...in our marriage. Sam and I argue so much. And the girls don't approve of me. At first, I thought everything was going to be fine, but then... I don't know what happened," she said with a sigh. "Somehow I disappointed them. There's no trust between us, and now with the baby coming, it will be even worse. I didn't handle any of this right."

Cal leaned forward and stuck his hand out as if to shake hands.

"What's that for?" she asked.

"Thought I'd introduce myself, because obviously you're a total stranger. What did you do with my feisty, independent sister?"

"Stop."

"I'm serious. You've always been a scrapper and a straight-from-the-shoulder—but a soft shoulder—kinda person. I've never seen you give up this way. It's not like you, Lynn."

"Maybe I'm just facing reality."

"Yeah? And maybe you're just lookin' for excuses. I got news for you, baby sister of mine. Bein' married is hard work. Damn hard work."

"I know that."

"Do you also know that not just you and Tyler, but *all* of the McKinney offspring, have had marriage problems?"

"But I thought you and Serena were happy."

"We are. But that happiness doesn't just fall like whatever that stuff is they talk about in the Bible—"

"Manna?"

"Yeah, like manna from heaven. We've had some sobering moments. And fight? Damn, but that woman is so hardheaded she'd argue with a fence post."

"Oh, and I suppose you're not?"

"I give as good as I get. Like I said, you're not the Lone Ranger when it comes to marital problems." He stopped and glanced down at his boots. "You know, I just had this conversation with Tyler not too long ago. I shoulda written it down."

"Cal, I appreciate what you're trying to do, but—"

"I got one question."

"What?"

"Do you love Sam?"

"Of course."

"Do you love his kids?"

"Yes. And that's two questions."

"So sue me. The point I'm tryin' to make here is that love is the basic ingredient, the only ingredient, you really need to make a marriage work, and you and Sam have got that in spades. As for the rest, I think you've been tryin' too hard."

"What do you mean?" In the background, she heard the phone ring.

"I think you've been tryin' to be everything to everybody, and that's not possible. Regardless of how perfect you try to be, you and Sam *are* going to fight once in a while. You and the kids *are* going to get in each other's faces now and then. Hell, if you didn't, it'd be a damn boring way to live." He reached over and patted her hand. "You gotta be who you are, Sis. You've gotta get back to being the woman Sam fell in love with."

Cynthia stuck her head in the door and said, "Lynn, phone call."

"Who is it?"

"Don't know. He said he wanted to speak to you personally."

"Maybe it's news about Allie," she said hopefully and headed for the kitchen.

Lynn put the receiver to her ear. "Hello."

"Hey there, Duchess."

Her knees went weak and all the color drained from her face. Sam was watching and knew something was wrong. In a split second he was by her side. Lynn looked up at him and mouthed, "It's him."

Instantly, Sam motioned for quiet in the room.

"You still there, Duchess?"

"Y-yes."

Through hand signals and mouthed words, Sam made Wayne Jackson aware of the caller's identity. Jackson immediately found an extension in order to listen in.

"I came by to see you, but you wasn't home."

"Is Allie all right?"

"Now, why would I wanna hurt a pretty little thing like that stepdaughter of yours? She's sweet as sunshine and soft as a kitten."

The last phrase conjured up a mental image Lynn would just as soon not have visualized, and she closed her eyes against the picture forming in her mind. "Please, bring her back to us."

"Happy to oblige."

Lynn's eyes snapped open. "You'll bring her back?"

"Only one hitch."

"Money? You want money. We don't have a lot of money, but—"

"I don't want your goddamn money. I want you!"

"What?"

"You heard me, Duchess. The little kitten for you. Even trade."

"Y-you mean . . . you'll return Allie if I—"

"That's right. You think on it. I been on this phone too long. I'll let you know the time and the place."

He hung up.

"What?" Sam demanded. "What did he say? What did he want? Money?"

Cal stepped up beside them. "Take it easy, Sam."

Wayne Jackson came back into the room. "I timed him. He was on for less than two minutes. Even if we'd been set up for a trace, we wouldn't have made it. But he'll call back, and when he does, we'll track him."

Sam ran both hands through his hair. "Whatever he wants, we'll give it to him. Anything. If he'll just bring her back."

Wayne looked at Lynn, trying to decide if she intended to keep Sam in the dark. But Sam caught the look that passed between them. "What is it? Something . . . that bastard said something—"

"He wants to work a trade," Wayne said, taking the decision out of Lynn's hands.

"What kind of trade?"

Again Wayne hesitated, only this time it was Cal who picked up the thread. "The son of a bitch wants to trade Allie for Lynn, doesn't he?"

"Yeah." Wayne Jackson's voice was deep and flat, and the silence that followed his answer could have filled up the empty Houston Astrodome.

"DON'T EVEN *THINK* about accepting that bastard's offer," Sam told Lynn an hour after the call from Tag. The FBI had arrived five minutes after she hung up and before he had an opportunity to discuss the outrageous offer. Now, in their bedroom while he was changing clothes in preparation to join the search, Sam snatched the first chance they'd had to talk about it in private.

"But, if that's the only way to get Allie back—"

"It's not the only way. The FBI are here now. They've got the phones tapped and ready to record when he calls again. Half of Claro County is standing in our front yard waiting to scour the countryside looking for Allie. We'll find her."

"But I could help."

"Not that way. Now, promise me that you'll stay out of it. I've got enough to worry about without adding you to the list."

At his unintentionally insensitive remark, something inside Lynn snapped. Eight months' worth of frustration and anger—eight months of trying to turn herself inside out to be what she thought he wanted—came boiling to the surface and spewed out.

"Stay out of it?" she all but screeched. "Stay out of it! Don't you dare treat me like some witless child, Sam Russell. I've let you get away with it since the minute I said 'I do,' but it stops. Right here. Right now."

In the process of buttoning his shirt, Sam stared at her as if she had lost her mind. Indeed, he thought that might be a distinct possibility, given the pressure she was under.

"Lynn—"

"No. This time you're going to listen to me, Sam." She got up and went to the other side of the bed to confront him. "I—" she poked a finger at her own chest "—am not your child. I'm *having* your child. And if you care one tenth as much about this marriage as you say you do, then you'd better wake up and listen to me, or you can kiss it, and me, good-bye."

"Sweetheart, you're upset. The stress is too much—"

"You're damn right the stress is too much. And don't call me sweetheart when you don't mean it."

"What are you—"

"I'm not your sweetheart. I'm another one of your sweet little girls. Except when we're in bed, of course. That's the only time you don't treat me like a child."

"Lynn!"

"And you're doing it again. Well, not this time, Sam. This time, it's too important. This time, we need each other too much. Allie needs us too much. Last night at Amanda and Brock's wedding, I thought we had a chance, that all we needed was to talk, to clear the air and tell each other how we feel. But we didn't get the chance, and now I can't wait for the right time."

She took a deep breath and plunged on. "Sam, I can't be Marta. I know that's what you want, but I can't. She was the perfect wife, the perfect mother. And it's only natural that you would compare the two of us, but I can't live with her ghost anymore. And I'll never be able to live up to her 'standard of excellence.' I'm not a clone, I'm a flesh-and-blood woman. All I want is to be treated like one, not just made love to like one.

"And while we're on the subject of love, I love Allie. She's not perfect either, and Lord knows we may never have the kind of mother-daughter relationship I would like, but I do love her. She's where she is at this very moment because of me. Now, that's a fact, not a child's assumption of blame. I have a right to worry about her. I have a right to help. And I have a right to be treated like a wife. I've got a father, Sam. I don't need another one. What I need is a husband."

Sam had long since stopped dressing. Dumbfounded, he simply stared at her, tying to assimilate everything she had told him.

He said the first thing that popped into his head. "Y-you think I want you to be like Marta?"

"Yes."

"How in the world did you ever get such an idea?"

"From you. Every day in a thousand ways."

He shook his head in disbelief. "I never—"

"Said it? No, not in so many words. But everything you did told me how much you missed her, how much you wished I was like her. So, that's what I tried to be. You told me once before we got married that she was quiet, unassuming. She let you make all of the decisions, she kept your house, raised your children, practiced medicine.... The woman was phenomenal—she did it all. How could anyone hope to live up to such a paragon?"

"Is that why you've been so withdrawn all these months? I thought it was due to the pregnancy, or maybe you were afraid of becoming a mother so soon. It never entered my mind that you were trying to imitate Marta."

"Well, I was. But it doesn't work."

"Of course it doesn't work. You could never be like Marta in a million years. And I don't want you to be," he added hastily when he saw the anger flare in her eyes.

Sam went to her and put his hands on her shoulders. "Sweetheart—and you are my sweetheart—I didn't fall in love with you because you reminded me of Marta. I fell in love with you because you *didn't* remind me of her. My mistake was falling back into some very bad habits." When she gave him a disbelieving look, he explained.

"Marta *was* quiet and shy. But that didn't stop her from being the most organized person I have ever met. She organized everything from her practice to her kitchen to our lives. And she did it so well, that— fool that I was—I didn't give her the credit she deserved. But she never wanted any credit.

"Don't get me wrong. She wasn't exactly a shrinking violet, but she liked things to stay simple and to run smoothly. She worked hard to accomplish that. And she told me. She liked for me to make all the decisions. I'm ashamed to admit that until she was so abruptly taken from me, I didn't realize how much I truly loved her. Or that our lives had fallen into such a comfortable balance that I didn't take the time to tell her how much I loved her.

"The day of the accident..." Sam paused for a moment, thoughtful. "The day of the accident, we had an argument before she was called on an emergency. First argument we'd had in ages. We both said some...hurtful things. The kind of things you want to take back almost the instant you say them. Then...two hours later I got word from the hospital that she was in the very emergency room she had just left. She was on her way home and a drunk driver... I never got the chance to apologize." He looked into Lynn's eyes. "Then later... I found out later that she had been to the obstetrician that day. Lynn, she was pregnant and I didn't give her that chance to tell me because of that stupid, senseless argument."

"I...I'm sorry," she whispered. "I didn't know."

"How could you? I've done my best not to talk about it, not even to *think* about it because I felt so guilty. I never even mentioned the baby to the girls. That's why I don't encourage Allie and Sandy to talk about their mother. Selfish, isn't it? Because I feel guilty, I've deprived them of their memories. But worse than that, with you, I've fallen into the same kind of sheltering husband I was with Marta. I *know* it's wrong, and *know* it has to stop. My only excuse is that I've had so much on my mind lately."

"What do you mean?"

He began to massage the spot where his hands rested on her shoulders. "I've kept some things from you. Financial problems."

"Sam—"

"It's complicated, but I promise to tell you everything later. I was wrong to shut you out. But right now the only thing you *have* to know is that even though I treasure my years with Marta..." With his thumbs he tilted her chin up until she had to look into his eyes. "I wouldn't trade one minute of the time since I opened Professor Bailey's door and saw you standing on the porch for all of those years with her."

"Y-you wouldn't?"

"No. I love you. You're my life. You, Allie and Sandy. And I don't want to kiss you or our marriage goodbye."

"And I love you. So much."

He took her in his arms and kissed her sweetly, tenderly, pouring all his love, all his commitment into the kiss, so she would know the promise was forever.

"Lynn, Lynn," he whispered, holding her tight. "Don't you see now why I can't let you offer yourself in trade for Allie? I can't bear the thought of losing you and this baby. Please, please promise me that you'll forget about this ridiculous idea.''

Lynn buried her face in the hollow of his neck. As much as she wanted to promise, she was afraid to, afraid she might have to break that promise.

CHAPTER TWELVE

BY THE TIME dawn made its first tentative peek over the horizon, Lynn was close to exhaustion, but no further progress had been made in the search for Allie. Except for a couple of FBI agents, Cynthia, Serena and Sandy, she was alone. Everyone else was participating in the search. Sam, J.T., Vernon and Carolyn, and several agents had led three groups out about midnight. The rest had gone with Cal, Ken and Wayne, plus more agents, before dawn's first light.

Cynthia had fallen asleep on the sofa, Serena slept in the extra twin bed in Sandy's bedroom and Lynn had slept—if an hour's worth of intermittent dozing could be called sleep—fitfully in her own bed. And still no news.

No news is good news, she kept telling herself, but it was cold comfort. *Why doesn't Sam call? Why doesn't Wayne Jackson call, or one of the FBI agents? Why the hell doesn't SOMEBODY call with some news?* She felt like doubling up her fist and hitting something—anything—as hard as she could. Lynn knew that if her frustration level was climbing, it must be worse for the scores of people out searching for her stepdaughter.

Thank God for friends.

Volunteers had been calling and coming in since word of Allie's kidnapping, and she wouldn't have been surprised to learn that half of Claro County was involved in the search by now. Of course, Wayne Jackson and the FBI were coordinating everything, but everyone was doing whatever they could, no matter how small. Rosa Walters from the Longhorn had offered to bring coffee and doughnuts for all the volunteers this morning, and follow up with as many sandwiches as they needed. Some of Val and Scott Harris's guests had joined in. Cal and Ken Slattery had even organized a group of searchers on horseback. Lynn was beginning to think the only people *not* out searching, were Amanda and Brock Monroe, and if they hadn't been on their honeymoon, they would undoubtedly have been involved, too.

Literally hundreds of people, and some of them had been at it for more than five hours without even a whisper of a break in the case. And this morning all the newspapers and TV stations would broadcast the details of the kidnapping, and a mug shot of Taggart. J.T. had set up a substantial reward for any information of Allie's whereabouts. Beverly, bless her heart, had offered to handle all of the public relations and interviews. Neither Lynn nor Sam wanted to talk to the press unless it was absolutely necessary.

Lynn walked to her bedroom window, and looked outside at the beginning of a new day, all fresh and sunny, full of promise and hope. Hope. Desperately, she clung to the hope that somehow this nightmare would end, and her family would be reunited. *Dear Lord, keep Allie safe, and send her home to us,* she prayed.

"Lynn?"

She turned around, and found Cynthia standing in the doorway. "Did you get any sleep?"

"Some. Any word?"

"No. And define 'some.'"

Lynn shrugged. "A few minutes, here and there. I'm okay. I don't think sleep is going to be much of a priority until we find Allie."

"I wanted to let you know that Rosa sent Tess Westlake over from the Longhorn. She brought one of those huge coffee makers, and Serena is downstairs getting it going. Tess said Rosa would be along shortly with the doughnuts, but in the meantime she sent some scrambled eggs and country ham, especially for you."

"Thanks, but I'm not hungry."

"Now, you listen to me." Cynthia shook a finger at her. "You're a McKinney and McKinneys do what they have to. And you have got to keep up your strength. I'm bringing that food up on a tray, and you're going to eat some, if I have to spoon-feed you the way I do Jennifer. You got that?"

"Yes, ma'am."

"Good. Now, sit down, and get off your feet."

Lynn did as Cynthia instructed, but a few moments later, was up again after deciding to check on Sandy. She expected to find her still sleeping, but was surprised to discover the ten-year-old wide-awake.

"Did they find Allie?" Sandy asked immediately.

Lynn sat down beside her on the bed. "No, honey, they haven't found her yet. But you know what?" She brushed back a swath of ginger-brown hair from the child's shoulder. "There are dozens of people out looking for her, so maybe we'll have some news real soon."

"Is Daddy with them?"

"He sure is. And my daddy is out with them. And Cal and a whole slew of hands from the ranch. Sheriff Jackson, lots of parents, even people we don't know, and they're all searching for Allie."

"That man that has her . . . is he gonna hurt her?"

Lynn fought threatening tears, knowing Sandy would be that much more frightened to see her fears. "I don't think he wants to hurt Allie. And we have to pray that he won't." It was a white lie, but for a good cause—Sandy's peace of mind.

"I prayed last night, and asked my mother to help find Allie."

Lynn put her arms around the child. "That's good, honey."

"Daddy told us that she's up in heaven, so I thought maybe she could see better from up there.

And maybe she could see Allie, and, you know, sorta look after her till they can find her."

"I'm sure she will." Acting on instinct, Lynn asked, "Do you think about your mother a lot, Sandy?"

"Sometimes."

"I know you miss her. When my mother died, I missed her so much that I slept with her picture under my pillow so I would dream about her every night. It made me feel closer to her somehow. You know the picture that I keep on my dresser?"

"Uh-huh."

"That's the very one I used to sleep with."

"She's pretty. Do you have other pictures of her?"

"Yes. As a matter of fact..." Suddenly Lynn had an idea that might make Sandy feel a lot better. "I'll bet you have pictures of your mother."

"Daddy put them in a big box, and put it in the attic when we moved here."

"Would you recognize the box if you saw it?"

"Sure."

"Then c'mon." Lynn grabbed her by the hand, and together they headed for the attic. Ten minutes later they were back in Sandy's room, the sought-after box in their possession.

Lynn lifted the lid with some trepidation, all of a sudden questioning whether or not her brainstorm was a good idea. Her hope was that Sandy could find a measure of comfort from seeing photographs of her mother *and* Allie, in happier times, but now she was faced with seeing Sam's first wife, and her own courage flagged. Sandy's did not. In fact, her eagerness doubled upon spying a snapshot of herself, Allie and Marta Russell.

"Oh, I 'member that one," Sandy said, delighted with her find. "It was Easter. See my dress?" She pointed to herself.

"It's lovely." But Lynn only had eyes for the woman with her arms around the two little girls. Marta Russell's most compelling feature was her eyes. Big, brown and looking soft enough to rival a cocker spaniel's, they were filled with love and pride for her children.

"This is when we went to the beach," Sandy said, pulling out another picture. "Look at Allie's pigtails."

What followed was a ten-year-old's version of the age-old ritual of remember-when. Sandy prowled through the snapshots and portraits—some of her mother alone, some of just mother and daughters, and some of the entire family. Lynn let her go through the photographic memories at her own pace, selecting which pictures she wanted to keep out, which to leave in the box. They decided not to return the box to the attic, but to place it in Allie's room so that when she came home, she could select her own favorites. They were still sitting together, photos scattered all over Sandy's bed, a half hour later when the bedroom door opened, and Sam peeked inside.

"Good morn—"

Lynn looked up, as startled to see him as he was to see her. She jumped up from the bed, sending snapshots tumbling to the floor. "Did you find Allie?"

"Is she okay?" Sandy echoed.

"We haven't found her yet, but we're narrowing the search area," he added quickly, making sure to keep his tone light, positive. "And it's looking good."

Lynn hoped the forced brightness in his voice fooled Sandy, but it didn't fool her for a moment. Neither did his tight smile.

"What are you girls up. . ." Sam's smile drooped. "Where did you get those?" he asked Lynn.

"In the attic. See, Daddy? All the pictures of you and Allie, and me and Mommy. Lynn said I could keep some in my room. Is that all right, Daddy?"

"Well, sugar, I'm not sure—"

"We've had a wonderful time, haven't we, honey?" Smiling, Lynn meant her words for Sandy, but her eyes were on Sam. "Sandy says she feels better now. She's going to keep out some photos of her mother and Allie so she can look at them when she says her prayers. That's a good idea, don't you think, Sam?"

"Y-yes. I suppose it is."

Lynn looked down at the girl. "Honey, I want to talk to Daddy for a minute."

Sam's heart almost skipped a beat. He wondered if Lynn even realized that she hadn't referred to him as "your daddy," as she usually did, but simply as "Daddy." The way a mother might speak to her child.

"Why don't you finish going through all this stuff, and when I get back, we'll put the box in Allie's room."

"Okay." Sandy gave them the first real smile they'd seen since Allie was taken.

Lynn took Sam's hand, and they walked out of the room.

"I don't understand," he said as soon as they closed the door behind them. "I know we agreed that the girls and I needed to talk more about Marta, but why drag out all those old pictures? Why now?"

"Because Sandy needed to feel close to Allie and to her mother. Marta's gone, and now Allie is missing. She felt isolated and alone, Sam. She needed to reconnect, and remembering happy times did that for her. I know you're upset, but—"

"No." Sam leaned his back against the wall and sighed. "No. I'm not upset. It was a very thoughtful thing to do. I've been so preoccupied with Allie, I haven't stopped to think how all of this is affecting Sandy." He gazed into Lynn's eyes. "Thank you. You're a born mother. A born parent."

"You look worn-out." She stroked his cheek with the back of her hand.

"I'm worried about you." He spread his hands over her abdomen. "And Junior."

"We're fine." She covered his hands with hers. "I think he's the only one who has gotten any sleep."

"Maybe he's getting his rest now because he knows in a month or so he'll need all that extra energy to demand his breakfast." Sam smiled. "Now you've got me saying 'he.'"

"But it is a boy, I just know—"

"You just know—" They finished together.

Lynn smiled back. "There's some cold scrambled eggs and ham downstairs. Want me to warm them up for you?"

"Only if we share them," Sam said, putting his arm around her shoulder as they walked downstairs.

As they came into the kitchen together, Wayne Jackson was quietly talking to Cal and J.T., both just in from searching.

"Did you find anything, Cal?" Lynn asked. "Anything at all?"

"Sorry, Sis. But we're goin' back out—"

"After you catch some sleep," Sam insisted, and Lynn agreed.

"Hell, I've stayed up longer than this, and ridden a couple of bad-tempered bulls to boot."

Serena walked up, and handed her husband a mug of hot, black coffee. "That's no brag."

Cal grinned. "Thanks, darlin'"

"Just the same, I wish you'd get a few minutes' rest before you go back out there," Lynn said.

Cal pointed his cup at Sam. "I'll rest when he does."

"Don't hold your breath."

"Great," Serena said, shaking her head. "They're dead on their feet, but the attitude is alive and well."

"What else did you expect?" Cynthia chimed in.

"Well," Lynn stated matter-of-factly, "if you're not going to rest, at least have something to eat."

"Now, *that* you talked me into," Cal said, and led the way to the doughnuts.

Cynthia hung behind, noticing that J.T. was in deep discussion with the sheriff. She waited until Wayne went outside, then joined J.T.

"Whatever you and the sheriff were talking about must have been serious. Did it have anything to do with Allie?"

J.T. glanced over her shoulder to where the others were gathered around the coffee urn. "I didn't want Lynn and Sam to know about this. Wayne just told me that the FBI has connected Taggart to the murder the other night down on Oak Springs in Austin. He beat that woman to death."

Cynthia was so shocked she didn't know how to respond to such news. "Th-they're sure?"

He nodded. "This ain't the kinda thing that'll raise Lynn and Sam's hopes, so I say we keep it to ourselves for a while. Wayne said he'd try to sit on the information as best he could."

"You're right. They don't need to hear this right now."

"Or ever, if I can help it." He took her by the hand, and pulled her arm through his. "C'mon, let's go over there with the others."

But before Cynthia and J.T. reached the others, the phone rang. The entire room went deathly quiet.

"Why don't you answer it, Mrs. Russell," said one of the FBI agents. "If it's him, he'll want to speak to you. Remember our coaching session. You had my instructions down cold. You'll do fine. Tell him whatever you think he wants to hear. Just try to keep him on long enough for us to get a trace. Take a deep breath and go for it."

Lynn nodded. With trembling fingers she picked up the receiver and said hello.

"Hey there, Duchess. You ready to talk trade?"

Sam moved up to stand beside her. "I—I'm not sure."

"'Course you are, 'cause that's the only way you're gonna get this little gal back. You know that, and I know that, so cut the crap. Now, here's how we do it. You got one of them mobile phones in your car?"

"Y-yes."

"Gimme the number."

"What for?"

"Don't play stupid, Duchess. Not if you want to find this little gal in one piece. You get my drift?"

Lynn licked her lips and called out the number.

"Now, I'll call you back—"

"No, wait! Why not just tell me now? Please, the sooner we make the exchange, the sooner Allie will be home where she belongs. Please."

"Oh, you beg real nice, Duchess. I'm lookin' forward to hearin' you beg some more when I get my hands on you."

She shuddered as though he *had* touched her. "Whatever you want, only please, let's get on with it."

"That's what I like. A woman that's—" There was a split second's pause before he said, "You bitch. You're trying to keep me talkin'. Well, it won't work." And he hung up.

"He hung up," Lynn said, tears gathering in her red-rimmed eyes. "He knew I was trying to keep him talking. Oh, Sam, I failed." She started to sob.

"Baby, shh. Don't, sweetheart—"

At that moment one of the special agents came bursting through the back door of the kitchen from the equipment van outside, carrying a map in his hand. "We got a partial fix," he announced.

"You found him?" Sam asked.

"No, sir, but we have a fix on his general location."

"What the hell does that mean?" Cal asked.

"It means we can narrow the search area down to a matter of miles rather than statewide, or even countywide."

"Where? What area?"

He spread the map of Claro County out on the table. "Here." He pointed to an area that was southwest of Crystal Creek.

"You sure those trackin' gadgets got this right?" J.T. asked.

"Positive. Why?"

"Because I know the area you're talkin' about like the back of my hand."

"And mine," Cal added.

And mine, Lynn thought.

"Can you take us to it?" the agent wanted to know.

"I damn well better be able to take you to it," J.T. replied. "It's my land. The son of a bitch has got her somewhere on the Double C."

AT LYNN'S INSISTENCE, the control center of the search was moved to the Double C. She wanted to be as close to Allie's possible location as she could. Besides, since the investigators narrowed the area, the search had taken on an aura of greater urgency. More volunteers had arrived, and the sheer organization of manpower was easier from a larger location.

With J.T.'s help, and a map of the area that not only included his property, but the Circle T and the Hole in the Wall as well, Wayne and the FBI agents marked off grids, and reassigned search parties. More men volunteered to go out on horseback, since a fair amount of the search area was inaccessible even by four-wheel-drive vehicles. A helicopter was also brought in from the Travis County Sheriff's Department.

In J.T.'s study, Sam, Cal, J.T., Wayne and several FBI agents were clustered around the map, discussing strategies, when Lynn decided to make her bid for a solution. She knew what Sam's reaction would be, but she also knew that if she could get the agents and other men to consider her plan, he *might* with the proper convincing, be willing to go along. It wouldn't be an easy job, but she was counting on him to see the logic of her suggestion.

"Excuse me," she said, the circle of males automatically making an opening at the sound of her voice. "I hate to interrupt, but—"

"You're not interrupting, sweetheart," Sam said, coming to her side. "This concerns you as much as anyone."

"I'm glad you feel that way, because I have an idea that I think might help bring Allie home."

"We're certainly open for suggestions, Mrs. Russell," Special Agent Rickman told her.

Lynn swallowed hard. *Here goes,* she thought. "Well, Tag's made no secret out of the fact that he wants to trade my stepdaughter for me, so...I thought perhaps you could use me to set up a kind of trade, only—"

"No," Sam said flatly. "Absolutely not. I won't let you do something like that."

"Sam," she said, her eyes begging him to understand, "Allie may not be of my flesh, but she's in my heart. If I can help—"

"No—"

"Mrs. Russell," the agent said, cutting Sam off. "We appreciate your making such an offer. And the idea is not completely without merit. But you, as much as anyone here, know what kind of terrain we're talking about. We don't call this the Hill Country for nothing. And no offense, ma'am, but in your current condition, you're not exactly—" Rickman searched his brain for a substitute for "graceful," and settled on "—at your best, mobility-wise. My primary responsibility is to find your stepdaughter and bring her back to you, safe and sound. My secondary responsibility is to you and your husband and all of these good folks who have volunteered their time and effort. And in all of this, I have to minimize risks whenever and wherever I can. In this instance, the risks outweigh any good that might come of it."

"But—"

Cynthia, with Lettie Mae right behind her, had only intended to stick her head in the door and see who needed more coffee, but hearing Lynn's offer, she stopped and listened. Over the heads of the other men, J.T. made eye contact with her, and motioned toward Lynn. It took only a second for her to get his drift. Obviously, he thought Lynn would be better off somewhere else. Ordinarily, Cynthia wouldn't have agreed, but in this case she did. Lynn was operating on the last of her energy. Cynthia was certain that Lynn, frantic with worry, and sleep deprived, had no idea just how irrational her suggestion sounded.

"Why don't we let them get on with their plans," Cynthia suggested, urging Lynn out of the room. "Lettie Mae and I could use some help with the food."

Lynn followed, glancing back only once to see that the men had already regrouped, having completely dismissed her and her idea.

As Cynthia and Lynn stepped into the hall on their way to the kitchen, the front door opened, and there stood Tyler and Ruth.

"Merry Christmas, everybody," Tyler said, smiling. "Looks like y'all started the party early."

At his side, looking considerably better than she had before she left Crystal Creek, Ruth, too, was smiling. "Merry Christmas, Cynthia, Lettie Mae. How are you, Lynn?"

"Tyler!" Lynn tried to smile back. "We're so glad you're home. Merry..." But the effort was too much, and she broke down and started crying.

Quickly Tyler ushered Ruth inside. "What the hell is going on?"

"Tyler? That you, son?" J.T. came out of the study. "I thought I heard your voice. Good to have you back."

"Yeah, good to *be* back. Daddy, what's wrong with Lynn? And what..." Astonished, he watched as first Cal, then Sam, then Wayne Jackson and a stranger filed out of his father's study. "What's going on around here?"

Sam tried to comfort Lynn as J.T. stepped forward in the role of spokesman. "Tyler, Allie Russell was kidnapped yesterday afternoon."

Ruth gasped and rushed over to Lynn, now sobbing quietly in Sam's arms. "I'm so sorry. What can we do to help?"

"You're just in time to saddle up, big brother," Cal said, happier to see his brother than he could ever express.

"Saddle up?"

J.T. pointed to the stranger standing beside the sheriff. "This is Special Agent Rickman of the FBI. He and Wayne are coordinating the search. When Taggart contacted Lynn, they were able to trace the call—"

"Taggart? Walt Taggart? That guy hired to train Lightning?" Tyler asked, shocked.

Since neither Lynn nor Sam seemed disposed to explain, Cal spoke up. "Yeah. Lynn caught him working Lightning over with a riding crop, and fired his sorry ass. He intended to make her pay, but when he got to the house, she and Sam were gone. He took Allie instead."

"Jesus," Tyler breathed.

"Look, boys," Wayne interjected. "If we're gonna make every minute count, we gotta get back out there. Tyler can be filled in as we go." He turned to Cal. "Slattery's bunch should be comin' in for fresh horses anytime. You ready?"

"Yeah," Cal replied. "Tyler, you with me?"

"Damn straight. Let me change, and I'll meet you at the stables." He started to leave, then stopped, and walked over to Sam and Lynn. "I—I don't know what to say."

"You don't have to say anything," Sam told him.

"We really are glad you're home," Lynn said, sniffing.

In an unpredictable show of affection, Tyler leaned over and gave his sister a light peck on the cheek. "Don't worry. We'll find her."

Five minutes later he met up with Cal in the barn. "Damn glad you're home," Cal said as he threw a saddle on a fresh mount.

"Yeah. Me, too."

"Does this mean you and Ruth are all squared away?"

"I don't know."

"What the hell does that mean?"

"It means I talked her into coming back to Crystal Creek."

"That's a start."

"Yeah, but things aren't...smooth. We're still not sure where we stand. We've got a lot of stuff to deal with."

Holding the reins of the horse he had just saddled in one hand, Cal used his other to slap his brother on the back. "What you've got is a second chance. Don't blow it."

BACK AT THE HOUSE, Lynn pulled herself together long enough to kiss Sam goodbye as the men dispersed. Cynthia had gone to feed Jennifer and Lettie Mae had returned to her kitchen, leaving Lynn alone with Ruth.

"Not exactly the kind of Christmas homecoming you expected, huh? I'm sorry we had to hit you with this two seconds after you opened the door."

"Don't you dare apologize to me," Ruth insisted. "I'm just sorry we didn't come home yesterday so we could have been more help."

"Well, you're here now. That's all that counts."

"Are you okay?" Ruth waved her hand as if to erase her words. "That was a stupid question. Of course you're not okay. No one would be under these circumstances. I'm sorry."

Finally, Lynn did manage a weak smile. "It's all right, really. No one knows quite how to act or what to do. I'm just grateful that so many people are around to help."

"From the looks of all the vehicles we saw outside, I'd say half the population of Crystal Creek is helping."

"I know." Lynn put a hand to her chest, and took a deep breath.

"You look exhausted. And no wonder. Here." Ruth helped her to a leather wing chair in the parlor. "Better?"

"Yes, thanks."

"You want me to get Cynthia or—"

"No. I'm fine." Lynn rested her head on the high back of the chair, and closed her eyes.

Ruth tried to look at her sister-in-law objectively, but it was difficult. In fact, now that she was unobserved, Ruth couldn't stop staring at Lynn's stomach. A part of her wanted to cry for the anguish she must be experiencing over the kidnapped child. But another part of Ruth wanted to shout how unfair it was for Lynn's baby to be alive when hers wasn't. Ruth knew she was reacting unfairly, just as she knew she shouldn't be staring at Lynn's belly. But she couldn't stop doing either one. She was still a long way from the end of her healing process, but for the sake of her marriage—and her sanity—she had gained a measure of control over her emotions. Now, seeing Lynn had brought those emotions close to the surface again.

Lynn opened her eyes. "I'm glad you're back. How are . . . things?"

"Better," Ruth said truthfully. "I agreed to come back and see if we could work some things out."

"Great! That's a start."

"Yes," she said, hopeful. "But I don't want to talk about me or Tyler right now. Is there anything I can get for you?"

Lynn licked her dry lips. "A glass of water would be great. Would you mind?"

Ruth smiled. "I'll be right back with it."

When she was gone, Lynn closed her eyes again. A few moments earlier when she had offered her suggestion, she had felt the same way she had as a child begging her father for a horse of her own to train. Predictably, he had told her she was just a little girl, and not capable of training a horse. Well, she had shown him, but that hadn't stopped the patronizing, then or now. *I'm not a fool. I know how awkward I am. I know I can't dash in and rescue Allie all by myself.*

Patronizing. Lynn even disliked the sound of the word. It was too close to pity to suit her. Despite her fatigue, anger flashed through her, compelling her to move. She rose from the chair, walked to the window and stared out over the lawn on the east side of the house. Knowing the anger was nonproductive, she let her mind drift, relax. As she stood, almost transfixed, without actually focusing on anything, a picture slowly formed in her mind.

A rock. Big rock. Flat on top, and extending far out like some kind of shelf. And a campfire.

Lynn blinked. She had seen the rock as clearly as if she had been standing in front of it. She blinked again, realizing she couldn't see it anymore. *Too tired. Your mind is playing tricks on you.*

But instinctively, Lynn knew her mind wasn't playing tricks. She *had* seen the rock. And what was more, she had seen that rock before. Years ago. When she was just a child. She and Cal had been there together. Lynn concentrated, trying to recall the memory.

Daddy was working cattle. Cal and I were playing. Playing. Playing... pirates! Cal and I were playing pirates on that rock! It was huge and it stuck out like the bow of a ship. We were pretending to walk the plank....

Suddenly, as clearly as she had seen the rock, Lynn knew *why* she had seen it. The reason reverberated through her heart and her mind like the clear, sweet tone of a beautiful bell.

She knew where Allie was.

Allie was somewhere near that rock. Lynn knew she was right.

It had been years since she had last been to that particular section of Double C land, but she could find it. And when she did, she would find Allie. Lynn had never been more certain of anything in her life. She *could* find it, and she would. By herself if necessary.

She turned, intending to find Sam and tell him about the strength of her feeling, but she had barely taken two steps when her belly seemed to harden instantly and a small, but decidedly sharp pain sliced through her.

THE PAIN WASN'T SEVERE enough to cause her to double over, but still she reached out and gripped the side of the wing chair to steady herself. *A contraction? It couldn't be.*

Slowly, the pain passed and her belly softened. She took a deep breath. Was it possible she was in the beginning stage of labor? *Of course not. It's too early. Must be Braxton-Hicks contractions,* she decided, remembering that Dr. Nate had told her to expect the muscle spasms. *Still, it wouldn't hurt to check with Cynthia,* she thought. *Cynthia will know.*

First she had to find Sam and tell him about the rock. She had to tell him so he could find Allie and bring her home.

But suddenly, all the joy she'd experienced over her vision of the rock a moment ago vanished. How was her revelation going to sound to Sam, Wayne and the rest of the men?

Like a hysterical woman.

Lynn sat back down in the chair. What if they could be right? What if this...*feeling* was nothing more than a delusion born of an overtired mind? But it had been so clear and the feeling so strong.

That's probably what all lunatics think when they hear voices and see visions. And you know where lunatics end up.

She sat quietly for several moments. Finally, she shook her head. "No. I'm not crazy. I *know* Allie is close to that rock." It might take the searchers hours to work their way to that section. *And God knows what Taggart could do to Allie in just a few hours.*

Still trying to play devil's advocate, Lynn asked herself what she would do if Sam didn't believe her. After all, it was a rather bizarre statement for someone to make. What if he didn't believe her?

Possible. Very possible, she had to admit. Then what? She had no answer, no plan B if Sam didn't believe her. But answer or no answer, plan or no plan, she had to talk to him before he left and at least try to make him understand.

And if he didn't?

I'll cross that bridge when I come to it.

CHAPTER THIRTEEN

BY THE TIME Lynn reached the stable area, Cal and his riders had already left. Sam and J.T. were preparing to go out in a topless four-wheel-drive CJ 5 Jeep that was considered part of the ranch equipment, and was nearly as old as she was.

"Sweetheart, you shouldn't be out here. You should be inside, resting," Sam insisted.

"I will. Later. Sam, I had a..."

The moment of truth had arrived, and almost as surely as she knew Allie's whereabouts, she knew that Sam and her daddy would never go along with anything so nebulous as her *feeling*. They would put it down to woman's intuition, probably agree to take a look just to pacify her, then forget it.

"What, sweetheart? You had what?"

"I had an idea about where to look. It's a strip of the Double C that runs along the backside of Aunt Carolyn's property. There's a big rock there. Sort of an overhang. It's big enough to hide a car or a truck. Cal knows where I'm talking about. We used to play there as kids. Will you check it out, Sam? Please, for me?"

"All right, if it will make you happy. We're going to search every inch of the area around here anyway."

"You promise?"

"I will, if you'll promise me something."

"What?"

"That you'll go back up to the house, and take it easy."

"I promise. Just please don't forget about that rock."

He nodded, hopped into the Jeep, and started the engine. J.T. came out of the stable and climbed in the passenger seat.

"Take care of yourself, punkin'", her daddy hollered above the noise of the old Jeep's engine. Sam shifted gears, and they raced off.

Please, Sam. If you've ever kept a promise in your life, keep this one.

She watched them, followed by several more four-wheel-drive vehicles, as they headed out toward the intersection with an east-west dirt road that would take them to the area where the big rock was located. She watched, and waited. And prayed, until...

Turn left. Go west.

They turned right, and headed east.

"No!" she screamed as the vehicles disappeared out of sight. "No. Sam, you promised."

But it was too late.

Half disheartened, and half downright angry, she turned and slowly headed back toward the house.

And had another pain.

This one wasn't any worse than the first one, but it certainly wasn't any better. Lynn tried to think how long it had been since the first pain had occurred and guessed it was more than a half hour ago. Maybe even forty-five minutes.

Lynn stared off in the direction Sam and the other searchers had disappeared. He *had* been humoring her.

Another pat on the head. *Go away, little girl, you bother me.*

After everything they had shared last night, she thought they had gone past that, and it was hurtful to think they hadn't. But even more hurtful was the knowledge that he had broken a promise. An important promise.

Undoubtedly, at least one of the vehicles was in communication with Wayne or the FBI through CB radios. What was she going to do? Call up Sam, and tell him he'd turned the wrong way? Yell at him for breaking a promise?

A surefire way to make him believe you're truly unbalanced.

No. If no one would believe her, no one would help her, then she would simply have to arrange it so that Sam had no choice but to go where she wanted him to go.

He would *have* to follow her.

FOR THE FIRST TIME in her life, Allie Russell knew what it was to truly hate someone. And to fear him.

Through a badly swollen black eye, she stared across the now dead campfire and the sleeping Tag. She wished he were dead. He was gross and ugly. And he had an ugly mind. But if he were dead, then no telling when, or if, anyone would ever find her. No matter, Allie thought. She still wished him dead.

He had returned last night madder than she had ever seen anyone in her whole life. Obviously drunk, he had stumbled around the camp, cussing and throwing things, and mumbling about getting even with Lynn. He had talked and cussed, mostly cussed. But when he talked, Allie wished he would go back to cussing because he talked about all the things he wanted to do to Lynn, once he had her. Even now, she almost got sick to her stomach remembering the horrible things he had said, the revolting descriptions he had recited. He'd laughed when she turned her head away in disgust.

And then, something had happened, something even worse than his cussing, worse than the mental images he had painted with his ugly words.

Without reason, he had suddenly yanked her off the cold ground, yelling at her to shut up. With both hands clutching her clothing, he held her in front of him, her feet dangling a few inches off the ground. At that close range, the look in his eyes was the most frightening thing Allie had ever seen. It was wild and cold, with so much hate in it, it seemed a separate being living inside Tag, raging to get out. Over and over, he kept screaming at her to shut her stupid mouth. Allie thought he had gone crazy because she was still gagged with the two bandannas. But he kept on and on until finally...

He hit her.

Her face felt as if it had exploded, and she literally saw stars in front of her eyes. Through vision already beginning to blur, she saw Tag raise his hand to strike her again, and the thought went through her mind that she was going to die. That he was going to hit her, and keep hitting her until she was dead.

But as abruptly as he had started, he stopped, cussing wildly. Then he tossed her back to the ground and stalked off into the darkness.

Allie had no idea what had caused him not to act on the rage she saw in his eyes. As she lay listening for his returning footsteps, she prayed to God to save her.

All her life, she had been taught that there was good in everyone, that no one was beyond hope. Now, she didn't think that was true. There was no hope for Tag. He had what Lynn called a black soul. The kind of soul that belonged in hell.

Thinking of Lynn reminded Allie of all the times the two of them had sat in the McKinney kitchen devouring Lettie Mae's goodies. All the times she had felt safe and happy. She wanted to sit in the kitchen again. Eat Lettie Mae's cookies again. And see her family again.

In her mind, she knew people were looking for her. Her daddy and Lynn, and probably lots of people. But in her heart, she was afraid they would never find her. Fear and hopelessness closed in on her, and she started to cry.

She cried and cried without ever making a sound, for fear it would wake the monster lying only a few feet away.

TO WORK PERFECTLY, Lynn knew her plan required two things: a clue and a witness. Planting a clue at the right time was easy.

"They've all gone out," she announced, when she came back into the kitchen after watching Sam and the others drive off in the wrong direction.

"Well, we're not completely alone," Cynthia said. "One of the FBI agents is still in his van, and J.T. asked Bucky to stay close in case we needed him."

"When will they be back?" Ruth asked.

"Cal told me they intended to work the grids in four-hour shifts, or until someone finds her," Serena explained.

Cynthia smiled and patted Lynn on the shoulder. "Which will be soon. I just know it."

She smiled back. "Me, too."

"Sure. They'll probably be reporting some good news before you know it."

"Absolutely," Ruth agreed, darting a glance at Cynthia and Serena. She couldn't speak for them, but judging from the way they were trying so hard to bolster Lynn's spirits, she surmised that the same thought was going through their heads as through hers. Namely, that the news might not be good. The unspoken fear hung in the air of the kitchen like the smell of something spoiled.

"I wish I could search for her myself," Lynn said. "You know, the time I did sleep last night, I, uh, dreamed about finding her. She was outside... somewhere. The only thing I remember is that she was close to a big rock of some kind."

"You mean, like a mountain?"

"No. More like a huge slab of rock big enough to hide under."

Cynthia's heart went out to Lynn. She was trying so hard to stay strong. "Often when we're under a lot of stress we have dreams we don't understand."

"I suppose. But it was so real," Lynn said, hoping she had conveyed just enough information for her "clue."

Serena rose from her chair and stretched. "You know what? I think we should do something besides standing around and staring at one another."

"I'm game," Cynthia said, agreeing with Serena's assessment that brooding was helpful to no one.

"Since it's a sure bet that Allie is almost as good as home, and tonight *is* Christmas Eve, I say we get a few pies baked. Maybe make some fudge."

"Yeah," Ruth chimed in. "I would love to learn how to make Lettie Mae's cranberry sauce."

"You better okay these ideas with Lettie Mae," Lynn suggested.

"You're right. I'll go ask her—"

"Ask her what?"

They all turned and found Lettie Mae standing in the doorway. "How long have you been standing there?" Cynthia asked.

"Long enough to know y'all are planning on takin' over my kitchen." She looked at the others, as if she was trying to decide whether or not to allow them into her inner sanctum. She knew what they were trying to do, and even though she couldn't abide a crowded kitchen, especially when it was hers, this was an exception. "All right," she said, shaking her finger at them. "But I give the orders."

So the women set about keeping themselves busy, and keeping Lynn's spirits up, all under Lettie Mae's sharp eye.

After ten or fifteen minutes of work, Lynn announced, "You know, I'm more tired that I thought. Maybe I'll just go into the parlor and put my swollen-almost-beyond-recognition feet up."

"Great idea," Serena said. "When the fudge is ready, I'll bring you a piece."

Lettie Mae pointed a spoon at Cal's wife and warned, "You ain't gonna get nothin' ready if you don't get back to choppin' those nuts in the food processor."

Serena saluted, and returned to her chopping.

For appearance's sake, Lynn headed into the parlor, then slipped around and through the door between the parlor and her daddy's study. In a matter of seconds, she was on her way to the stables.

"Hi, Bucky," she said when she strolled in. "How's Lightning?"

At the sound of her voice, the big horse stomped his feet, and tossed his head in greeting. Lynn reached out to stroke his nose and the animal quieted. She had missed him. Had it only been a day since she had seen him last? It felt like weeks.

Bucky glanced up from working on a piece of tack. "Howdy, Miz Russell. Why, he's fine as wine. Eatin' good, runnin' good."

"Is he behaving himself?"

"Well, he ain't bit me yet."

Lynn smiled. "I'm glad to know you're minding your manners," she said, scolding the horse gently.

"Uh, I'm right sorry to hear about that little girl of yours," Bucky said a little awkwardly. "I hope they find her real soon."

"Thanks, Bucky. So do I."

He frowned. "You ain't thinkin' about ridin' out to look for her, are ya?"

"Not on a horse."

With a nod of agreement, Bucky went back to working on the tack. Lynn continued to pet Lightning, talking to him in a soft voice. After several minutes she idly asked, "Bucky, do you know where there's a big—I mean, really big—rock around here, shaped like a boat?"

He thought for a moment, then snapped his fingers and said, "You must be talkin' about Shiprock, over on that section back of Miz Townsend's—I mean Miz Trent's—place. The top's flat and comes to a point like one of them ocean liners. That how come they call it Shiprock."

"On the backside of Aunt Carolyn's place, you say?"

"Yes'm."

"How long would it take me to drive out there?"

"Maybe a half hour. Forty minutes, tops."

"Thanks, Bucky."

"Any time, Miz Russell."

Lynn walked out of the stables, went straight to Sam's pickup and got in. She deliberately backed the truck out, making a wide arch to ensure that Bucky would see her leaving and in what direction she traveled. Sure enough, when she was almost even with the open end of the stables, Bucky glanced up, and waved.

Lynn waved back, put the truck in gear and drove off.

Now she had her witness.

CYNTHIA WAS the first one to notice Lynn wasn't in the parlor. After checking the downstairs bathroom and several other rooms, she came back to the kitchen. "Did any of you see Lynn leave the house?" she asked the other three women.

Serena looked up from stirring a batch of rich chocolate fudge. "No, why?"

"I can't find her."

"Maybe she went down to the stables to see Lightning," Ruth suggested. "Want me to check?"

"You're up to your elbows in cranberries, missy," Lettie Mae reminded her.

"No," Cynthia said. "I'll go."

Soon Cynthia came tearing back into the kitchen, her face flushed, and breathing hard from running. "She's gone."

Lettie Mae looked up. "Whatdaya mean, she's gone? Where'd she get off to? And what's got you so red-faced?"

"That dream. That damn dream she told us about," Cynthia said, trying to catch her breath. "The one about the big rock."

"Oh, that was just a—"

"Bucky said she asked him if there was such a rock close by. He told her it sounded like the place they call Shiprock."

"Why, nobody's heard of that place in years," Lettie Mae said, growing more concerned by the minute. "Why on earth would she want to..."

Ruth, Serena and Lettie Mae all seemed to arrive at the same conclusion at about the same moment.

"Oh, good God," Lettie Mae said. "She's done gone off to find that child."

"I'm afraid so," Cynthia confirmed, between trying to restock her lungs with air and calm her heart rate.

"What are we going to do?" Ruth asked.

"Serena," Cynthia said, "go get that FBI agent, and tell him what's happened. Tell him to get on the CB, and contact Sam and tell him to come back. Now."

When Serena had taken no more than two steps, Cynthia added, "And tell him to find the group of searchers that Nate Purdy is with. We may need a doctor before this is all over with."

LYNN HADN'T GONE FAR before she had another pain. This time, it was longer and sharper. She eased her foot back on the accelerator. As much as she wanted to drive like hell to the spot where she knew Allie was being held, she realized that she needed to give Sam time to follow her.

Surely, by now Cynthia or one of them has discovered I'm gone.

Lynn knew the first place they'd look was the stables.

Please, Bucky, don't let me down.

Taking into consideration the time it would take to get a message to Sam and for him to turn back and head in her direction, she calculated that he would be approximately twenty minutes behind her. She needed to slow down even more, so she'd waited until she reached the bottom of quite a high hill, then pulled off on the edge of the dirt road and looked around in order to get her bearings. Now was not the time to get lost, she reminded herself.

But it had been years since she had even thought about this part of the Double C. Some of the landscape had changed and she wasn't as certain as she had been when she left the ranch. Thinking that being inside a vehicle might be affecting her perception, Lynn opened the door of the truck, and slipped out of the front seat. Her swollen feet hit the hard-packed earth with a thud, and...

Suddenly water gushed from her body and down her legs, making a dark spot as it seeped into the ground beneath her feet.

Oh my God!

Before she could form her next thought, another pain seized her abdomen.

Shocked, Lynn instinctively took short, quick breaths until the pain passed. With its passing came the realization that these were not Braxton-Hicks contractions, and that she was very probably in labor. But the baby wasn't due for a month.

It's too early. Something must be wrong!

She glanced down at her damp clothing and shoes, wondering what to do next. She knew that she had to get back to the ranch, but how much time did she have? Lynn glanced at her watch. What if the pains started coming fast, too fast? What if she couldn't get back in time?

Stop it, right now! Don't panic. She forced herself to take deep, calming breaths. *Get a hold on yourself,* she cautioned.

Lynn searched her memory, mentally thumbing through the many books she had read on childbirth and prenatal care. The mental exercise helped calm her.

Okay. Breathe deep, But not too deep. You've probably got hours to go before this baby is born.

Unless something went wrong.

You're okay. You're okay. Don't panic and you'll stay okay.

And then she remembered the mobile phone.

Thank God.

The back of her maternity jumper was soaked, but she did her best to arrange the material so that she wouldn't be sitting on the worst of it, then climbed back into the truck, and pulled out the phone. With trembling fingers she dialed the ranch, and waited for the answering ring. But when she finally got the ring, she could barely hear it. The static was so bad, it drowned out the voice of whoever answered the phone.

"Hello," she yelled into the receiver. "This is Lynn. I need help. Hello. Can you hear me?"

But all *she* heard was static. She disconnected and tried again. This time she didn't even hear the ringing, the static was so fierce.

She *had* to get back to the ranch, but somewhere out there—maybe only a mile or so away—poor lit-

tle Allie was waiting to be rescued. Lynn was torn.
The thought of anything happening to her baby ter-
rified her. But the idea of being so close to finding
Allie and then turning away was breaking her heart.

Another pain seized her. Lynn glanced at her
watch.

Twenty minutes since the last one.

That wasn't too bad, was it? Women didn't go
from twenty-minute intervals between contractions
right to delivery, did they?

"Easy does it," she said aloud in her best coaching voice. "Focus, focus. Breathe, breathe." A few
more seconds and the pain was gone.

How could she focus when her mind kept going
back to thoughts of Allie in God knew what kind of
shape, hoping and praying for someone to find her?
And she was so close. She knew it.

Lynn knew she had to make a decision. Time was
running out.

Sitting there in the truck, at the bottom of that hill,
Lynn had never felt so alone in her whole life. How
could she play God, choosing one life at the possible
expense of another?

Gently, she stroked her stomach and prayed.

Please, dear Lord, help me.

Unceasingly, she prayed the same words over and
over, until finally, when she stopped, they seemed to
echo in her ears. And as the echo faded into silence,
she heard another sound.

The sound of engines.

Car engines. Truck engines.

Lynn's head snapped up. She glanced in her rearview mirror and started to cry. *They're coming. Thank you, Lord. They're coming.*

They were possibly a half mile back, but indeed headed straight for her position. Lynn recognized the Jeep Sam and her daddy had driven off the ranch, and her heart leaped for joy.

Now, that's something to focus on, she thought as another pain reminded her that time was slipping through her fingers. The pain had passed by the time the Jeep pulled up even with the pickup.

Sam jumped out of the Jeep, and practically ran around to her door. "What the hell are you doing out here?"

"I know where Allie is," she said, no longer caring if he thought she was crazy or not. "I saw it. Don't ask me to explain. I *saw* her near a big rock that jutted out like the front of a ship."

Seated in the Jeep, not five feet away, J.T. said, "Shiprock?"

Lynn nodded.

"What is she talking about?"

"It's a place about two or two and a half miles from here, but—"

"The rock ledge extends far enough to cover a truck or a tent, right?" she asked anxiously.

"Maybe." J.T. was beginning to think maybe his older daughter wasn't as crazy as she sounded.

Her arm resting on her door, Lynn leaned forward to look her husband directly in the eyes. "She's there, Sam. Don't ask me how I know. I just do. Find her. Please, please. You promised me."

Sam gazed into the troubled eyes of his wife and knew that regardless of how bizarre the idea sounded, she believed it with all her heart.

"What have we got to lose?" he said, and gave her a quick kiss. "We'll go check this place out, but—"

"Now?"

"Yes. But since we're talking about broken promises, you broke yours when you decided to come tearing out into the middle of nowhere like this."

"I know, I know. And I'm sorry, but—"

"Will you please go back to the ranch now?"

"Yes, but—"

"No, buts," he said, walking back to slide behind tne steering wheel of the Jeep. "Turn that truck around, and get going."

She started to tell him if he didn't stop interrupting her, he would be a new father before she could tell him she was in labor. But the Jeep was already moving on down the road. A string of Jeeps and trucks roared past in pursuit.

Lynn sighed and leaned her forehead against her arm. Maybe it was just as well she hadn't told Sam that she was in labor. He would have been torn between wanting to stay with her, and going to find Allie. And there had been enough emotional push and pull in her family today to last a lifetime.

Slowly, she turned her vehicle around and headed back to the ranch. A mile down the road she had another contraction. She looked at her watch. Ten minutes since the last one.

APPROXIMATELY a mile before they reached the point J.T. estimated to be their destination, all search vehicles were waved off the road, and engines killed. They couldn't afford for the noise to alert Taggart in case he might escape. Or worse, retaliate against Allie. Cal and Ken had been contacted by CB radio and informed of the plan to check out Shiprock. They were on the way on horseback.

"How long will it take them?" Sam asked, growing increasingly anxious. He hadn't completely bought Lynn's theory, but he sure as hell bought her conviction. And as he had pointed out to Lynn, they had nothing to lose.

"Another fifteen, maybe twenty minutes. They had changed to fresh horses so that'll help."

"You think there's a possibility that Lynn's hunch is right?"

J.T. shrugged. "I've certainly heard crazier. And to be truthful, if I was looking for a place to hide, that's as good a one as you're likely to find. It's good cover, and a straight line of sight to the road."

"That's not good news. How will we be able to get close enough?"

"Cal and Ken can come around behind the rock without being seen," J.T. assured him. "Question is, what do we do once we know Taggart is there?"

Sam knew what he was going to do. He was going in to get his daughter.

"If you're thinkin' about ridin' in to rescue to Allie, you better think again."

"Why?" Sam asked, perturbed that his father-in-law had read him so easily.

"What if Taggart's got a gun? You won't be any good to Allie dead."

"I've thought about it."

"And?"

"And . . . I don't know."

"Of course, I'm a fine one to talk. Can't say I would do different if it was Lynn or Jennifer," J.T. had to admit. "But—" he pointed to the approaching vehicle that carried the head of the FBI team "—at least see what Rickman has to say before you go off half-cocked."

As it turned out, Rickman had a lot to say—most of it not what Sam wanted to hear. J.T.'s idea that Taggart might have a weapon was echoed by Rickman. And that meant no civilians. FBI and local law officers would be the only ones to face Taggart. Period. End of story.

Sam was furious until J.T. made him realize that, in his rush to get to Allie, her own father could do more harm than good. The trained professionals were more objective and therefore less likely to make mistakes. Rickman stood by while the elder McKinney delivered the same speech he had intended to lay on Sam Russell. The only thing he could have added was that there was always the possibility that he might not get his daughter back alive. He had worked his share of kidnap cases and he usually had a feeling going in if the subject was alive or not. In this case, Rickman was convinced the girl was still alive. This bastard, Taggart, still had delusions of a trade, and that was Allie Russell's life insurance policy.

"Sam," Rickman said when J.T. finished, "the bottom line here is that you want your daughter back safe. We can do that with a minimum of fuss because we're trained to do it. To put it bluntly, you'd be in the way. And we won't have time to stop and bail your butt outta trouble when we're nose-to-nose with this creep. I know it's hell to have to stand to one side and wait, but that's what you've got to do."

"All right," Sam finally agreed. "Anything as long as I can hold her again."

Rickman held out his hand for Sam to shake. "Hang on just a little while longer and I'll personally put her in your arms."

CHAPTER FOURTEEN

LYNN HAD another contraction before she got back to the ranch. Cynthia, Lettie Mae and Serena were waiting for her on the front steps.

"I oughta take a switch to your backside for runnin' off like that," the woman scolded. "You plum scared the daylights outta us. Now, get outta that truck, and get yourself in this house."

"Can you wait until this contraction passes?" Lynn asked, breathing hard.

"The good Lord have mercy," Lettie Mae cried, rushing toward the truck, with Cynthia not two steps behind.

"How far apart are the contractions?" Cynthia asked.

"About eight minutes apart, but a half hour ago they were twenty minutes apart."

Lettie Mae and Cynthia exchanged knowing glances.

"I'll make sure Nate Purdy is on his way," Serena volunteered, and promptly hurried inside.

Cynthia and Lettie Mae helped Lynn from the truck and into the house. Deciding the stairs would be too strenuous at this point, they had her lie down on the wide extra-long leather couch in J.T.'s study.

"Nate's service said he's on his way here," Serena said, joining them a moment later. She glanced from Lynn's face, tense with pain, to Cynthia's. "What do you think?"

"I think," said Cynthia, "that it may be too late for the hospital, and that Nate Purdy better get here quick."

"Damn quick, unless I miss my guess," Lettie Mae agreed.

"WHAT THE HELL is taking so long?" Sam paced back and forth in front of the Jeep.

"Take it easy, son. They've only been gone for a few minutes." J.T. wished he could offer his son-in-law more comfort, but the truth was, he was nervous himself.

Not fifteen minutes ago, Special Agent Rickman and his men, along with Wayne Jackson and his deputy, had headed toward Shiprock, taking a circular route. On horseback, Cal, Ken and several others had worked their way around the back of the rock, and were positioned and waiting. Using walkie-talkies, Rickman had instructed the riders not to make a move of any kind until he and his men were in position on either side of the location. And every minute since then had ticked away like a slowly dripping faucet in the middle of the night. Interminable. And nerve-racking.

J.T. knew Rickman was armed, and he supposed his agents were, too. And Jackson, of course. The question in his mind was whether Cal and Ken were armed. Tyler hadn't had enough time to get a weapon, and neither Cal nor J.T.'s foreman was in the habit of carrying a gun. But he suspected at least one of them—possibly both—had included a weapon when they collected their gear for the search. It was bad enough that poor little Allie was in danger, but the possibility of an exchange of gunfire made J.T. sweat.

On an impulse, he approached the agent Rickman had left in charge. "Mind if I use your walkie-talkie to contact my son and the men on horseback?"

The agent looked as if he wasn't thrilled about handing over government equipment to a civilian, but he did.

J.T. hit the Talk button on the walkie-talkie. "Cal? Cal, can you read me?"

"We gotcha, Dad. What's up?"

"That's what we want to know. Can you see anything from where you are?"

"There's a campsite for sure, but can't tell much else. I'll tell you one thing, though. I'll never doubt my kid sister again. She was right on."

"Is Tyler with you?"

"Yeah."

There was a long pause before J.T. said, "Don't either of you take a notion to be heroes, you hear me?"

There was another equally long pause on Cal's end of the line. "I hear you, Dad."

"McKinney?" Rickman interrupted. "Get off this line."

"Pick one," Cal quipped.

"The elder," Rickman returned.

"Guess that puts me in my place," J.T. said, handing the walkie-talkie back to the agent.

Instantly, Sam was at his side. "Any news?"

"Nothing new."

J.T. looked toward the spot where Sam's daughter and two McKinney sons waited. He certainly hadn't made any emotional declaration as far as his sons were concerned, but he hoped the fact that he had said anything at all wasn't lost on Cal. He glanced at Sam, worried sick about his child, and he was no less afraid for his own. He thought about Lynn and little Jennifer, and how precious they all were to him. And he wondered why God, in his infinite wisdom, often brought a man to the brink of losing so much before he realized just how much he had.

Just then, the crackle of the walkie-talkie and Rickman's voice told them the waiting was almost over. Several seconds later, they heard gunshots.

J.T. put his hand on Sam's shoulder, and both men silently prayed.

BY THE TIME the searchers were called in from all sectors and the good news was passed along, Sam and Allie were almost back at the Double C.

Sam still couldn't believe he was holding his daughter in his arms, that she was actually sitting in his lap, her arms around his neck.

"We're almost to the ranch, baby. Almost home," he whispered against her bruised cheek.

As soon as Allie had caught sight of her father, she had begun crying, and she'd hardly stopped since. As for Sam, the instant he saw her, his knees had gone weak, and he, too, had started to cry.

Then they had held each other and cried.

And every mile of the way back Sam had thanked God that his child was safe and for the most part at least, physically unharmed. Her eye was badly swollen, and the bruise on her cheek was an ugly one, but Allie had insisted those were her only injuries. As much as he hated to add to Allie's distress, Sam had finally been able to question her, and was satisfied that she hadn't been raped or sexually molested in any way. Of course, he wanted a doctor to check her over, and he realized that she might need to talk to a counselor about her ordeal. But the most important thing was that she was alive and safe.

The second most important thing, as far as Sam was concerned, was the fact that Walt Taggart was dead.

Rickman and his men had gone into the confrontation with every intention of taking Taggart alive so he could be brought to justice, but in the end, Taggart had made the decision for them by going for his gun. The results had been quick and final.

J.T. whipped the Jeep into practically the only vacant spot in front of the McKinney ranch house.

"There weren't this many cars here when we left," he commented, killing the engine.

With Allie still in his arms, Sam swung his legs out of the Jeep and headed toward the front door. But before they had reached the top step of the porch, the front door flew open, and Sandy, Serena and a half dozen others, including Carolyn Trent, Beverly Townsend and Reverend Howard Blake, came rushing out to surround them. Everybody talked at once, trying to kiss and hug Allie. Sam had to work his way into the house, but he didn't mind.

"Lynn!" he called. "Sweetheart, where are you?" By now, he had set Allie down and she was being smothered with affection on all sides. "Lynn—"

"What's all the hollerin'?" Lettie Mae said, grinning from ear to ear.

"Where's my wife?"

"She's upstairs in her old bedroom. Plumb tuckered out, but I expect she'll be real happy to see you. You better get on up there and see what's been going on."

Sam couldn't imagine what the McKinney cook was talking about, but he was in too big a hurry to question her. He took the stairs two at a time. "Lynn," he called, rushing down the long hallway.

"We found her. She's gonna be all right." He opened the bedroom door...and his heart felt as if it had hit the pit of his stomach.

Dr. Purdy was standing on one side of the bed, and Cynthia was on the other. Lynn, looking pale and tired, was propped up on pillows in the middle of her bed.

Nate Purdy saw the color drain from Sam's face and knew the young father had assumed the worst. He smiled. "Hold on there, Sam. This ain't as bad as you think. I wouldn't want you to pass out before you've had a chance to meet your son."

Sam's eyes widened. He looked from the doctor to Lynn.

She was smiling and weeping at once.

For the first time he noticed the blanketed bundle in her arms. His throat went dry. His gaze met hers. "But...how?"

"The usual way," Nate quipped.

"But he wasn't supposed to get here for another month," Sam said, dumbfounded by the news and unable to take his eyes off Lynn. She was more beautiful than he had ever seen her.

"He showed up early. He's a real go-getter. Eight pounds and two ounces. Pink from head to toe, with a fine set of lungs. Just the way I like 'em." Nate clapped Sam on the back. "Congratulations, son."

"Th-thanks," Sam muttered as he slowly made his way toward the bed. "It's a...a..."

"Son," Lynn finished for him. She lifted the corner of the blanket to reveal a wrinkled, red-faced baby. "Sam Russell, say hello to your son, Hank."

"Hank," Sam breathed, awestruck at the sight of his child. He swallowed hard. "Wh-when—"

"About an hour ago. Sam—Allie? Is she all right? Taggart didn't—"

"She's fine," he assured her. "She's got an ugly black eye and some bruises, but she's okay, Lynn. Physically okay, I mean." He glanced up at Cynthia and Nate Purdy as they headed out of the room. "Doc—"

"I'm on my way to check Allie over, Sam."

"Thanks—"

"Sam." Lynn tugged on his sleeve. "Sam, what about Taggart? What happened?"

Gently he brushed a wisp of damp bangs away from her forehead. "Before I tell you what happened, I want to ask you to forgive me."

"Sam—"

"No," he insisted. "I broke my promise to you. And it makes my blood turn cold to think what might have happened to Allie if you hadn't followed your instincts. You were right and I was wrong." He reached for her hand. "Oh, Lynn. I've been wrong about so many things. I don't want a carbon copy of Marta. I want you exactly as you are. I love your sweet spirit and your joy for life. I love you. Now. Forever. And that's a promise I will keep."

"I love you, too," Lynn whispered as he brushed a tear from her cheek. "And I believe in us, but Sam, I have to know that you won't ever keep anything from me again."

"I won't ever again. That's another promise I intend to keep. And we'll work out the money problems somehow. Together. But if I've learned nothing else the last few days, I've learned how fragile life is and how much we take for granted. The important thing is that we're all together and safe. And we're going to stay that way."

"But Taggart?"

"He won't hurt Allie or you, or anybody ever again. He's dead."

Lynn wasn't shocked or thrilled by the news. The only important thing was that Allie was safe. "Did...did...oh Sam, did she see him..."

Sam nodded. "She'll probably need to talk to someone—you know, a professional—about this."

"We'll see that she gets the very best help we can find. Please, Sam, I want to see Allie. I need to see her."

He nodded, still a little dazed by everything that had happened. He leaned over and kissed Lynn, then kissed his son, a smile finally wreathing his face. "I'll be right back."

Seconds later, Sam, Allie and Sandy were standing in the doorway. Immediately, Lynn's gaze went to Allie. Her heart nearly broke when she saw the

SOMEWHERE OTHER THAN THE NIGHT 299

evidence of Taggart's brutality, and she was glad the man was dead.

The girl stood there half in, half out of the room, as though she wasn't sure of her welcome.

Still holding little Hank cradled to her, Lynn held out her other hand. "Allie, oh, Allie..."

Before she could finish whatever she had intended to say, Allie was across the room and in Lynn's embrace. "I'm s-so s-sorry," the girl sobbed.

"Shh, shh." Lynn patted her back. "You didn't do anything to be sorry about."

"B-but none of th-this would have h-happened if...and it was s-so...I was s-so scared and..."

"Oh, sweetheart." Heedless of the tears streaming from her own eyes, Lynn drew back enough to one-handedly wipe the tears from the child's dear face. "I just thank God that you're all right. That you're home where we can hold you and love you." She looked directly into Allie's eyes. "Where *I* can hold. Where *I* can love. Allie, Allie," she whispered again, drawing her close. "I love you so much."

Her declaration seemed to open the floodgates and Allie sobbed and sobbed while Lynn held her for what seemed like forever. Sam and Sandy had joined them on the bed and they were all touching Allie, stroking her, comforting her.

Allie's ordeal had been traumatic and would undoubtedly leave some emotional scars. She would need time to heal. They all would. And now Lynn knew they would do it as a family. Her family.

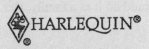

MILLION DOLLAR SWEEPSTAKES (III)

No purchase necessary. To enter, follow the directions published. Method of entry may vary. For eligibility, entries must be received no later than March 31, 1996. No liability is assumed for printing errors, lost, late or misdirected entries. Odds of winning are determined by the number of eligible entries distributed and received. Prizewinners will be determined no later than June 30, 1996.

Sweepstakes open to residents of the U.S. (except Puerto Rico), Canada, Europe and Taiwan who are 18 years of age or older. All applicable laws and regulations apply. Sweepstakes offer void wherever prohibited by law. Values of all prizes are in U.S. currency. This sweepstakes is presented by Torstar Corp., its subsidiaries and affiliates, in conjunction with book, merchandise and/or product offerings. For a copy of the Official Rules send a self-addressed, stamped envelope (WA residents need not affix return postage) to: MILLION DOLLAR SWEEPSTAKES (III) Rules, P.O. Box 4573, Blair, NE 68009, USA.

EXTRA BONUS PRIZE DRAWING

No purchase necessary. The Extra Bonus Prize will be awarded in a random drawing to be conducted no later than 5/30/96 from among all entries received. To qualify, entries must be received by 3/31/96 and comply with published directions. Drawing open to residents of the U.S. (except Puerto Rico), Canada, Europe and Taiwan who are 18 years of age or older. All applicable laws and regulations apply; offer void wherever prohibited by law. Odds of winning are dependent upon number of eligible entries received. Prize is valued in U.S. currency. The offer is presented by Torstar Corp., its subsidiaries and affiliates in conjunction with book, merchandise and/or product offering. For a copy of the Official Rules governing this sweepstakes, send a self-addressed, stamped envelope (WA residents need not affix return postage) to: Extra Bonus Prize Drawing Rules, P.O. Box 4590, Blair, NE 68009, USA.

SWP-H1294

Fifty red-blooded, white-hot, true-blue hunks
from every State in the Union!

Look for MEN MADE IN AMERICA! Written by some
of our most popular authors, these stories feature fifty
of the strongest, sexiest men, each from a different state
in the union!

Two titles available every month at your favorite
retail outlet.

In December, look for:

NATURAL ATTRACTION by Marisa Carroll
(New Hampshire)
MOMENTS HARSH, MOMENTS GENTLE by Joan Hohl
(New Jersey)

In January 1995, look for:

WITHIN REACH by Marilyn Pappano (New Mexico)
IN GOOD FAITH by Judith McWilliams (New York)

You won't be able to resist MEN MADE IN AMERICA!

If you missed any Crystal Creek titles, here's your chance
to order them:

Crystal Creek™

#82513	DEEP IN THE HEART by Barbara Kaye	$3.99	☐
#82514	COWBOYS AND CABERNET by Margot Dalton	$3.99	☐
#82515	AMARILLO BY MORNING by Bethany Campbell	$3.99	☐
#82516	WHITE LIGHTNING by Sharon Brondos	$3.99	☐
#82517	EVEN THE NIGHTS ARE BETTER by Margot Dalton	$3.99	☐
#82518	AFTER THE LIGHTS GO OUT by Barbara Kaye	$3.99	☐
#82519	HEARTS AGAINST THE WIND by Kathy Clark	$3.99	☐
#82520	THE THUNDER ROLLS by Bethany Campbell	$3.99	☐
#82521	GUITARS, CADILLACS by Cara West	$3.99	☐
#82522	STAND BY YOUR MAN by Kathy Clark	$3.99	☐
#82523	NEW WAY TO FLY by Margot Dalton	$3.99	☐
#82524	EVERYBODY'S TALKIN' by Barbara Kaye	$3.99	☐
#82525	MUSTANG HEART by Margot Dalton	$3.99	☐
#82526	PASSIONATE KISSES by Penny Richards	$3.99	☐
#82527	RHINESTONE COWBOY by Bethany Campbell	$3.99	☐
#82528	SOUTHERN NIGHTS by Margot Dalton	$3.99	☐
#82529	SHAMELESS by Sandy Steen	$3.99	☐
#82530	LET'S TURN BACK THE YEARS by Barbara Kaye	$3.99 U.S. $4.50 CAN.	☐
#82531	NEVER GIVIN' UP ON LOVE by Margot Dalton	$3.99 U.S. $4.50 CAN.	☐
#82532	GENTLE ON MY MIND by Bethany Campbell	$3.99 U.S. $4.50 CAN.	☐
#82533	UNANSWERED PRAYERS by Penny Richards	$3.99 U.S. $4.50 CAN.	☐

(limited quantities available on certain titles)

TOTAL AMOUNT	$
POSTAGE & HANDLING	$
($1.00 for one book, 50¢ for each additional)	
APPLICABLE TAXES*	$_____
TOTAL PAYABLE	$_____
(check or money order—please do not send cash)	

To order, complete this form and send it, along with a check or money order for the
total above, payable to Harlequin Books, to: **In the U.S.: 3010 Walden Avenue,
P.O. Box 9047, Buffalo, NY 14269-9047; In Canada: P.O. Box 613, Fort Erie, Ontario,
L2A 5X3.**

Name: _____

Address: _____ City: _____

State/Prov.: _____ Zip/Postal Code: _____

*New York residents remit applicable sales taxes.
 Canadian residents remit applicable GST and provincial taxes.

CCREEKB10

HARLEQUIN®